THE CURSED QUEEN

THE LYRIAN ALLIANCE

BOOK 1

COLLEEN FORBES

THE LYRIAN ALLIANCE

BOOK 1

This book is a work of fiction. Names, characters, places, and incidents are the product of the author's imagination or are used fictitiously. Any resemblance to actual events, locales, or persons, living or dead, is coincidental.

Copyright © 2020 by Colleen Forbes
All rights reserved.

The scanning, uploading, and distribution of this book without permission is a theft of the author's intellectual property. If you would like permission to use material from the book (other than for review purposes), please visit www.colleenforbes.com

Thank you for your support of the author's rights.

Cover Designed by Damonza.com
Formatting by Enchanted Ink Publishing.
Map Illustration by Hanna Sandvig: www.bookcoverbakey.com

Printed in the United States of America

To my dog, Lila.

Faithful companion.
Constant distraction.

CHAPTER 1

*R*avenna was bored. She looked around the room at all of the nobles in attendance who were helping to plan the upcoming Alliance Ball. She knew that the men and women here were capable of making it spectacular, and they didn't really need her there, did they?

Of course they did. As the queen of Lyra, the monarch of the largest country on the continent, it was her idea to host the ball to celebrate the upcoming new alliance between the neighboring countries at the palace in Lyra's capital. She had wanted a way to show that her country didn't pose much of a threat, despite being the largest one. She just didn't want to be part of the party's planning committee.

"Your Majesty, did you hear what was said?" Ravenna snapped back to attention at her uncle's question. She dropped the piece of her skirt that she realized she had been fiddling with. Her Uncle Damien and everyone else were waiting expectantly for her.

"Yes, I think that it's a wonderful idea to give a toast at the beginning of dinner instead of at the end. Thank you, Lady Russel, for the suggestion." The noble lady nodded her head at the recognition.

"Now, if you will excuse me, ladies and gentlemen, I must be off to another appointment. Please continue the good work that you have been doing. I look forward to seeing it all come to fruition." Everyone got up and bowed to her as she exited the room. Her uncle followed right behind.

"Ravenna! Where are you off to?" Damien demanded. Ravenna turned around and looked up at her uncle. He and her father had shared the same tall build, blond hair, and blue eyes. But while her father's eyes showed kindness and patience, his twin brother's eyes were hard and calculating.

"I have an appointment with Cress for another fitting for my ball gown."

"Why wasn't I told of this?" Damien seemed to be just shy of yelling, but he held back with clenched teeth.

Ravenna's eyes flashed with irritation as she replied, "As regent, I didn't think you needed to know all of my comings and goings."

"Do you think I want to continue to be your regent? As long as you insist on having this curse on you, the monarchy will be in a state of unrest. You have no prospective husband and no hope of having an heir."

Ravenna could feel a headache coming on. It was the same argument over and over again with her uncle. It wasn't like he was wrong about the problems arising due to the curse, but somehow he had gotten it into his head that she could simply make it stop at will.

It was also no secret that some of the nobles who were

in line to the throne would be more than happy to take the throne for themselves. There had even been suspicious accidents that had caused serious injuries to some of those farther up the line. Just a couple of weeks ago, one of her distant cousins on her mother's side had been unexplainably shot. Thankfully he hadn't died, but it only seemed like a matter of time before one of these "unexplainable occurrences" turned deadly.

"I will try my best to find someone to break my curse. Now, I must hurry before I'm terribly late." Ravenna turned around and went to find her favorite seamstress.

CHAPTER 2

"Ravenna! I need you to stop moving!" Cress looked up from her kneeling position on the floor at the queen in exasperation.

"Sorry, Cress," Ravenna said as she straightened back up so the seamstress could finish adjusting the dress's length. Tatiana, who was also sitting in the room, covered her mouth to hide a smile from her goddaughter.

"After all of these years having to get your dresses hemmed, you still can't figure out how to not fidget while waiting?" Cress admonished.

"I can't help it if I get antsy after a long day of meetings," the queen sighed as she thought of her previous conversation with her uncle.

"What's the matter?" Tatiana asked.

Tatiana and Cress had become some of Ravenna's most trusted confidantes. After her parents' death a year ago, they were her source of comfort and companionship during Ravenna's time of grief and transition to queen.

Ravenna looked into the mirror and saw how heavy with worry her face appeared. She replied to Tatiana, "Uncle Damien brought up again that I need to marry. Which of course I know, but it does feel hopeless."

Tatiana pressed her lips together.

"I'm sorry, dear, that it has gone on for this long," she finally said. "However, there's always a chance that you could meet someone at the ball."

Ravenna didn't look convinced. "I am almost eighteen years old and have gone through twenty-five different suitors. Who could possibly be left?"

When she looked over at her godmother, she saw Tatiana frowning. "I'm sorry, Tatiana. Please don't think that this is your fault. I asked for this and will deal with the consequences of the nobles' infighting myself. I could always appoint any one of cousin Irena's future children. That would make her happy with me." Ravenna muttered the last part. Tatiana nodded, but Ravenna could still see that Tatiana's expression hadn't smoothed out.

Ravenna thought back to that day in the flower gardens. She had found the fairy basking with her eyes closed in the midday sun on her favorite bench: the one that got the most sunshine during the day.

"Hello, Ravenna," she said without opening her eyes. Ravenna stopped walking.

"How did you know it was me?"

"I always know when my goddaughter is around. It comes with the territory of being a fairy godmother." Tatiana opened her eyes and smiled. Ravenna never forgot that Tatiana was a fairy. Not really. Otherwise, she wouldn't be seeking her out now. It's just that Tatiana didn't usually flaunt the fact that she was a fairy. For the sixteen years that Ravenna had known her, she was simply Tatiana. She had been her mother's best friend, and she was like an aunt to her. She was someone she trusted.

"You know why I'm here then?" Ravenna said, lifting her chin.

"Yes, child, I do. You want me to cure your broken heart and never let it break again." Ravenna relaxed when she heard that she didn't have to explain herself. "I can't cure your broken heart, but I can protect you from wasting your time on someone who won't love you."

"That's the same thing. If I know he's safe to love, then I won't suffer like I do now." Ravenna had recently gone through her first heartbreak, and she thought she had experienced all the suffering that the world had to offer. But life constantly offered pain with its joys. It wasn't what Hoseenu had designed, but He allowed pain in order to strengthen those He loved.

Tatiana peered at Ravenna for a long moment before she said, "I have a potion already made for you." She pulled out a small vial containing dark red liquid that almost resembled blood.

Ravenna reached out to take it, but Tatiana held it back.

"So eager to curse yourself that you won't even wait until I tell you what it will do? You might not like what it'll do to you. For it is, indeed, a curse." Ravenna's face felt hot as it turned red from the gentle rebuke.

"Why do you call it a curse? It's supposed to keep my heart safe."

"If you drink this, whoever decides to pursue you will be transformed into a dog. The only way he will become human again is if he gives up trying to woo you or if you truly love each other."

Ravenna frowned. "How would we know when we love each other if he is a dog?"

"You will know because each night you'll be able to have dinner together with him as a human. And every night he will ask you to marry him. Every night if you say no, or if you both do not love each other, then he will be transformed back into a dog." Tatiana watched as Ravenna processed the information.

"I'll do it." She took the offered vial. She drank the potion in one gulp and then sat, waiting expectantly.

"You're not going to feel any different. You're not the one who's going to turn into a dog," Tatiana chuckled as Ravenna started to blush.

"How am I supposed to know that it worked?" Ravenna asked.

"You'll just have to wait until someone tries to court you," Tatiana told her, with a hint of amusement in her voice.

Ravenna slumped forward in her seat. Tatiana leaned over and gently lifted Ravenna's face with her hand.

"Don't worry, my dear. Curses always make their presence known in a grand way. Besides, you know that my magic is usually more subtle."

"I'm not sure I'd call keeping Lyra running smoothly subtle," Ravenna snorted. "You moved an entire flood away from our farmlands!"

Tatiana chuckled, "True, but those are the exceptions. It's usually keeping pests controlled and listening to Hoseenu for wisdom to advise your parents. Speaking of which, I need to go and speak with them."

They both stood up from the garden bench and walked inside together before they each went their separate ways.

"I don't understand why Damien keeps pushing you

to marry. I'd have thought your uncle would be happy to be regent," Cress piped up, speaking around a pin that she held in her mouth, drawing Ravenna's attention back to the present.

"Maybe he thought that he'd have more power than he actually does?" Ravenna shrugged. "It doesn't matter. Getting married would help put the country at ease. Ouch!"

"I can't avoid pricking you if you keep moving. Now stay still!"

Ravenna was thankful that she only received a few more pricks before her session with Cress was done.

The queen's chambers were a midnight blue with silver highlights: a reflection of the night.

Ravenna had always loved visiting her mother here. Even though they were now hers, the rooms still didn't seem to belong to her, and it felt as if they still waited for her mother to return.

Ravenna missed her parents. They had been crossing over the mountains to attend the coronation of Wilderose's new queen when they were attacked and killed by raiders at the border, leaving their sixteen-year-old daughter as the new queen of Lyra.

Ravenna crossed the room from the four-poster bed to the window seat where her mother used to brush her long dark hair and tell her about Hoseenu, who created their world and continued to watch over them. She sat down and looked through tear-blurred eyes at the stars twinkling in the distant sky.

Lyra was a monarchy designed to be ruled equally with a king and a queen. No one monarch was greater than the other. They were supposed to be united and pave a way for the whole country's people to feel equal and have representation. The oldest child of the king and queen was always the next in line, no matter if it happened to be a son or daughter. At the death of a parent, the prince or princess would take the throne. The new king or queen was expected to be married or marry soon after. Any new monarch who was not already married would have a regent king or queen of lesser authority. This was usually a parent or the next closest relative who was already married, so as to not be eligible for the throne. This made way for a new generation of rulers. Ravenna still had not married, and she had no one to blame but herself.

She needed to show strength in the public's eyes. Even though she had not yet found her king, she was still a capable queen on her own. She was someone who could do the duties designed for two people by herself with only minor assistance from her uncle. With the signing of the new alliance treaty coming up, perhaps her people would feel safe and secure.

"Please, Hoseenu, tell my parents that I'm sorry for the mess Lyra is in. I know that You are always listening, so please give me wisdom on how to keep peace." She paused as she thought about the ambassadors that would start to arrive the next day. "And I know that I don't deserve this, but please let one of them be my king."

CHAPTER 3

Lyra's capital resided at the top of a hill. Liam's view from the hilltop across the way gave the Second Prince of Wilderose an advantageous position to calculate how long it would take him to reach the castle. As the morning sun peeked over the hills, he figured he would arrive just in time for lunch.

Liam felt like he was eighteen going on fifty. He had been traveling for over a week and was exhausted. His mind wandered back to when his sister, the Queen of Wilderose, first came into his office back at their castle.

"The Queen of Lyra has proposed that all of the countries in the known world sign an alliance treaty," Sophia said as she leaned on the chair across from his desk.

"Oh?" he replied, not even looking up from one of the latest reports about raiders attacking a merchant caravan to the south.

"I want you to represent Wilderose."

That drew his attention to his sister.

"Why me? You know that I don't have enough time as it is, doing the one job that I promised father I would do. Now you want me to play ambassador as well?"

"That's the exact reason why I want you to go. You don't have enough time to do anything that you enjoy doing." Sophia walked around the chair and slid into its seat. "You used to love the idea of traveling to all of the different countries and exploring. Now all you do is sit here and read reports."

"That's not true. I also visit the areas that have been attacked to look for clues," Liam sniffed. Though he couldn't hide his smile at his obviously weak attempt at arguing with her. The look of satisfaction on her face showed him that she knew she had won.

"When do I have to leave?" he sighed good naturedly.

"Next week. You're my favorite brother!" Sophia jumped up and went around his desk to hug him.

He laughed, "I'm your only brother."

"I guess that just means it's lucky for you that we didn't have any more siblings after you were born," Sophia said as she laughed too.

Liam smiled at the memory. She was right. This would be the most time he'd had to explore since their father's death a year prior. However, the week leading up to his departure would also include thinking up ways to try to ask Lyra for help with the raiders. It had been almost year since the former Lyrian king and queen had been killed by said raiders. He was surprised that Lyra still hadn't demanded justice or done anything to acknowledge that the culprits remained free. He hoped that he could get their help, if not the help of some of other countries, after signing the treaty.

Once he got settled into his room in the Lyrian castle, Liam looked in the mirror and saw how unkempt his red hair and beard had become while traveling. He immediately groomed himself back into looking like a prince before he left his room to roam the castle halls.

The halls had tall ceilings and large windows to let the sunlight in. Tapestries hung from the walls showing scenes from Lyra's history, as well as of Hoseenu creating the world.

Liam turned a corner and caught sight of some children engaged in a game of knights and dragons. As soon as they noticed him watching, they froze in place.

"Please don't stop on account of me. Actually, could I join your game?"

One of the little girls holding a toy sword widened her eyes. "You want to join us?" she asked incredulously.

The others seemed to be just as skeptical since a boy added, "But you don't even live here!"

Liam took a closer look at the children, who he figured must belong to the servants working at the castle. They were well fed and had clean clothes made from practical cloth, but the garments were extremely well worn.

"It's been a while since I've had a chance to fight a real dragon," Liam shrugged.

The children took some time to talk amongst themselves. Once they had decided, the first girl who had spoken announced, "You can play with us. But you have to be the dragon and we will be the knights that will defeat you!" And with that, they charged at Liam and tackled him.

Liam let out a few roars and playfully picked up each of

the ten or so children to swing each one around before picking up the next child, causing several of them to giggle in a way that was unsuitable for knights. After several rounds of this, Liam collapsed onto the ground in surrender.

"I've been defeated!" he declared. The children cheered in triumph at the news.

As Liam got back onto his feet, he asked them, "I suppose that you all must know everyone who belongs here and all of the ins and outs of the castle, don't you?"

Again, the same little girl, who seemed to be their designated spokesperson, replied, "We know everything and everybody in the castle!"

"Great! Because after being a dragon, I get extremely hungry. Could you show me to the kitchen?"

Without waiting to see if their new friend was following them, the children rushed down the corridor. "I'm Liam," the prince introduced himself to the apparent leader of the ragtag bunch, who didn't seem to be older than ten.

"My parents named me Cordelia, but my friends call me Cori. And you are a friend, so I don't want to hear you say Cordelia!" She turned and gave Liam a deathly glare, and he quickly assured her that he wouldn't dream of saying the name.

"Good. And that's my brother, James. He's five, but we let him play with us, or else he would have to help mama and papa clean if we didn't." She shuddered at the thought of forcing someone to clean with their parents. Liam had to hide a smile behind his fist as he nodded in understanding.

After they had been walking for what felt like forever to the hungry prince, they came to a giant doorway. Cori threw open the door with all of her might and yelled, "Cook! We need food for our guest!"

Cook, a middle-aged woman with graying hair, currently poured tea into a cup for a silver-haired woman sitting at the counter.

"Cori! What did I tell you about making a ruckus?" She looked up and glared at the little girl who, Liam was impressed to see, seemed unbothered by the cook's scowl.

"To not make one if it's not important. But this is important! Liam's hungry and we can't let our dragon go hungry!"

The woman at the counter chuckled, "That does sound important, Cook. Perhaps we could make some more tea and have a little bit of bread and cheese." Cori cleared her throat. "Oh, and a couple of cookies, of course," the woman added, smiling.

"Alright. But if any of your parents be complainin' that you didn't eat your dinners because you were too full, this will be the last I hear 'bout needin' cookies." Cook gave a fierce glare to the children.

"Hooray! Thanks, Cook! Thanks, Tatiana!" The children shouted and began finding places to sit and wait for their treats while Cook went to fetch more cups and plates.

"Something tells me that this isn't the first time, nor will it be the last time, that Cook gets talked into doing something like this," Liam said as he sat next to the woman who the children had called Tatiana.

She laughed, "You're right about that, Sir Dragon."

"Liam. My name is Liam. Cook wasn't the only one talked into doing something today," he winked.

"Well, it's nice to meet you, Liam. You don't sound like you're from around here?"

"No, I came today from Wilderose." He shifted in his seat. He wasn't sure if it would be considered appropriate for a foreign prince to be having tea in the castle kitchen with the servants' children.

"I see, then you must be Second Prince Liam of Wilderose."

He looked over at his violet-eyed companion in surprise. She smiled. "I'm Tatiana, the queen's fairy godmother."

"It is an honor to meet you, Your Excellency," Liam stammered as he scrambled to remember how to properly address a fairy.

"Please, none of this 'excellency' stuff. I'm just Tatiana."

Liam observed her skeptically. Wilderose's royal family did not have a fairy godmother, but he knew from historical accounts that when a family did have one, they were not *just* some simple fae with simple magic. They were more powerful than that. He didn't know how powerful exactly, but he knew enough to know that no matter what, this fairy deserved his respect. She nodded in approval as if she could read his thoughts.

"Liam, you seem to be a good and kind man. I have heard about you, that you are faithful to your sister, the Queen of Wilderose, and that you do not take your commitments lightly. I need help from someone like you and wonder if you could assist me."

"I am honored that you've taken notice of me," Liam said slowly. A fairy godmother for another royal family asking for help from a foreign prince was not a common occurrence, and it made him wary. He continued, "What do you need done?"

Tatiana rested her hand on the one that he had wrapped around his mug of tea.

"I want you to break my goddaughter's curse." Tatiana gave him a warm, motherly smile.

Liam stilled. She was asking him to do the impossible.

No one else had been able to accomplish the task. Why did she think that he could? He glanced up at the ceiling, hoping an answer was written there that wouldn't potentially offend the most powerful being he had ever met. Seeing none, he looked back at the fairy godmother.

"I can see how that is something that you would want help with. Are you sure that you would want me to do it?" He asked cautiously.

"You would make a good partner for Ravenna and a good king for Lyra."

"But you just met me," Liam couldn't help but point out.

"Yes, but I saw how you interacted with the children and won them over. They're not an easy bunch to fool. You were humble enough to not flaunt your title to who you presumed to be a kitchen servant girl. And this observation is solely from today alone. That sort of character doesn't come overnight, am I right?"

Liam couldn't answer. If he didn't know better, he would have suspected that Tatiana had deliberately asked those children to play in that hall for him to find. Then again, she very well could have. He looked over at Cori eating her tea and cookies and decided that if he could get a moment alone with her, he'd ask the little girl about it.

"My sister would have to be consulted first," Liam said.

Reaching into a pocket hidden in her dress, Tatiana pulled out a parchment paper.

"I have already been in contact with the Queen of Wilderose. Here is her agreement to free up your duties so that you may take the time to break the curse."

Liam narrowed his eyes while reading a letter that seemed to be in his sister's handwriting. He looked back up at Tatiana.

"How?" was all that he could come up with.

She gave a secretive smile. "I am the fairy godmother of the royal family of Lyra. I look out for the good of Lyra. As I have said, you are loyal to your sister. You wouldn't have agreed to do this without letting her know. I have ways to send missives that are faster than any messenger."

"Why is she agreeing to this? And what if I had said that I wouldn't even try?"

"I have also informed Her Majesty that if you were to successfully break the curse and marry Ravenna, it would mean that you will have joined the royal family. As such, Wilderose would come under my protection for the duration of your lifetime." Then Tatiana gently added, "Hoseenu has blessed you with a selflessness that few people have. You put others before yourself."

Liam rubbed his face with his hand. He couldn't just leave Sophia on her own while he tried to court a queen that others had failed at wooing. A queen who people had started to say had a heart made of stone. Then again, having a fairy godmother look after Wilderose would be a huge boon. Even if it was only for his lifetime. He sent up a small prayer to Hoseenu that he'd be blessed with a long life. That was when he realized he was already committed to breaking the curse. If it meant that this would take some of the weight of leadership off of his sister, then he was going to be the last man to try to marry the Queen of Lyra.

Liam tilted his head back and blew out a deep breath. "Very well, I will break the Queen of Lyra's curse."

Tatiana broke out into a huge grin. "Thank you for your sacrifice, Your Highness!" And with that, she called farewell to Cook and the children and left Liam alone to let it sink in what he had promised to do.

CHAPTER 4

It was the day of the ball, and everyone was working hard to ensure its success. Ravenna had gone from meeting to meeting making sure that everything was ready for tonight. Cook had needed to make sure that some of the menu substitutions were acceptable. The Minister of Music had been in a panic after one of his violinists could no longer play due to breaking his hand in a fall. Little last-minute fixes added up and kept her busy all day.

Ravenna massaged her temples. *Maybe I should have hired someone to handle overseeing the ball*, she thought when she was finally alone.

She hadn't even had time to greet every guest individually, but she figured she would at least try to see everyone who could celebrate the alliance between all of their countries. There were a few she had to greet personally, like Irena and her betrothed, Crown Prince Titus of Faircoast. It had been awhile since she had seen her cousin, and just as long since Uncle Damien had seen his daughter, so she made it a priority for their sake to greet the family. Their welcome went as well as to be expected. Titus said something tactless about Ravenna's last suitor, and Irena not so subtly hinted that Ravenna looked haggard and was ruining her chances of finding a husband, which led her uncle to reiterate all the ways that the curse was causing problems for Lyra...the typical family reunion.

A knock at the door brought Ravenna out of her musings about the ball.

"Come in."

Cress, carrying the dress that Ravenna was to wear tonight, opened the door.

"Here, let me help you." Ravenna walked across the room, took the dress from Cress's hands, and started putting it on.

"It fits perfectly! You did a wonderful job." The forest green dress contrasted her pale skin and dark hair beautifully. The skirt reached all the way to the floor and had sleeves that became bell shapes right past her elbows.

"Thanks, Ravenna. Another dress to help my growing reputation. It also helps that my star client and model is absolutely breathtaking in them," Cress said with a wink.

"Don't be silly. Your dresses would look good on anyone. Although, I will gladly take credit for being your 'star client.' I owed you one, remember?" Ravenna teased. Cress didn't join in her mirth.

"You might have 'owed me one,' but you have gone above and beyond in getting the court ladies to want to buy dresses from a mere castle seamstress." Ravenna grew quiet as she remembered how excited Cress had been to design her wedding dress only to never have a chance to show it off publicly.

When she finished getting ready with Cress's help, she glimpsed in the mirror and saw a tired woman looking back at her. She was the youngest ruling sovereign in the alliance, but the weight of a leadership that was meant to be shared with another person was starting to show.

Cress looked over at her friend. "Your parents would be proud; you know that, right?"

Ravenna sighed, "I hope so. It was a year ago today that they died. I thought it would be fitting to host the celebration of the countries' alliance on the anniversary of a day that could have turned into war."

"It is fitting," Tatiana said as she stepped through the doorway. The women turned around and looked at the fairy. "They had worked so hard to create an alliance, and you will see that dream come true."

Ravenna smiled at Tatiana, but she then turned to Cress and said, "Cress, you better hurry up and get ready. You don't want to be late for your dress's debut."

"You're right! Look at the time! I'll see you both in the ballroom!" And with that, the dressmaker dashed out of the room.

Tatiana and Ravenna smiled fondly after their friend, but Ravenna's smile dropped first as she sat at the window seat.

"I'm not sure I can do this. Despite everyone's willingness to sign the truce, there are still high tensions among different countries. Plus, I have accidentally insulted a good number of the men out there." A self-deprecating half-laugh escaped her. Tatiana joined her on the seat.

"Your mother was just as nervous before going to official events. Right up until the end."

Ravenna gave her a side glance of disbelief.

"Truly! She was a good queen and always conducted herself with poise and dignity. But no one knew she was terrified of insulting the wrong person and inadvertently causing a war. You have managed even more. We have not only *not* gone to war, but you have joined all the countries together. Despite insulting twenty-five men." Tatiana playfully shoved Ravenna's shoulder, causing the queen to smile again.

"You're right," she said, then added with a knowing grin, "As usual."

A knock sounded at the door, and Damien entered. Ravenna immediately straightened. "Are you ready?" Damien asked.

"Of course," she replied with a firm tone and accepted her uncle's arm to escort her down to the ballroom.

CHAPTER 5

    Liam didn't usually pay attention to décor, but when he saw the ballroom, even he couldn't help but notice the glowing extravagance of the crystal chandelier, the silver-and-gold rug, and the silk table cloths.

    When the herald announced the Queen of Lyra and the Regent King, he fixed his gaze at the top of the stairs for his first glimpse of the woman he had agreed to risk so much for.

    She was beautiful. Liam took in her petite features and her almost-black hair. Her eyes looked like they were made of emeralds. He could see her firm determination in them.

    The crowd below quieted. Those of lower ranks than she bowed low while the kings and queens in attendance nodded their heads to their host.

    As soon as they came to the thrones, she announced, "Thank you to everyone who was able to come and represent each of our countries. It is with great honor that on the memorial of my parents' deaths their lifelong dream of unity has been fulfilled. Even though our shared past has been riddled with war and distrust, I am hopeful that, starting today, our shared future will be one of peace and friendship."

Everyone in the room clapped and cheered, and as soon as the queen sat down, they resumed their conversations and dancing. Liam decided to walk over to the refreshment table to grab something to drink. He picked up a glass of wine - maybe some liquid courage would help him approach the queen. As he turned around, someone bumped into him. Not wanting to spill his drink on whomever he had bumped into, he just let them fall.

"I'm so sorry! Here, let me help you up."

Liam was mortified when he saw who the person was as he helped her off the floor. Of course, it couldn't have been just anyone, but Queen Ravenna herself. Coincidentally, he was just about to go look for her. Not that he knew what he was going to say when he found her. How does someone ask another person, a person who one hasn't met before, to more or less marry them? Was he supposed to go up to her alone and ask? Did he have to make a grand announcement in front of everyone? When did the whole turning into a dog happen? He had to admit that he wasn't looking forward to that part.

"Thank you," she said as she took his hand and got up.

"I'm Liam, the Second Prince of Wilderose. It is, erm, an honor to meet you, Your Majesty." He bowed.

"You can just call me Ravenna," she told him.

Now he had to make amends for her first impression of him as some clumsy prince. His sister was going to kill him. He cringed while he apologized to Ravenna. At least he had a good first impression of her. She had laughed off the situation despite everyone staring at them and a few of the Lyrian palace guards giving him glares.

"Would you do me the honor of a dance? I would like to show you that Wilderose does train their royalty to be more graceful than what you have seen." He smiled at her, hoping that she would accept his invitation despite the obvious hesitation on her face.

"I suppose you may." The corner of her eyes crinkled with her smile.

"Thank you, Your Majesty," he said with a bow.

"It's Ravenna. I'll give you a dance; however, if you end up stepping on my feet, I will have to assume that Wilderose's royal training is lacking." She had a twinkle in her eye as though she was losing a battle with herself to hide a smile.

"Trust me, you'll not be disappointed." Liam hoped at least.

He led her out onto the dance floor as soon as the next song began. While they danced, he tried to make as much conversation as he could while also making sure he didn't step on her feet.

"So...what do you like to do?" This was going to be more awkward than he had initially thought. Maybe this was a bad idea, but he had made a promise to a fairy godmother. A fairy godmother who would be able to look after his sister and their country.

"That's an odd question for a queen," Ravenna's brows furrowed.

"Just because you're a queen doesn't mean you're not a person with her own interests too," he retorted. His sister was definitely going to kill him for how casually he was talking to their strongest ally. Thankfully, he could see the beginning of a smile on Ravenna's face.

"I like to go walking in the woods. What about you?"

"I used to love horseback riding in the forest with my father. It felt like we would discover a new section every time." He smiled wistfully at the memory before he continued. "I know that the Wilderose court had sent a formal condolence for your parents' deaths a year ago, but after your speech tonight, I want to add to it personally. My father died shortly before they did, and there are still moments when it feels fresh. It's very apparent that you feel the same about your parents' death."

"Yes. It was - is - very hard. Is there something you want?" A little bit of wariness had slipped into her voice.

"What do you mean?" Liam asked, slightly taken aback.

"People only try to empathize with me before they ask for some sort of favor." Ravenna's eyes narrowed.

With a pained whisper, as though he regretted his next choice of words, he said, "I want to break your curse."

Then, just like the twenty-five men before him, a dog stood in his place.

CHAPTER 6

*L*iam wasn't used to being so low to the ground. He had been a good head taller than Ravenna, and now he only came up to a few inches above her knees. He felt crowded in, and he could feel his new tail tucked between his back legs. From what he gathered, he had long, wavy fur that he suspected was red due to his previous hair color. He also had long, floppy ears. Was he a red setter?

Looking up at Ravenna, he saw that she appeared resigned. To his embarrassment, a whine escaped from him that tried to convey his apologies at causing yet another major spectacle at one of the most important events of the century. He should have thought this through more.

"We should leave for somewhere more private," Ravenna told him. "You're the first one in months that decided it was a good idea to propose in a crowded area."

She didn't sound happy, and Liam couldn't really blame

her. If the roles had been reversed, he would not be pleased with some stranger turning a night that was supposed to be a celebration into a catastrophe.

He followed her through a slightly hidden door next to the thrones. Her uncle's face was beet red with anger and he looked like he was going to follow them, but Ravenna went up to him and whispered something to him that made him stop in his tracks and turn back to the crowd.

As soon as they were alone, she turned on him. "What were you thinking asking to break my curse in the middle of a dance?"

He tried to answer her, but all that came out of his mouth was one big, "Woof!"

She sighed as she pinched the bridge of her nose. "You have to speak to me through your mind." She turned to look at him and continued, "It is a little difficult to get used to, but you know how you speak internally to yourself?"

Liam tilted his head.

"It's the same thing, but louder. Or at least that's what the others have said."

I'm sorry, Your Majesty. I was originally hoping to ask for an audience with you this week, but since you were right there, I thought it was as good a time as any.

"It wasn't as good a time as any!" Ravenna's hands started to fidget with her skirts as she continued, "Why does Wilderose want a marriage alliance anyway?"

He struggled with his natural inclination to speak with his mouth instead of with his thoughts, so it took him a while to say, *It's complicated.*

"How is it complicated?" Exasperation filled her voice.

I did not come here with the intention of asking to marry anyone. However, due to recent unforeseen circumstances, I made a promise to myself that I'd break this curse.

He then laid down on the floor and put his head on his front paws. He felt exhausted and didn't know what else he could possibly say. He thought back to his conversation with Tatiana, which he'd learned had been set up by the fairy, and realized that he had assumed she had had a similar conversation with Ravenna. He had apparently assumed wrong.

Ravenna seemed to be equally as tired as she slumped into a nearby chair.

"Well, I guess we'll have to make the most of this. It seems like some of the palace guards have already. They were exchanging money when we walked out."

Erm, they were doing what?

She replied with a thin smile, "The staff and some of the nobles like to make bets when someone decides he would like to try his hand at winning the throne." She closed her eyes and pinched the bridge of her nose again. "How much do you know about the curse?"

I know we have to fall in love for it to break.

She opened an eye to peek at him.

"You don't claim to already love me?" she smirked.

I'm no expert, but from what I gather, it doesn't happen in a day. At least not the true love that Hoseenu created.

"At least you don't have any delusions. Do you know about the part where you'll be human during dinner, but you will be forced to ask me to marry you afterward?"

I do now. He was startled to feel his tail wag in amusement on its own accord. He quickly glanced behind him and saw that his new appendage was indeed moving as if it had a mind of its own.

"You also know that this can be over for you whenever you want? At any point, you can always tell me that you no longer want to pursue me, and you'll no longer be a dog," she quietly added. His tail stopped wagging, and he turned back to meet her gaze.

I'm well aware of that, but I made a promise to break the curse over you. *Not over me.*

She shifted in her seat as she slowly added, "Traditionally, whoever is courting the Lyrian monarch is also courting the throne."

A huge sigh escaped him.

"Is something wrong?"

I will be honest with you. Growing up, it was my sister who was expected to take over the Wilderose throne. In case something were to go dreadfully wrong, I was given some preparation, but it was never my desire to be a king.

She gave him a confused look. "Then what was your desire?"

To be an explorer. It's why I was head of the military. There was more traveling involved. There was the opportunity to see every part of Wilderose.

"Well, if it helps, part of my job as queen does involve traveling, so if I have to go somewhere, you will have to come with me."

Liam nodded his head as best as he could.

"Let me show you to your new rooms. You will be staying in the king's chambers that connect to the queen's. It was decided a few suitors ago that since I'm the only one that can understand whoever is courting me, it made sense that I should be close to where he is staying. After you settle in, I should probably get back to the ball." He got up to follow her out of the small room's back entrance and into the hall.

"I'm surprised that Tatiana hasn't shown up," she said more to herself than to Liam. He decided to keep quiet.

When they got to the king's chambers, she opened the door for him. It was spacious, adorned in red and gold.

"That's the door connecting to my room if you need anything tonight," she said as she pointed. She hesitated at the door. "I'll have someone get your things from your guest bedroom."

His ear flickered toward her to acknowledge that he had heard her, but he thought to add, *Thank you, Your Majesty.* He started to head toward the bed.

"It's Ravenna," he heard her say before she walked back to the ballroom.

CHAPTER 7

*I*t seemed like everyone was waiting for her return to the celebration. As soon as Ravenna walked in, people lined up to ask her about her new dog...err, suitor. The sole member of the Wilderose's royal family that she had met before that night was Queen Sophia, and that had been a little less than a year ago at Ravenna's coronation.

The only information she had about the Second Prince of Wilderose was what her advisors had told her during debriefings of the various neighboring sovereigns, which was that he led the Wilderosian military. Other than that, there hadn't been much to learn about him.

Before anyone else could approach her, Cress pounced on Ravenna. "Well, this made for a memorable night!"

Ravenna groaned as she made her way toward Damien, "It wasn't supposed to be remembered for this!"

"Just think of it like this: now all of the future children

learning history will have something much more interesting to focus on instead of the whole known world forming an alliance together," Cress teased.

Before Ravenna could come up with a good retort, Damien stormed up to her.

"This is outrageous! We wanted people to see Lyra as a strong ally, not to remind them of past insults." Ravenna glanced around the room at the people staring at her uncle yelling at her.

"Uncle, you are only the regent king. Not actually the king. I would advise you to remember your place before your queen who is more than merely your niece."

Damien took a step back at the queen's icy tone. He bowed low and exited the room, followed by Irena and Titus who had followed behind Damien when he came to her. Irena smirked at Ravenna before walking away. Anger and embarrassment turned Ravenna's cheeks red and hot when she realized that this was yet another example of her not measuring up to her fair cousin.

Ravenna glanced over the guests who still lingered. Most tried to make it seem like they hadn't noticed what had transpired, but several gawked unabashedly.

"Thank you for coming tonight. It has been a privilege to host all of you. I will see you tomorrow for the signing of the alliance treaty." And she left the room unaccompanied for the first time as queen.

Again she found herself sitting on the window seat looking out at the stars. Ravenna had peeked through the doorway into her father's old rooms to see the dog prince sleeping heavily on the bed. It seemed that the transformation on the first day always sapped the energy out of her suitors. He likely wouldn't wake up until noon the next day.

It's a good thing that the treaty meeting doesn't start until after lunch, Ravenna thought to herself. She and her advisors had assumed that most people wouldn't go to bed until late after the ball, so they decided it would be better to have everyone meet later in the day. Hoseenu knew she needed the extra rest in the morning.

As Ravenna whispered prayers to Hoseenu, asking Him for wisdom, Tatiana quietly opened her bedroom door and joined her on the window seat.

"You have been curiously absent this evening," Ravenna wryly pointed out.

The fairy shrugged and changed the topic. "What do you think of him?"

"I'm impressed. You have picked out a fine prince for me." She laughed at Tatiana's surprised face. It didn't happen often that she could shock her godmother and friend, but when she did, she relished it.

"Oh, come on. He had no reason to pursue me and wasn't planning on it before he arrived. *Someone* must have persuaded him."

"I didn't want you to reject him if his reason for doing it was because I asked him to," Tatiana explained.

"It doesn't really matter to me why he's doing it. He's convinced himself that he's going to break the curse and that we'll fall in love." Ravenna couldn't hide her sardonic tone. She didn't believe him. Several of the other suitors had said the same thing, or something similar, when they first activated the curse. And yet the longest had lasted three weeks. Long enough to get her hopes up...but not long enough for them to fall in love.

"I know that you have given up on breaking the curse, but will you give him a chance at least?" Tatiana's eyes pleaded with her to say yes. She gazed out the window and, not for the first time, wished that her life could have turned out differently. She hadn't always been this cynical.

"I always do."

Tatiana exhaled in relief. "You should get some rest. Good night."

"Good night."

As soon as her godmother left, she went to bed. While she laid there in the dark, she let her tears roll down her cheeks, remembering the first suitor that had rejected her all the way up to the twenty-fifth.

Ravenna had been a couple of weeks away from turning seventeen years old when someone first decided to court her after the curse had been put in place.

He at least had the decency to wait awhile after my intended wedding, Ravenna thought ruefully to herself. She had been with her parents in the throne room that day, listening to the Crown Prince Titus of Faircoast who had begun his speech about a marriage alliance. The southwest neighboring country had a strong history of trade with Lyra. They provided pearls and fish in return for fresh produce. It would be advantageous for Faircoast to have a marriage alliance with her; Lyra was their only neighbor, and on top of this, was a source of trade routes to the rest of the countries surrounding them. Lyra functioned as a centralized hub for trade, and it would be economical suicide to not be in their good graces.

Before Prince Titus's speech, Ravenna had hoped that Lyra's status would be enough to prevent any ill feelings once her curse was discovered. She hadn't told anyone what she had done. Tatiana was the only other person who knew about it. Ravenna sat on her throne next to her parents' thrones and shifted uncomfortably. She had thought she would be able to tell them before anyone proposed the possibility of a marriage alliance, but her luck had not held... for here stood a powerful man about to turn into a dog, and only she knew it.

"So, with your permission, I would like to officially ask your daughter, the Princess Ravenna of Lyra, for her hand in marriage."

Before her parents could even answer one way or the other, a cloud of smoke swirled around Titus. Once it had cleared, a small beagle stood in his place. Everyone froze in shock for a moment before all at once the throne room erupted into chaos.

The accompanying dignitaries from Faircoast were shouting at the Lyrians for endangering their prince. The beagle, who was actually Titus, started barking, and the Lyrian court officials protested that they could not possibly be at fault. King Tristan and Queen Katherina looked over at their daughter, who was slowly slumping lower on her throne. She hoped beyond hope that she could disappear from their disappointed gazes.

"Be quiet." A woman's voice rang out and immediately the noise stopped. Tatiana stepped into the middle of the room, drawing everyone's attention to herself. "Your Majesties, I would like to explain if I may."

"Go right ahead, Tatiana. It seems like you are the only one of us who is informed." Ravenna watched as her father tried but failed to hide a scowl.

"Thank you, Your Majesty." Tatiana bowed her head at the king to show to the Faircoast court that he was still the one who deserved respect.

"Ravenna has been cursed to prevent her marriage to anyone unworthy of becoming her king. I took it upon myself to provide the terms and conditions and was waiting for the right moment to inform Your Majesties. However, I regret that I may have waited too long, and I wish to formally apologize to you and to the Crown Prince of Faircoast." At this, she bowed her head to the Lyra monarchs and to the beagle prince.

"And what of the crown prince?" the Faircoast ambassador shouted. "We cannot return home to our king and queen with their son as a dog!"

"Ravenna can communicate with him to see whether or not he wishes to give up on trying to marry her. If he wishes to still pursue her, he will become human again during dinner each night with the princess. If he does not, he will return to his human form." Ravenna peered over at Titus, who continued his barking.

This is ridiculous! An insult to Faircoast! Ravenna heard Titus say. She expected someone from Faircoast to agree with him, and when nobody responded, she realized what Tatiana had said was true. She was the only one who could understand him.

"May I speak with Prince Titus alone?" she asked.

"Your Highness, are you alright with that and, er, could you perhaps nod your head?" The Faircoast ambassador asked the beagle. He was obviously uncomfortable talking to a dog, even if it was his very own prince. The beagle nodded in affirmation and walked over to Ravenna, who was already heading toward the door before anyone could stop her.

As soon as they were out in the hallway in front of the throne room, Ravenna got onto her knees to look at the transformed prince who had started growling at her.

"I'm sorry about this. I didn't realize that your annual visit was to propose a marriage alliance. Otherwise, I would have stopped you from asking."

It seems like I'm not the only one who wasn't aware of what might happen, Princess. Ravenna could tell by the way he held his nose up in the air that Titus thought that she had handled this incompetently.

"No, you are not. However, if you no longer wish to marry me, this will be over for you as of tonight. If you choose to decline, since we are going to be the future rulers of our respected kingdoms, I would like to offer you a marriage alliance. But not with me." At this, Titus seemed interested. Ravenna had been right to assume that no matter what sort of insult he felt toward himself, he still wouldn't risk the economic security of his people.

I'm listening.

The throne room was still tense when Ravenna and Titus walked back in. With her head held high, Ravenna spoke confidently to everyone still in the room. "We have reached an agreement. Titus will give up his pursuit of my hand in marriage and will return to his human form tonight. As for a peace treaty, he is still inclined to have a marriage alliance with any one of my cousins who are willing."

She glanced over at her Uncle Damien, who stood next to his brother and Irena. Despite her father and uncle not being originally from a noble family, her uncle had married a duchess, and since Irena was a blood relative to Ravenna, she had inherited a title of her own. Her rank would not be an insult to Faircoast. There was the added bonus that Irena would no longer be around to make Ravenna's life miserable. Not that she would admit that to anyone.

"As cousin to the princess, I accept whatever marriage alliance that she deems suitable," Irena called out. Damien nodded his head at the opportunity to have a future king as a son-in-law.

"Then it is decided." King Tristan took control of the situation before anyone from Faircoast could argue. "Let us go to the dining hall to celebrate the union between our two countries!" And with that, everyone filed out of the throne room.

"Don't think you have been let off the hook, young lady," Queen Katherina whispered to her daughter. "Your father and I would like to have a word with you after dinner." Ravenna lowered her head in response and continued to follow everyone to the dining hall.

When they arrived at their table, Prince Titus was no longer a canine and had a look of relief.

"I am glad to see you that you are all right, Your Highness," the queen said.

"As am I, Your Majesty," Titus replied, seemingly still a little sore over the short incident. "And I regret to inform you, Your Highness, that I formally no longer wish to pursue your hand in marriage," he added to officially meet the terms of ending the curse for himself.

"No regrets needed, Your Highness. I am sure that we'll continue trading with you in the future," Ravenna said to remind him of where his country stood compared with hers.

She saw her uncle approach their table, escorting her cousin. Titus's eyes widened as he took in the beautiful young woman that was to be his wife. Titus's smile grew when Irena came to the table.

"I'm extremely sorry for the ordeal that my cousin put you through," Irena cooed within earshot of Ravenna, "but I can't say that I'm disappointed that it has resulted in our betrothal." She gazed up at Titus through her long eyelashes.

"My dear, you are a far greater prize than I could ever imagine." Titus kissed Irena's hand, and Ravenna saw the smug look Irena shot her way. She sighed. *He* really had been the only one to ever tell her that she was worth more than her beautiful cousin.

The pain in her chest that had never truly gone away since *he* left became tighter at that memory. It was just another lie that she had wanted to be true.

After everyone had eaten their fill and left the dining hall, Ravenna followed her parents to the king's chambers. As soon as the door closed, her father started talking.

"First, I do want to say that we are proud of how you handled this...unfortunate situation. You managed for our countries to still be united instead of both of us losing a valuable trade alliance. It is a sign that you are going to become a good queen." Ravenna wanted to relish the praise from her father, but her parents were not finished.

"However," her mother started, "you should have warned us that you were cursed. When exactly did this happen?"

"Five months ago," Ravenna mumbled.

"You've had plenty of time to tell us." Her parents' disapproval weighed heavily on her.

"I'm sorry, Mama, Papa. I should have told you as soon as I asked Tatiana for the curse."

Her parents wearily made eye contact with each other

before her mother spoke again. "We forgive you, but why did you do it?"

"I didn't want to live through what happened last year again." Ravenna couldn't meet her parents' eyes when she replied. King Tristan and Queen Katherina quickly reached over to hug their daughter.

"Well, what's done is done. It seems like you have gotten your wish," Tristan ruefully said. "Am I correct to assume that you're not going to curse yourself again? We'll only have dog princes running around, right? No cats?" her father asked with a twinkle in his eye.

"No cats. Just dogs," Ravenna laughed.

"Well, then I guess we should be thankful for small mercies. Can't have hairballs in one's breakfast!"

"Tristan! That only happened once!" Katherina exclaimed. "And besides, I haven't even owned another cat ever since. You should really let it go."

"My dear sweet queen, if I hadn't eaten the hairball with my eggs, I would gladly let it go. I swear your cat hated that I was trying to court you."

Ravenna giggled to herself as she listened to her parents' banter. She knew it was their way of trying to cheer her up and let her know that all was forgiven. They seemed to think that her curse was punishment enough.

CHAPTER 8

Liam woke up to loud noises coming from the room next to his. Weren't castle walls supposed to be soundproof? The sun had just barely risen. He groaned and tried to roll over when he realized that his arms and legs didn't feel right. He opened his eyes and saw fur covering his appendages.

This isn't a dream. He also realized that castle walls are usually soundproofed for human ears, but dog ears were a different story. He stood up, but he then fell back down on the bed. His whole body felt sore, as if he had gotten run over by a horse.

The door between his and Ravenna's room opened. She had already dressed and looked wide awake and ready for the day.

"Good morning. Would you like to join me for breakfast?" She was a morning person, he realized with horror.

Was this what the rest of his life was going to be like if he broke the curse? Waking up to an early bird's greeting? He heard a dog whimpering and, with shock, noticed that the sound came from himself.

"Are you alright?" Ravenna questioned, looking puzzled.

Yes, I'm fine. I would love to join you for breakfast.

She didn't look completely convinced but let the matter drop.

"I can lead you to the family dining room." She stepped aside to give him room to walk through the door between their bedrooms.

Hoping that he'd be more successful this time around, he got up and jumped off the bed. He gave himself a moment to make sure he wasn't going to fall again and then followed Ravenna through her room and out into the hallway.

They were quiet on their walk to breakfast. When they got to the breakfast room, they found Tatiana already drinking tea at the table.

"Good morning, you two."

Is everyone a morning person here? Liam wondered to himself as he watched the women hug each other.

Good morning. He greeted the fairy less enthusiastically with a slight nod.

"I'm sorry, love, but only Ravenna can hear you right now."

Ravenna gave him an apologetic look for forgetting a detail as important as that.

Then how am I going to communicate with anyone? he asked the queen.

She cringed. "During dinner, you can talk with anyone since you will be human, but during the rest of the day, you can ask me to speak to anyone you desire."

If he wished to talk with anyone, was he really expected to be around her all the time? This was going to be more challenging than he thought. How was he supposed to learn to love this woman without ending up resenting her first?

The next unexpected challenge arrived with the food. He could smell eggs, sausage, and toast. The servant girl bringing in the trays of food looked at him and hesitated with two bowls: one filled with water, the other filled with food. He jumped into a chair next to where Ravenna sat to convey that he might physically be a dog, but he was going to eat with the humans. Out of the corner of his eye, he saw Ravenna wince. As soon as the bowls were placed before him, she said, "I'm sorry. I should have offered you your seat first as my guest."

The seating situation was figured out, and he started eating his breakfast. He gave up trying to eat it politely and let himself wolf it down as the dog he was. Same with letting decorum go when he drank water. There was no helping that water got everywhere and dripped down his muzzle as he lapped it up.

While they ate, Ravenna rattled off the day's schedule.

"Today is a bit unusual in that it's the day after a ball. That means everything is set later in the day so everyone who has to do business will be awake and aware of what's going on."

Then why are we up early?

He couldn't hide his annoyance when he realized that everyone else in the castle was still asleep in bed and he had to be surrounded by morning people.

Ravenna apologized when she noted his irritation. "I'm sorry. I didn't think that you would want more sleep. You had been asleep for ten hours, and I thought that you would want to know the usual routine."

Liam mentally kicked himself. They were strangers. They didn't know what it looked like to share life together, let alone how the other person woke up.

You're right. I do want to know what the schedule is. He watched her expectantly, trying to convey that he was willing, and waited for her to finish.

"Right. After lunch is the treaty signing. Um, since you won't be able to hold a pen, a paw print would be a sufficient signature." He huffed out a dog's version of a laugh at that.

When word was sent to my sister that I was going to attempt to break the Lyrian curse, I'm sure she didn't think about the consequences of it. Please do not invite her to visit anytime soon.

"Why ever not?"

I want to have time to think through all of the possible pranks I'll have to avoid.

"I'm sorry, but are you implying that the Queen of Wilderose is a prankster?" Ravenna started laughing uncontrollably, then added, "Are you serious?"

Dead serious, he deadpanned.

"Then I guess we won't be inviting her over." She wiped tears from her eyes. He honestly didn't see how she could laugh so hard over this.

"I'm sorry, but your sister has always been considered the most dignified queen on the continent. I can't imagine her doing anything fun."

Don't all public figures have a secret life of some sort?

She sobered at his statement. "Yes, you're right." Then she quickly continued with logistics. "After the treaty has been signed, there will be a feast, and then, thankfully, everyone starts to leave tomorrow. We won't have any meetings on that day, and the following day is the day of rest. I can show you some more of the surrounding area then."

The thought of exploring caused his tail to wag. He caught Ravenna smiling when she saw his tail's reaction. He wasn't used to having all of his emotions on display, and there didn't really seem to be any way to hide them.

What do normal days look like? he asked her.

"They begin early, but thankfully that means that as soon as dinner happens, that's it for the day. It's usually one meeting after another: state affairs, daily reports, potential court cases, etcetera. It changes day to day."

Liam resigned himself to early mornings. This really was going to be the rest of his life.

Tatiana broke her silence and said, "Ravenna, you both have some time between now and midday. Why don't you show Liam around the flower gardens?"

He wasn't sure why, but Ravenna tensed when Tatiana mentioned the gardens.

"I think that you would be a better guide for that. You are the one that spends a lot of time out there. Besides, there are a few more things that I need to prepare before the signing."

Tatiana sighed, "Very well. Liam, we're being dismissed, so we might as well get going."

She got up from the table, and Liam realized that he really was expected to follow her. He wasn't exactly looking forward to another one-sided conversation with the fairy, but he also realized that his private needs weren't going to be met inside, so he begrudgingly left the table as well.

Ravenna physically relaxed when they had both gone. It had felt like years since she'd gone into the flower gardens, and she didn't really think she was ready to face the memories left from *him*. She knew it was silly, but that didn't mean it wasn't true. Talking with Liam wasn't so bad as long as she stuck with logistics. It was unfortunate that she was expected to talk to him about personal things.

She was curious to learn more about him and his family after hearing about his father and sister. She just wasn't looking forward to having to share her own personal life with him. After all, it was only the first day of his curse. Too soon to give any part of herself to him. For all she knew, he would give up today or tomorrow once it fully sunk in what being a dog really meant. He depended on her for his voice. For Hoseenu's sake, he had to relieve himself outside. Rain or shine. Although, fortunately for him, it was sunny today.

She got up from the table and headed toward her office to go over the treaty once again. As she walked past a window overlooking the gardens, she saw Tatiana and Liam step out of the castle.

Hoseenu, I don't think I can hope again. It would be better to hold my heart close until some time has passed, she prayed as she left the window.

CHAPTER 9

The castle gardens were beautiful. Spring was about to arrive, and Liam could see some of the buds starting to grow on the different plants. When they first got outside, Tatiana had thankfully given him some privacy, but now they were walking silently side by side on the garden path until Tatiana broke the silence.

"Thank you again for doing this. I know it's not easy for you, and you'll just have to trust me that this isn't easy for Ravenna either." Liam waited for her to continue. "I know you are the one that has to be physically changed, but you see, you are the twenty-sixth suitor Ravenna has had. She's used to being disappointed and will probably keep you at a distance for quite some time."

Liam internally shuddered. That wasn't exactly encouraging to hear.

"I'm telling you this now so you have a better idea of what you're up against."

Tatiana stopped walking and observed a rose bush, still bare from winter. "You're going to have to discover a lot about Ravenna on your own, but I will be here to help you both when you need it."

Liam could tell there seemed to be more that Tatiana wanted to tell him, but that it wasn't her place to share. He wondered for the first time where the curse originated. None of the rumors he had heard mentioned anything about where it had come from, only that a couple of years ago a prince tried to pursue Ravenna and had subsequently turned into a dog. Then it kept happening to anyone else who wanted to marry into the Lyrian royal family through the current queen.

He gave a soft whine to tell her that he understood and got a small smile from the fairy in return.

"Let's head back inside, shall we?" They turned around and headed back toward the garden's entrance.

Ravenna sat at the head of the long table in the meeting room with Liam by her side. This time he had passed on the opportunity to sit in a chair so as to not draw even more attention to himself. He figured it was less conspicuous for a dog to be sitting on the floor.

She was pleased to see everyone in attendance. In total there were eight countries represented in the room. Besides Lyra and Wilderose, there was Faircoast, Clearford, Ironedge, Silvermeadow, Harmon, and Leadvan. Not all countries had a history of peace among them, so it was a gift from Hoseenu that everyone could remain in the same room two days in a row without any sort of name calling, let alone bloodshed.

"Before we sign, I want to reiterate that we are promising each other that our countries will be united together. If anyone decides that they no longer wish to be a part of this treaty, then they can leave now with no fear of reprisal." At this, she gave everyone in the room a chance to speak up. When she saw everyone give some sign of agreement, she looked at Damien, who stood by the door with the rest of the advisors, signalling him to pass over the document that went into more detail of what this alliance would look like.

It had taken months of drawn out meetings and lots of letters back and forth for everyone to be happy with the wording. However, Ravenna was just thankful that they would now rally together in times of crisis and that any disputes one country had with another would not pull in the whole continent.

Taking a pen, she dipped it into the ink pot and signed her name. After everyone had signed, she passed the paper to Liam, who took his paw, dipped it into the ink, and stamped it above the spot reserved for Wilderose.

Once the cheering had subsided, Ravenna rose from her chair. "Now let us feast," she declared, and led the way to the banquet hall.

As soon as Liam was seated next to Ravenna, he transformed back into a man. He decided right there and then to never again take his body for granted.

"It feels great to be back again, doesn't it?" Crown Prince Titus of Faircoast said and slapped Liam on his back.

"Yes, it does." Liam grimaced at the pounding.

"I didn't even last a day. Thankfully, though, my efforts weren't wasted, and I will still get to marry into the Lyrian line," Titus said as he looked over at his soon-to-be wife Irena, who was talking with Clearford's empress.

"You were one of Ravenna's suitors?" Liam asked, despite the fact he didn't really care to engage with the man.

"I was the first." Titus threw back his shoulders and stood up straight. It was as if he took pride in the fact.

Liam thought that it'd be worth boasting more if he was the last. Liam thanked Hoseenu for the small mercy that for now he was human and could hide his emotions better.

"I see you have met my future cousin-in-law," Ravenna said, glancing over at Liam when Titus turned his attention back to his betrothed.

"Yes, I have. He leaves tomorrow?"

She gave a sly smile. "That's the plan, but if you desire his company so much, we could always ask him to stay longer. It would give Irena an opportunity to spend more time with her father since she'll have to return to Faircoast soon to coordinate her wedding."

"No. I'm sure they will want to get back to Faircoast as soon as possible. I hear weddings need a lot of attention."

She snorted at his hasty reply. "It's alright. There will be other visits for you both to reconnect."

This was the true Ravenna, the one he had danced with the night prior. One with a sense of humor and wit instead of merely duty. He found himself wanting to see more of this side of her.

One of the other monarchs had taken her attention

from him, so he decided to replenish his plate at the buffet table. Before he could finish his selection, a feminine voice spoke to him.

"Good evening, Your Highness."

Liam looked up and saw Irena standing beside him. "Good evening." He tried to sound cheerful, but after having to talk with her betrothed, he wasn't sure what to expect.

Her smile widened at his acknowledgement, and Liam couldn't help but notice her beauty. Her long blonde hair sat delicately around her shoulders and her wide blue eyes seemed to sparkle.

"How are you doing with everything going on? You must be exhausted," Irena purred as she put her hand on his upper arm. Liam tried not to pull back, but instead made his best effort to keep his composure at her forwardness.

"I'm doing quite well. Thank you for your concern." He paused, but continued after a moment, "And yourself?"

"I'm just so worried for my dear cousin," she said as she ran her hand down his arm. He shuddered.

"Is there something wrong with Her Majesty?"

"You're the twenty-sixth suitor. Before you came along, there was talk that she was going to give up breaking the curse. This could possibly break her spirit." Irena peered up at him through her long lashes.

"I assure you that your cousin is in good hands. I have decided to be her last suitor."

A flicker of disappointment flashed on Irena's face, but it was replaced with a smile before Liam could be sure that he had even seen it.

"Well then, that's wonderful news."

Irena turned to go back to her seat. Liam watched the future Crown Princess of Faircoast saunter away for a moment before walking back to his own spot next to Ravenna.

As soon as he sat down he quickly ate his second serving.

When Ravenna noticed that Liam seemed to be done eating, she leaned over and whispered, "Are you ready to leave, or do you need to talk to anyone else?" Liam looked over at her in confusion, but then realized that he had forgotten that this was just temporary. He was going to turn back into a dog. He shook his head, and as soon as she got up, he grabbed her hand and heard the words, "Your Majesty, will you marry me?" come out of his mouth involuntarily.

He noticed that she seemed to become very tired before answering with a simple no. As she walked out of the banquet hall, he found himself a red setter once again and followed her out.

CHAPTER 10

Ravenna woke up early to birds chirping outside of her window. Yesterday had gone better than she could have hoped. No one had made any snide public comments about the curse, and everyone had been willing to sign the treaty. She was looking forward to her day of nothing.

Then she remembered that she had a dog to take care of. She closed her eyes as if she could shut out her new responsibility. She wanted to hide away somewhere...maybe even visit Cress while the seamstress worked on her personal projects during her day off. What was she supposed to do with him all day?

Getting up, she took a moment to sit on the edge of her bed to collect her thoughts. She laughed to herself when she remembered her prayer to Hoseenu about asking for someone in attendance to break the curse. Well, here was someone trying, so she should be a better sport about it. Not for the first time, nor for the last she reckoned, she regretted how foolish she had been when she acted out because of her broken heart.

When she had finished getting ready, she opened the door between her room and Liam's. "Good morning," she said. A growl came from the bed.

She paused. "Do you want breakfast, or no?" Another growl. She sighed, "You need to project your thoughts. I don't understand dog."

Go away. Too early. Too early? It was already an hour after sunrise. She closed the door and walked out to the dining room to get breakfast alone.

"Good morning, Ravenna. Where is your prince?" Tatiana greeted from the table.

"He said it was too early."

Tatiana burst out laughing. "So that explains his sour mood yesterday!"

Ravenna stared at her in disbelief. "I would have thought it was because he was turned into a dog," she muttered.

"I'm sure that's part of it, but he seemed in better spirits after he had time to wake up," Tatiana said with a final chuckle. "How are you this morning?" Tatiana looked at Ravenna, who seemed to be more relaxed than she had been in the months leading up to the ball.

"I would have said great, but I still have a furry situation to figure out." Before Tatiana could comment, Ravenna quickly added, "But enough about him, how are you doing?"

Tatiana raised an eyebrow at her diversion, but let it slide. "I'm always happy when winter comes to an end and I can spend time among the flowers in the gardens." Ravenna cringed. She had walked right into another uncomfortable subject.

"That's nice for you," Ravenna muttered as she tried to muster up some sort of enthusiasm for her former favorite part of the castle.

"You know, enough time has passed. It's not healthy for you to keep avoiding it. Plus, you have lost your beautiful glow and are as pale as a ghost. You need to be outside!"

Here we go again. Ravenna knew Tatiana was right. She recognized that it was interfering with her life, but she wasn't ready to face the flower gardens quite yet. They still held too many painful memories of *him*.

"I get outside! I go to the forest whenever I have time and the weather is good." Which was true; it was just that those conditions were met infrequently.

"Then you should take Liam with you today." And just like that, Tatiana had rounded back to the other topic Ravenna was trying to avoid.

"Fine. You win. After I eat, I'll go check on him and see if he actually wants to spend time with the person who ruined his life."

Tatiana put her fork down. "Ravenna, you are being too hard on yourself."

"Am I though? He was human before he met me! He would be going back home if he hadn't *somehow* gotten it into his head that he should be the one to break the curse." She focused her narrowed eyes pointedly on Tatiana when she said this. "How is he supposed to love me if this is just some sort of obligation that he's been asked to fulfill?"

Tatiana leaned over to put her hand on Ravenna's. "Ravenna, part of true love is the commitment to keep loving the person that you have chosen to love. It's like nothing you have experienced before, and it will be worth it. I promise."

Ravenna sighed. "I've never asked you before, even though I should have a long time ago, but have you ever been in love?"

Tatiana smiled sadly. "Yes, I have, and it was worth every bit of hardship and pain that came with it. But it was a long time ago and is not important right now."

Before Ravenna could press Tatiana for more, the door opened and one of the castle girls came in with Liam following her.

"Here you go! I found the queen. Don't forget that you promised to play with us later." She looked sternly at the red-furred dog.

"Woof! Woof!" Liam replied, wagging his tail enthusiastically and spinning around in circles. The little girl, Cori, if Ravenna remembered correctly, laughed with joy.

"See you later, Liam! Bye, Tatiana! Bye, Your Majesty!"

"Goodbye, Cori," Tatiana called out while Liam barked his own goodbye. Ravenna barely managed a wave, and as soon as Cori left the room, she turned to the dog prince.

"What was that?"

Cori heard me trying to get out of my room and offered to help me find you. In return for an afternoon of knights and dragons, of course.

Ravenna winced at the thought of Liam being locked in his rooms.

"I'm sorry. I should have had someone make it so you can open the doors on your own. This really should have been done a long time ago." The other twenty-five other suitors hadn't stuck around long enough to make it seem worthwhile to change the door handles, but if Liam was really as stubborn as he seemed about breaking the curse, perhaps it would be a good investment.

It worked out this morning, but it would be nice to be able to use a door without assistance. He started eating hastily from the bowl that a servant had placed in front of him.

"How do you know Cori?"

I ran into her and several of the other castle children my first day here. They know every inch of this castle! He sounded so impressed, and Ravenna remembered what he had said about his penchant for exploring.

She quickly glanced over at Tatiana and then looked back at Liam, who was still wolfing down his food. "I was wondering if you wanted to go out into the forest with me today."

Liam stopped eating and looked up at her. *Other than knights and dragons, my time is all yours.*

Ravenna released a breath that she hadn't even realized she had been holding. "We can go after you finish eating."

When Liam was done, they both got up to go.

"Have fun, you two!" Tatiana called out. Ravenna rolled her eyes in response, and Liam let out another bark. Ravenna was still not sure what to talk to him about. She still didn't want to tell him anything personal about herself, but they couldn't walk for hours and say nothing.

Liam interrupted her thoughts with a question. *Do we need to tell your guards that we're going out?*

"I don't have personal guards. All parts of the castle's entrances and exits are guarded. This part of the forest is actually on walled-in castle grounds, and soldiers patrol all of the walls. If we were to go through any of the wall gates, then some of them would come with us." When he didn't answer right away, she looked over at him.

"Is something wrong?"

That doesn't seem like enough security for a queen. He added a growl to emphasize his point.

"I got tired of people following me around in my own home." She was confused why he was so worked up over the matter.

Maybe it's different in Lyra, but Wilderose is surrounded by raiders, and anyone who even looks like they might be wealthy is a target. It has been my job for the last couple of years to try to solve the problem, but until then, Sophia always has a personal guard to keep her safe. Including in her own home.

Raiders from Wilderose had killed her parents. She had assumed that the raiders lived in just that one mountain pass at the border of the two countries, not throughout the whole country.

"I thought that they were contained."

They were for a bit, but they started to become a real concern around a year ago. Another growl showed his frustration.

Ravenna realized that this prince wasn't as frivolous as she had originally thought. He was serious when it came to solving problems.

"Is there anything that can be done while you're in Lyra?"

It was my hope to draw your attention to it, Your Majesty. However, my sister has someone else looking into it for the time being.

All of a sudden, before she could tell him yet again to call her by her name, he stiffened. His head and ears perked up as if he had heard something. She looked around, confused. There wasn't anything there that she could see. He dashed off quickly into the bushes.

"Liam! Where did you go?" Ravenna pleaded. After she shouted for him a couple more times, he came back out of the underbrush, panting and wagging his tail.

"Why on earth did you run off like that?" she demanded. He became somber and looked up at her.

I don't know. There was a scent, some sort of animal or something, and I had to discover where it came from. I couldn't control my actions.

He sounded frustrated that he had done something that a human wouldn't do, so she let the matter drop. Instead, she offered him a chance to become human again.

"You can always go back to Wilderose, you know. You don't have to stay like this. You can find out who is behind the raiders and stop them." She turned her head away to hide the fact that she was afraid he would actually give up. It had only been two days. Why should she feel so upset?

Liam looked down at his paws and sighed, *No, I believe that this is just as important as stopping the raiders.*

Ravenna didn't know how to respond, so she just petted the top of his head to acknowledge that she had heard him and then continued walking. Liam followed closely behind.

CHAPTER 11

After returning from their walk, Ravenna went to her room to have some time to herself. She wasn't sure if she was happy that Liam was still going to try to break the curse or upset that her hopes just kept getting higher and higher. The more she hoped, the more it would hurt when those hopes inevitably fell.

"Hoseenu, you have answered my prayer to have someone from the ball try to break the curse. But I am scared of the pain this will cause. My ability to trust is very small."

A knock interrupted her, and when she called, "Come in," Cress walked through her door. Her friend took one look at the queen and, plopping herself onto Ravenna's bed, called out to a servant in the hall to bring them a tray of tea and some lunch.

"Want to tell me what's got you mumbling to Hoseenu while you pace back and forth?"

"What makes you think I was doing that?" Ravenna gave a wry smile.

Cress snorted, "I've known you for years, and that's what you do when you're working out a problem." Ravenna lifted an eyebrow. "And I could hear you on the other side of the door," Cress admitted.

"Were you pressing your ear up to the door or something?"

"Maybe," Cress offered reluctantly, but then she sharply added, "Stop trying to change the subject! Otherwise I won't let you have any of the treats that I'm sure Cook will add to the tea tray." Cress tried to make herself look firm and menacing but failed when she couldn't hide her smile.

Ravenna laughed, "You are the only one in the country able to threaten the queen and get away with it. I don't know why I put up with your attempts to keep me from my own food."

Cress broke out into a grin. "Because you love me, and you know it. Also, I am going to become a famous dressmaker, and the nation wouldn't be too pleased if I were exiled to another country. My dresses would be labeled as a foreign good, and it would make them more expensive. You would have to deal with the anarchy that would result from forcing them to pay such high prices for their favorite designs!"

Ravenna's smile faded away, and she started pacing once again. "I already have anarchy."

Cress frowned. "What do you mean?"

Ravenna sighed, but before she could explain, a servant came in with the tray of tea and sandwiches.

When the servant left after pouring the tea, Cress looked expectantly at Ravenna. After adding a little cream and then taking a sip of some calming tea, Ravenna continued,

"Remember a couple of months ago when Lord Rook got shot in the leg with a crossbow?"

"Yes, but it was an accident," Cress frowned in confusion.

"That's what I had originally thought as well, but he's not the only one to have something like this befall him. Remember? Lady Winter's saddle slid off her horse while she was riding. After several more of these accidents, I decided to investigate." She took another sip of tea.

"And?" Cress asked impatiently.

Ravenna smiled to herself, knowing how much suspense drove Cress crazy. Creating that anticipation every so often was one of her little pleasures in life.

"And I found out that in every situation, there is strong evidence that the accidents were a result of sabotage."

Cress inhaled sharply. "You really do have treason on your hands; but why is it happening?"

"I don't know, but the only common theme is that the nobles being attacked are the ones who have the most claim to the throne if something happens to me before I produce an heir."

"So if, Hoseenu forbid, you died, someone would already have an advantage in a possible civil war for the throne?"

Ravenna set down her tea and began to pace some more. "Perhaps, but whoever is doing the actual sabotaging has to be extremely incompetent."

"What do you mean?"

"No one has actually died. Lord Wentworth did break his leg when it fell into a hole in the cabin of his ship, but there's no reason to suggest that he would have died from it. Lady Elliot accidentally ate an apple that was cooked into her food. Even though everyone knows that she is allergic and it gives her a rash, it's not a serious enough allergy to kill her. The other cases are similar. It's like someone knows enough about each person to know their habits and weaknesses, but it's only enough to cause them pain."

Cress continued to watch Ravenna pace back and forth as she hopefully asked, "Maybe it doesn't have anything to do with the throne?"

"I thought it could be so, but so far, all eight people are directly in line. There are several other nobles that have ancestors that were rewarded with nobility or have bought titles themselves, and none of them have become targets. I need more clues."

"You know..."

Ravenna could already tell that she wasn't going to like what Cress was going to say next. "You do have a new dog running around who could sniff them out for you." Ravenna definitely didn't like what she had heard.

"No. The Prince of Wilderose has his own problems to deal with. Not including the one involving being turned into a dog. Besides, I can't let a foreign prince know that there is some sort of tension going on inside the Lyrian court. It could possibly lead to a weakness being exploited."

"Alright, if you say so...but aren't you supposed to fall in love with him? Doesn't that mean being vulnerable with him?" Cress said in annoyance.

Ravenna thought about how Liam had admitted to her earlier that day that Wilderose was suffering with raiders.

She pushed it out of her mind and said, "Yes, but it hasn't even been a week yet. He could find out, decide that it's too much, and then leave." She was mad with herself when her voice cracked as she said "leave." She didn't care if he left. She had been taking care of herself well enough without her own king. It didn't matter if there were times when she wished that she could be vulnerable without worrying that her vulnerability would be used against her.

Cress could tell there wasn't anything she could say to change the queen's mind. "You don't have to tell him now, but if the accidents continue and he's still around, then you should let him know. He's also being tested to see if he'll make a good king for Lyra, and he'll need to know at some point," she couldn't help but add.

Ravenna finally sat down again in defeat. "You're right. If he is still a dog in a couple of weeks, I'll tell him what's going on. But you have to admit it is too soon right now." She arched her eyebrow at her friend, daring her to contradict her.

Cress laughed then said, "I'll admit that maybe I was a little too eager to get you to open up to your new suitor. I'll back off now."

"Good."

Cress got a wicked gleam in her eye. "But first, you have to tell me what he's like! I've only seen him during the ball. I thought he looked pretty attractive. What do you think?"

"Cress!" Ravenna's face flushed as she turned bright red.

"Admit it! You do think he's good-looking!" Cress tossed one of Ravenna's pillows at her.

Throwing it right back, Ravenna said, "Fine, you win. He is handsome."

"I knew it!" Cress crowed, as Ravenna laughed at her friend's enthusiasm.

After they had caught each other up on the rest of their lives, Cress looked down at her near-empty teacup and said, "I should get back to work. Have fun with your dog prince!"

Cress took a last sip of tea, got up, and left Ravenna's room. Ravenna shook her head at her friend's playful humor, but at the same time, she was thankful that her mood was always lifted after a visit from the famous dressmaker.

CHAPTER 12

Liam found Cori and the other children playing in the hallway near the kitchen.

"Doggy!" James had spotted him first and rushed over to him. He started petting the top of Liam's head. "Good doggy," he whispered. Liam sat down and calmly wagged his tail to stay in the five-year-old boy's good graces. It wasn't long before the rest of the children saw the dog and rushed over to pet him. Some of the children he gave big sloppy dog kisses, and he barked happily when they shrieked in response.

"Now that our dragon is here, let's go play!" Cori, the constant leader of the ragtag bunch, declared. The rest shouted in agreement, and Liam barked his own enthusiasm at getting to play again with the children.

While they were playing, he didn't notice Tatiana strolling down the hallway to the kitchen. When the children decided that it was time for a snack break, he was surprised by an extreme case of déjà vu when he saw the fairy with another cup of tea, sitting in the same spot as the day he had met her.

"Hello, Cook. Hello, Tatiana." Cori shouted as the group walked into the kitchen.

"Hello. Did you have fun today?" Tatiana asked. They all gave various declarations of affirmation and automatically headed to the where Cook kept the cookies. Liam wasn't sure if he should follow them or not. He knew dogs weren't allowed in kitchens, but he wasn't *just* a dog. He was still a prince.

Cook looked over at him and sighed in resignation. "Come on in, Your Highness. It would be bad form to ban the future king from his own future kitchens."

Liam bowed his head in respect.

"But I don't tolerate messes, so if I catch you trackin' in fur or mud, you'll be out before you can even sniff that dog nose of yours. Prince or no prince, you'll be treated like all the humans around here." With a satisfactory nod to herself after saying her piece, she walked toward the children to dole out their afternoon snack.

"No one is allowed to create a mess in her domain. She is queen here," Tatiana told him as she pointed to a bowl filled with water as if he had been expected to come in eventually. Gratefully, he lapped up the water. He hadn't realized how thirsty he was. That's when it finally sunk in what Cook said about him being the future king, and he started choking.

The children paused to look at the dog coughing, not really sure how to help him, until he finally stopped. He felt some embarrassment at looking even more undignified than he already felt as a dog, but it couldn't be helped.

"So, Your Highness, did you have a nice walk with

Ravenna?" Tatiana continued talking as if he hadn't just made a scene.

He hadn't really taken the time to think about his morning spent with the queen. He had been so caught up by the thought of his limited impulse control as a dog that he hadn't considered much else before finding the children. As he thought back now, he remembered how that lack of control over his new instincts also meant he was more tuned in to the feelings of those around him. He had helped calm Ravenna when she felt guilt over his situation, and he had been calm around James when the boy greeted him. It wasn't a bad consolation prize, all things considered.

Tatiana cleared her throat to get his attention. He didn't know how to respond so he just nodded his head. His thoughts drifted back to Ravenna, and he considered the fact that she wasn't comfortable around him. That much was obvious. When it wasn't just the two of them, he could see that she was intelligent and was more aware about her country and its neighbors than some of the other leaders he had met. True, she hadn't known the full extent of the situation in Wilderose. But he had diligently been trying to cover up the problem from the other nations because he had been suspicious that one of his neighbors was behind it.

She was someone who didn't demand respect, but she had definitely earned it by standing firm in her beliefs and being gracious to all. He just couldn't figure out why it gave her so much tension that he had activated the curse. He wished he had paid better attention to the details of the curse, but even then, there weren't many that Lyra had willingly shared. The curse had started nearly two years ago, and by the time he took command of Wilderose's military and defense, all of the truth had been diluted with gossip. He planned to ask her about it during dinner tonight.

Tatiana had turned back to Cook, who was predicting snow that night. Liam laid down in front of the fire to listen and watch how the two of them interacted.

"I tell you, Miss Tatiana, there'll be snow."

"But there wasn't a cloud in sight this morning."

"Aye, but when the weather turns toward snow, I can feel it in my left knee. If it were just my right knee, then I know it'd just be a drop of rain. But the left knee. That means snow. Has meant snow since I broke it trippin' over a fire log thirty years ago," Cook grunted while she kneaded some dough.

"Then you're probably right. You haven't been wrong yet, so I'll tell the rest of the castle staff and the groundskeeper to prepare." Tatiana finished her cup and took it over to the rest of the dirty dishes.

"Thank you again for the cup of tea and your company, Cook. I'm sure I'll stop by in the next few days."

"Always a pleasure havin' you around, Miss Tatiana. The scallywags always seem better behaved when you're here."

Turning toward Liam, Tatiana asked, "Your Highness, would you care to join me as I talk with the rest of the staff?"

He got up and followed her out of the kitchen.

As they walked, Tatiana explained, "Eventually, you should know all of the important people in the castle. I have always held the role of something like a housekeeper and advisor to the current king and queen. If they are busy or in need of rest, it falls on me to make sure that Lord Chamberlain knows what is expected of the castle and the grounds. Otherwise, I'm involved with domestic and foreign affairs to help best serve the king and queen. We'll just let Lord Chamberlain know about the incoming snow. Cook was right in that it's going to be a late winter storm."

Liam followed after her, wondering how long she had held this unofficial position. He knew that as far back as all documentation on Lyra went, Tatiana had been mentioned either directly or in passing.

They arrived at an open office door. A small man sat behind a large desk with stacks of books and papers on it. He hadn't noticed the two of them standing in the doorway until Tatiana knocked on the open door. Looking up, the man squinted at them and quickly rummaged around his desk, looking for something.

"Your glasses are on your head, Lord Chamberlain," Tatiana pointed out. Reaching up to pat his head, Lord Chamberlin found his glasses and put them on.

"Thank you, Tatiana. I never seem to put them in the same spot." He regarded the fairy and the dog scrupulously. "Hello, Your Highness. It seems that you are the favored suitor if Tatiana has brought you here." Liam still didn't know how to respond to people casually talking to a dog that couldn't talk back, so he kept up his habit of nodding his head as an answer.

"What sort of emergency brings you here?" the Lord Chamberlain asked Tatiana.

"Why, Lord Chamberlain, whatever makes you think we didn't want to enjoy your lovely company?"

"Because you never *just* visit me unless you want to add more work to my plate. So, my dear lady, out with it."

Tatiana seemed more amused than offended by his behavior. "There's going to be a big winter snow storm tonight. You should probably let everyone know."

"Couldn't you have told me this yesterday?" Lord Chamberlain groaned. "The groundskeeper has already started getting everything ready for spring, and the maids have just begun airing out the spring linens."

"Weather isn't that easy to predict. I'm just a fairy, not Hoseenu. Besides, I needed to know what Cook's left knee had to say on the matter."

Liam was impressed with her casual tone. He was beginning to think that maybe more countries should follow Lyra's example of being less formal with each other.

"You needed to…?" Lord Chamberlain slowly started to ask, but then shook his head and said, "Nevermind. I only wish Hoseenu would give you a little bit more of a warning."

"I'll let him know that you asked," Tatiana replied. "Well, it's almost time for dinner, and we don't want His Highness to be late."

"No, we most certainly do not," Lord Chamberlain mumbled distractedly to himself. He had already started creating a list of what needed to be done before the snow fell.

"I'll let you head inside the dining room. It will only be you and Ravenna unless there's some sort of official event. She should be in shortly. Goodbye, Your Highness." And with that, the fairy left Liam in front of the door. With no way for him to enter on his own, he lay down in front of the door and waited for the queen to arrive.

CHAPTER 13

If I weren't the queen, I could run down these halls and no one would judge me for it! Ravenna thought to herself. She was late to dinner, and all she could do was walk at a brisk pace with her head held high as if she didn't have a care in the world. In reality, she was running behind because she kept mulling over the suspicious accidents. Her room currently looked like a windstorm had blown through it with all of the reports of the different incidents and her notes on them scattered about. It wasn't until Tatiana had knocked on her door and said Liam was waiting for her that she even remembered that this was going to be their first time alone together with him as a human.

When she turned the corner, she saw the dog prince lying asleep in front of the dining room door. She was trying to decide on how to best wake him up when he jumped up suddenly as soon as she got close to him.

Good evening, Your Majesty. He bowed his head to her.

"You can use my name."

Liam walked into the room as if he hadn't heard her. His continued refusal to use her name was causing a nagging feeling like she had forgotten something. As she followed him to the table, she made a mental note to herself to take some time later to refresh her memory about Wilderosian customs.

Like the previous night, the dog turned into a human as soon as he sat down. Ravenna heard him breathe a sigh of relief at his transformation as she sat next to him at the small dining table. Before they had a chance to speak, a few servants came in and placed trays of food in front of them.

As soon as they left, Ravenna saw that Liam looked like he was going to say something, so she quickly jumped in, "How was knights and dragons?"

He was startled by her abrupt question and took a second to answer. "These knights are very good at slaying the dragons. They haven't lost to a single one yet," he chuckled.

She smiled at the image of the castle children climbing all over him.

"What did you end up doing afterward?" she asked before taking a bite of the chicken on her plate.

"Tatiana had me meet Lord Chamberlain. Apparently it's going to snow tonight."

Ravenna took a look out her window and saw that clouds had covered up the clear skies from earlier that day. She couldn't help but feel a little excited. Lord Chamberlain and most people who worked on the castle grounds hated the white stuff, but she loved it. Everything looked so fresh and new afterward. It was breathtaking.

"I take it you're a fan," Liam smiled at her.

"Hmm?"

"You started to get this huge grin on your face as soon as you heard the word 'snow,'" he pointed out.

"Is there something wrong with that?" she asked, a little too defensively.

"Nothing. It's quite beautiful, and it's nice to see a fellow kindred spirit. Not too many adults find enjoyment in something they deem extra work." His eyes twinkled.

"Then, if you like, after service tomorrow, we can go outside and enjoy it for ourselves," she shyly offered.

"That sounds like a marvelous idea, Your Majesty!" He smiled.

Ravenna frowned when he again didn't say her name. "Why don't you call me by my name?"

He seemed to not have heard her. He took a sip of water and said instead, "Tell me how the curse came to be."

"It's a long story that I would rather not get into right now," was the politest answer she could come up with.

"Then I'm afraid I can't answer your question just yet either." He smiled with a wink after taking another sip of water.

They ate in silence after reaching a stalemate on conversation topics. Again Ravenna finished eating first and waited for Liam to finish.

"Your rooms and the common areas should now be modified so you can enter and leave without hands," she said as soon as he was done eating.

"Thank you."

She noticed that his green eyes filled with resignation at the thought of being turned into a dog again. Guilt reared its ugly head. She couldn't say she had enjoyed their awkward dinner, and she wanted to leave as soon as possible, but this was the only time he had to be human.

"What are your thoughts on chess?" she blurted out.

Liam looked at her quizzically. "It's alright." His eyebrows furrowed as he tilted his head.

He seemed confused by her change of topics, so she hurried to explain, "We could play tomorrow, if you would like, or a game of Tables during dinner. Unless you want to play another game, or maybe you don't like games. That's fine if you don't." She could hear the slight panic in her voice as she started babbling.

When her parents first had her start attending meetings with them as the future queen, they had worked hard to find a balance between either being completely silent or constantly talking when she was nervous. For a while, there had been no middle ground. She was better at controlling her tongue now, but sometimes it didn't want to be controlled. Like in this moment of trying to find a way to make dinners more pleasant for Liam...

He chuckled and held up his hands. "Slow down, Your Majesty. I enjoy playing games. Let's start with a game of chess tomorrow."

"Great! I'll bring a set."

Ravenna got up to go when Liam grabbed her hand like he had the night before.

"Will you marry me?" The words were forced and fell flat. They both knew her answer already. It was just a part of the curse that made him ask.

"No, but I will see you tomorrow at service."

She started to leave the room, and she heard Liam sigh as he found himself no longer human before he followed Ravenna out.

CHAPTER 14

The next morning after service, Ravenna and Liam walked side by side away from the castle's chapel, which was a small building with an entrance from the castle courtyard. Ravenna loved service days, especially the quiet meditations about the works of Hoseenu. Sometimes it was the only peaceful part of her week - not many people usually went to service. Tatiana, Cook, Cress, and a few of the other castle residents were regular attendees alongside her, but it was rare to ever see more than them.

Once she had asked her parents why Uncle Damien and Irena didn't come with them. Her parents had looked at each other before her father answered and explained that Uncle Damien used to, but after Aunt Isabella died, he was too angry at Hoseenu to go to His services.

Ravenna didn't remember her aunt since she was only a baby when Isabella had died, shortly after Irena was born.

She had felt sad for her uncle and cousin who still showed how much they missed their wife and mother by the fact that they couldn't continue going to a place that reminded them about Hoseenu, who could have made Isabella live. Now, as she still mourned the loss of her parents a year later, she could empathize with her uncle and cousin.

I have never been in a small chapel before. The one that the Wilderosian royal family goes to is almost as big as the palace, but it loses the feeling of intimacy that Lyra's has. Liam noted.

"There's a bigger one near the marketplace outside of the castle. The size varies from the city to the county. However, I do agree with you that I prefer the intimacy of smaller chapels. It's less distracting for me to meditate, and it truly feels like being with family," Ravenna said.

The snow was still falling from last night. Servants had cleared out the courtyard so people could easily walk around, but as soon as Ravenna and Liam got to the edge of the forest, the snow became deep enough that it covered half of his legs. Liam started jumping through the snow to be able to get through it. When he heard Ravenna laughing at his antics, his tail started to wag, and he began to exaggerate his movements to delight her even more.

When they managed to trudge through the snow a little ways away from the castle, Ravenna fell onto her back. Liam immediately went over to her to make sure she was alright, but stopped and tilted his head when he saw her move her legs and arms from side to side.

She laughed at his confused look. "I'm making a snow

angel!" She got up to show him the impression of a woman with wings left in the snow.

Liam flopped onto his back and wiggled in the snow, but because he was a dog, his four legs stuck up in the air. When he got up, all that was left in the snow was the impression of a circle. Ravenna continued to laugh, and Liam realized he was starting to become addicted to the sound of her feeling carefree and relaxed.

"We should make a snowman!" Ravenna cried out. Liam looked around at the snow. He wasn't sure if it was snowman snow. It seemed too powdery, and powdery snow wouldn't stick together. However, he soon felt a snowball hit him on his shoulder, proving his theory wrong. He shot a look at the Queen of Lyra, who was innocently whistling and looking away from him. What had changed in her overnight? She had been standoffish until she suggested that they play games during dinner. Now she was throwing snowballs at him and acting like a child during her first snowfall. He decided to not question it and just let himself enjoy her having fun.

That's not fair! I can't get you back! He regretted reminding her about the curse as soon as he spoke. Her face fell, and she looked as if she was about to apologize, so he immediately ran over to her, scraped some snow up with his tail, and flung it toward her. The snow burst in her face. She dropped her mouth in surprise.

Got you! he cried and ran away as soon as he saw her bend down to scoop up another snowball.

"I'm going to get you for that!" she called out after him.

Only if you can catch me! He could hear her squealing in delight during their snow fight. After a while, he noticed her starting to shiver despite her many layers.

Come on, let's go inside and get warm.

"But we didn't build a snowman!" He couldn't believe it. The Queen of Lyra was pouting. Was she flirting? He could feel himself smiling as much as a dog could.

I'm sure the snow will be better to make a snowman later, and right now you're freezing! He leaned up against her leg and he could feel how cold she was.

She smiled. "You're right. It's been a while since someone has agreed to come out with me into the snow. Cress hates being even remotely cold. I guess I wanted to try to get it all done in one go."

They trudged their way through the forest and back to the castle. As soon as they got inside, they went to the kitchens. Cook was again making something that smelled delicious while Tatiana sat at her usual seat at the counter drinking her tea with a plate of cookies in front of her.

"You both look like you had fun out there," she said to the two of them, who each wore grins on their faces.

"And you're wet!" Cook exclaimed as she saw the puddles forming from the water dripping off of them. "You, dog! Go lay by the fire. And you, girl! Out of those wet things this instant! Can't have Her Majesty catchin' a cold, now can we?" she hollered.

Liam quickly obeyed the queen of the kitchen and started to dry off by the fire. Ravenna was no different. She knew who ruled this part of the castle, so she took off her coat, mittens, gloves, boots, and wool overdress to hang in front of the fire. She was left in only her shift. Cook handed her a cup of tea and pointed to the stool by the fire for her to sit on while she warmed up. She could hear Cook muttering to Tatiana something about them being worse than the children.

Where are Cori and the others?

Ravenna glanced over at Liam whose head had popped up.

"Service days are for families to spend together, so I imagine Cori and the rest of the children are with their parents and siblings. They're probably playing outside too," she answered.

"They haven't gone outside yet. I heard Cori askin' around for her dog friend to play in the snow," Cook told them while she stirred a pot of soup. "I said that he was off with the queen and would be up for playin' later. If that be alright with you, sir." Liam wagged his tail in response.

He looked over at Ravenna. *Would you want to join? We could build that snowman of yours too.*

Ravenna nodded. "After we have something to eat. We forgot about lunch." Cook, always on top of things, was bringing them bowls of soup.

"Now, don't you be burnin' your tongues. Wait for it to cool off first," Cook said and then went back to the counter to begin the next round of food preparations.

As soon as they had finished eating and could feel all of their limbs again, the two went right back outside to find the children and to build a snowman. It wasn't hard to find Cori and her group of family and friends. They could hear squeals of delight coming from the other side of the castle wall. Going through the castle's open gates, they saw the children sledding down the hill leading from the castle to the village marketplace. When Cori spotted the queen and the dog, she called over to them to join in on the fun.

"You gotta try this!" she cried out right before she went down the hill on a wooden sled.

Liam looked over at Ravenna. *Shall we join them, Your Majesty?*

Ravenna's face lit up at the prospect of sliding down the snow.

"I haven't gone sledding in years!" she exclaimed as she raced toward the line of children waiting their turn for the sleds. Liam followed closely behind.

When it was their turn, Ravenna offered for Liam to sit in front of her on the sled since he didn't have a way to hold on to her otherwise. After he jumped on, she sat down and scooted toward the edge of the hill. The next moment they were soaring down the slope. Ravenna shrieked in exhilaration. Liam tried to hide the fear that had crept up; since he didn't have any hands to hold on to the sled, he felt like he could easily fall off. However, when they reached the bottom, he got off with his tail wagging and jumped around in a circle when Ravenna asked if he wanted to go again.

They took several more turns going down the hill. Each of the children demanded to be partnered up with one or the other of them. On their last run together, the sled veered off the track and headed toward some trees. Ravenna tried to steer them away, but she wasn't able to control the sled. Moments before hitting a tree, Liam turned around, caught Ravenna's coat in his mouth, and jumped off the sled, pulling Ravenna with him. Right as they hurled off the sled, it crashed into the tree and splintered.

Are you all right? Ravenna could hear the desperation in Liam's voice.

"Just a little shaken up. What about you?"

I'm okay, but maybe we should call it a day?

Ravenna spotted the broken sled.

"Yeah, we should, but we need to give them a new sled.

It's supposed to snow some more tonight, and I'm sure that they'll want to do this again tomorrow," she said, right before a guard ran down the hill to check in on them. The children could be seen at the top of the hill looking down at where they were lying in the snow.

"Your Majesty! Your Highness! Are you hurt?" the guard shouted as he headed toward them.

"No, we're alright. We can't say the same for the sled though," Ravenna called up as she got off the snow-covered ground. Instead of walking toward the guard, she first went to get the sled. Liam walked beside her to make sure she could walk properly and wasn't hiding any sort of injury.

When they got to the top of the hill, Ravenna apologized for breaking the sled.

"I'll make sure you get a new sled while this one is being fixed." The children hugged her tightly. James started crying, so Liam pressed himself against him as Ravenna watched on.

"What's wrong?"

"He was just scared that you and Liam were hurt even though I told him that queens don't get hurt when they have princes to save them," Cori said.

Ravenna gave a rueful smile. "I'm sorry to have scared you, James, but I'm okay. You don't need to be scared anymore. But Cori, I need to tell you something." The young girl leaned closer to her. "Just because I am a queen doesn't mean I can't get hurt. I still have to be careful. Just like you have to be careful. There won't always be a prince to save the queen."

"Oh, but who is supposed to keep the queen safe then?" Cori asked.

"Herself, mostly," Ravenna answered with a sigh. After

a pause she added, "And brave people like you." Ravenna tickled Cori's stomach until the girl began giggling uncontrollably.

"Now, let's get inside. It's time for dinner," Ravenna said and led the little group back toward the castle.

CHAPTER 15

Ravenna and Liam sat at the dinner table, all of their attention on a game of chess. Ravenna still had most of her pieces, and Liam was down to his king, queen, and one rook. Liam looked up from the gameboard to see Ravenna frowning in concentration as she twisted her dark hair up into a bun and held it with her hands.

"What did you mean when you told Cori that queens don't always have princes to save them?" Ravenna looked up in surprise, not expecting Liam to disturb her while she was planning out her next move.

"I meant just that. The queen has to save herself. She can't always expect a prince to come and save her." She moved a bishop, hoping that Liam would go back to focusing on the game.

"Why not? Shouldn't she expect to receive help when she needs it?"

Ravenna scowled as Liam's rook took a knight. "I never said that a queen couldn't ask for help when she needs it. She should just be able to save herself so she won't end up in a helpless position if no one is around to rescue her." She moved her rook.

"Check," Liam said, as he used his queen to take her rook. "That's fair, but you seem like the kind of person who wouldn't ask for help even if help is available."

She could feel him looking at her, but she refused to meet his gaze and moved her bishop again.

"Check," he said once more, moving his rook to take the bishop.

"No. I'm not the kind of person to ask for help even if it's available." She sighed, "I want to be perceived as strong, and not some damsel in distress." She moved her queen.

"Needing help is not a sign of weakness. Admitting that you can't do everything is actually a sign of strength. It builds trust." Liam moved his king and declared, "Checkmate."

Ravenna stared at the board. She scowled at Liam. Eventually she got up and said, "We have an early start tomorrow, so I'm going to go to bed."

Before she could leave, Liam kneeled in front of her and held her hand. "Will you marry me?" he asked. He looked resigned and exhausted despite his earlier win.

"No." Her answer was tinged with some regret. After a couple days with Liam, she was able to tell that he was a good man, but that still didn't change the fact that they didn't love each other.

She waited for his transformation back into a dog to complete, and they walked out of the room together.

Ravenna sat in her bedroom's window seat. The clouds covered the stars, but the snowfall was beautiful. Ravenna's mood now reflected more of the cloud cover than the picturesque falling snow: she hated how unsettled she felt after the conversation with Liam at dinnertime. She hadn't meant for it to seem like she would tell a young girl that asking for help was a sign of weakness. She just knew how awful being vulnerable was and how easy it was for that vulnerability to be exploited.

It reminded her of *that day* in the marketplace with Cress. They were oblivious to the hustle and bustle around them as Ravenna watched Cress take a closer look at some thread in a stall. Suddenly, Cress screamed as a loose horse galloped straight toward Ravenna. Right before the horse could trample her, a hand grabbed Ravenna's arm, pulling her out of the way and right into the embrace of the arm's owner.

Ravenna had read stories about tall, dark, and handsome men saving princesses, but never before had she experienced it for herself. Until today.

"Are you alright, Your Highness?" the man asked.

"You saved me."

She internally winced at how trite that sounded. Of course he had saved her. She didn't just happen to find herself wrapped in the arms of attractive strangers for no reason.

His smirk made her want to disappear out of embarrassment, but his voice was calming.

"And I'm glad I did. It would be bad form for a soldier to let the crown princess get injured right in front of him." The soldier stepped back with a bow. At his words, she noticed that he was indeed wearing a soldier's uniform.

"Thank you." She tucked a hair behind her ear as she finally said what she should have from the start.

"May I escort you back to the castle, Your Highness?"

"Ravenna! Are you okay?" Cress shouted, running over to the pair.

"Yes. Thanks to him." Ravenna pointed to the soldier who nodded his head to the princess's friend.

"Oh, thank Hoseenu! You were in danger, and I didn't know what to do! There were so many people crowding the street that I couldn't even reach you! Your parents are never going to let you come out with me ever again! I just know it!"

"Cress...Cress!" Ravenna shouted to distract her friend from her ramblings. "They will. They love you! My savior has offered to escort us back to the castle so that nothing else will happen."

Cress frowned in confusion as she observed the man, but then shook her head before saying, "That's a relief!"

The trio walked back to the castle. Cress led the way, but kept glancing back while the soldier and Ravenna fell slightly behind her.

"Your friend obviously cares about you. That's a good sign for the future of the country."

"How so?"

"Well, it must mean that you are kind and worth being loved. A queen like that gains loyalty from her subjects who will prosper under her rule."

Ravenna blushed at the praise. When she looked shyly up at her rescuer, she was surprised to see him gazing fondly down at her. He had the most beautiful blue eyes she had ever seen, a stark contrast to his dark brown hair and scruff. He smiled when he noticed her looking at him. She quickly turned her focus back to the road.

When they reached the castle gate, the young soldier bowed to the two friends.

"Ladies, I will now leave you at your destination."

"Thank you, sir," Cress said and walked through the gate.

"Yes, thank you for everything today." Ravenna felt like it was inadequate, but she didn't know what else to add.

She had started to follow Cress inside when she heard, "Ravenna, wait!" and felt the handsome soldier's hand on hers.

"I was wondering if I could see you again?" he asked, rubbing the back of his head with his free hand.

She smiled brightly. "Yes, you may."

"Great! How about I meet you in the castle gardens tomorrow night? There shouldn't be any runaway horses there," he said with a wink.

"I will be there." Ravenna's voice was breathless. She walked through the gate and her heart started to pound faster than when she thought the horse would trample her. She couldn't wait to tell Cress what had happened.

"I was a fool," Ravenna said to herself, emerging from the memories of the first and last time she had allowed herself to be enamored by a rescuer.

CHAPTER 16

Ravenna woke up earlier than usual. It was even too early for the birds as it was still dark outside. She lay in bed for a little while longer, thinking through her day. She had a few meetings with the court council to talk about new policies; they were supposed to go over funding for Lyra's schools. It was going to be another battle with a few members of her court. Some of them, like her Uncle Damian, wanted to put more funding into their military. Others backed up her idea that for their country to continue to prosper, they needed to invest in their children's education. While it was a good idea to invest in the armed service during times of war, their military was sufficiently funded, even if an unexpected attack were to come. School funding wasn't the only item on today's agenda, but it was currently the biggest one.

Ravenna groaned as she rolled out of bed. While she got dressed, she debated whether to wake Liam now or later. Breakfast wouldn't be ready for another hour, but she hadn't had a chance to fill him in on the day's agenda. After remembering his comment the other day about it being "too early" an hour after sunrise, she decided to give him a little bit longer to sleep. She walked over to her favorite window seat and took in the sight of the landscape below. The snow from the night before had covered all the tracks from yesterday.

She bit her lip, thinking about the previous day's events. She didn't like feeling indebted to Liam for pulling her off the sled before it crashed into the tree. It was too similar to how she had felt when *he* had saved her the day they first met. However, she couldn't deny that she had enjoyed the time spent letting her guard down and playing in the snow with Liam.

"Hoseenu, what am I supposed to do with him?" she prayed. So far, he was the most determined of all the suitors to break the curse. He gave off the impression that he didn't want to be king, which had been the motivating factor for the previous men. However, would that be a reason for him to give up? It seemed like he loved his life back in Wilderose, along with all the responsibilities he had there. Would the burden of becoming king actually cause him to stop trying to break the curse?

When dawn's first light appeared on the horizon, Ravenna decided to give her thoughts about the curse a rest and wake the dog prince up. She knocked on their shared door and opened it when she heard a muffled growl.

Liam was lying in the middle of the king's bed with his eyes firmly closed.

She hesitated. "Good morning."

A huff was all she got in return.

"I need to talk to you about today's schedule." Another growl. Ravenna walked over to the window and pulled back the curtains to let in the morning light. She heard movement behind her and thought it meant that the bright sun was enough to get him out of bed. But when she turned around, she saw the tip of a red-furred tail poking out from under a blanket.

"Come on. We need to get going," she exhaled in frustration and pulled the blanket off of the prince. He didn't even budge. "So this is how it's going to be," she sighed as she briskly walked out of the room only to return with a pitcher of water. "If you do not get up at once, I swear I will pour water on you."

What is it with morning people disturbing everyone's sleep? Liam moaned as he gave up on the idea that she would leave him in peace. She just smiled as he jumped off the bed.

They were the first ones to breakfast. Liam hadn't spoken during their walk and just barely made it without running into anything. Ravenna had had a hard time not outright laughing at him. It wasn't until after he had eaten some of the food placed before him that he seemed a little bit more aware of his surroundings.

"Are you ready to hear about what we have to do today?" she asked him. He nodded his head once and went back to eating. Ravenna set down her tea and informed him that they were expected to attend a meeting with the nobles of the court council to go over the previous week, possible new policies, and any updates for this week's schedule.

"You won't be expected to contribute this week, but eventually the court would like to hear anything that their potential future king might have to say about the topic of discussion." *If he stays that long,* she added to herself. Before

Liam could reply, Tatiana walked in and called out, "Good morning," as she sat at the table.

"Good morning, Tatiana. I'm sorry we can't stay and eat with you, but we should probably start walking to the council room," Ravenna said as she got up from the table. Liam followed suit.

"That's all right. Good luck getting the votes you need!"

Ravenna smiled in acknowledgement and left the room with Liam.

What votes? Liam asked as soon as the door closed.

"The court council is reviewing the new budget that I proposed and will vote to either approve it or have it revised."

Is this normal? Ravenna could hear the confusion in his voice.

"No," she sighed. "The court council only has to vote when a queen and king are split on a matter. Laws, policies, and budgets get passed if both rulers think they should be. If they do not agree, then the court council will vote on the matter."

But there is no king of Lyra.

"No, but if a king or queen is not married, a temporary partner is found for them. Usually a married next of kin."

Why married?

Because Lyra is complicated, Ravenna thought to herself, but she answered, "Lyra's government is jointly ruled by a king and a queen to show the people that both men and women are valued equally. It gives way for equal opportunity of voices to be heard, unlike Ironedge, which is ruled only by men, or Silvermeadow, which is ruled only by women. Due to this philosophy, the king and the queen are encouraged to freely choose their partner out of love instead of choosing because of political gain. If they have not married before their coronation, the council will choose a regent queen or king for them. To make it clear that it is temporary, the regent has to be married, or related to the sovereign, and someone who is well acquainted with how the royal government works. My uncle has filled that role for the last year."

They walked a little farther in silence until Liam spoke up. *It seems that, like most philosophies, it is good in theory, but difficult in practice.* He didn't comment on how he would be expected to rule with her. He continued, *I think that would drive my sister crazy. She appreciates simplicity.*

"How does Wilderose not end up becoming ruled by a tyrant? It seems like an easy way for someone who is corrupt to take complete control." Ravenna had wondered about this since she first learned about the different countries' forms of government.

Thankfully, Sophia is only a tyrant to me, Liam joked as his tail wagged, and he panted happily. *She has a big heart and takes looking after the wellbeing of Wilderose seriously, listening to the needs of the people and her advisors. However, there have been ancestors that have been more selfish and have tried really hard to become tyrants. They don't live too long though.*

"What do you mean?"

There is no official record that the royal family of Wilderose is cursed, but every king or queen that tries to take advantage of their power always ends up dying mysteriously shortly after three abuses of power within a year.

"But what if the abuse comes from misguidance or a lack of knowledge?"

It doesn't seem to affect rulers who fix their mistakes. From what we can tell, there is some sort of warning that comes before death. My father and sister have hinted that there is no way for someone to get away with ignorance, and that Hoseenu always makes it clear one way or another. Before Sophia puts anything into law, she has several advisors go over her proposals to weigh out the benefits. There have been occasions when she listened to one advisor's opinion that seemed like a good idea, but she later revoked it because it was discovered it would do more harm than good.

Before Ravenna could ask any more questions, they arrived at the council hall. She stood up straighter, and with her head held high, she walked into the room. Liam walked in beside her as regally as possible for a dog. The men and women who were already seated around a long oval table stood up and bowed. They did not sit back down again until after Ravenna and Liam took their places at the head of the table.

Ravenna noticed that Damian had yet to arrive. Normally he showed up before her or walked in with her. As soon as the thought crossed her mind, he entered the room.

When the room had settled, she opened the meeting. "As you are now all well aware, during the Alliance Ball, the Second Prince of Wilderose decided to try to break my curse. He will be accompanying me to all of my meetings unless one of you thinks there is a topic that would be best addressed without him present. In such a case, you may request a vote for him to leave the room." Everyone nodded.

"As for today's agenda, we will be following up on how the Alliance Ball and Treaty went, as well as voting on the budget proposal. Then we will go over the usual regional reports. If no one else has anything to add afterward, we will adjourn." Ravenna looked over the room, praying to Hoseenu that it would be a relatively short meeting, ending around lunch time instead of going until afternoon tea.

When no one brought forth any other topics of discussion, she continued, "Other than the announcement of another suitor, the Alliance Ball went smoothly. There were a few tense moments between Clearford and Leadvan, but no one declined to sign the treaty. As to whether or not the countries will honor it, only time will tell."

Ravenna saw some of the council members exchange wary glances. She wasn't the only one who harbored skepticism about some of the other rulers' expected participation when they would eventually be asked to offer assistance to their allies. She just prayed their allegiance wouldn't be tested anytime soon.

"Now, as for this year's budget proposal, since it was designed with my Uncle Damien, the regent king, and we have not yet come to an agreement..." Ravenna trailed off as she tried hard not to scowl. She didn't want to give away how angry she still was over her uncle's refusal to privately negotiate the budget. She finished, "We need to have the council's vote for its approval."

"What were the disagreements again?" Lord Wentworth asked. He was one of the younger lords on the council, and Ravenna had noticed that he was easily distracted. She would have to eventually talk to him about paying closer attention to these meetings.

Before Ravenna could answer, Damien took the question as his cue to speak. "There were cuts to the military's portion of the budget. Now that we have to also take responsibility if any of our allies declare war, we must maintain a strong military!" Some of the council members murmured in agreement.

"We have entered a time of peace. I proposed that it would be better to spend the money on the schools so Lyrian children can have the best education possible. It will help Lyra in the long run to have more people grow up literate and advance different parts of the economy." Ravenna could see her point was also well received based on the few nods around the table.

"What future could they possibly have if we no longer have a military to protect our children? It would be all for naught."

"That is why I have included a contingency plan. If, for some reason, we have only managed to have a short term of peace, the funds that would have gone toward the schools will be redirected back to the military." She again prayed it would never come to that. She had worked so hard to build up relations with the neighboring countries so they would be willing to sign an alliance, but for some reason, her uncle acted as if they were on the brink of war. She made a mental note to find out if he had received any sort of intelligence she wasn't aware of.

When Damien didn't have a rebuttal, the other members of the court council took the time to read through the rest of the budget proposal.

As soon as they finished, Lady Elliot spoke up, "If the rest of my fellow council members are ready, I would like to set into motion the vote. All of those in favor?" More than half of the members raised their hands. When those who opposed raised their hands, Ravenna saw that the most of them were Damien's allies.

"Then it is settled: the queen's budget will be put forth into motion," Lady Elliot declared.

Congratulations, Your Majesty. Ravenna had momentarily forgotten Liam's presence. He had been so quiet. She looked over at him sitting beside her and smiled.

"Thank you," she whispered.

When she glanced at Damien, she could see that he was trying to remain composed, but his face was red, and there was a hardness in his stare. When he saw that she was looking at him, he gave a curt nod, got up, and left the room, slamming the door on his way out.

Everyone stopped talking and stared at the closed door that Damien had just exited through. It was rare for anyone to leave so abruptly during a council meeting. Ravenna cleared her throat and said, "Lord Wentworth, would you like to begin with your region's report?" The young lord looked a little uncomfortable, but he started going over current events in the eastern part of Lyra.

CHAPTER 17

As the meeting droned on, well past lunch, Ravenna noticed, she started to wonder about her uncle's recent behavior. When she first became queen, they agreed on everything. Now it seemed like they needed the council's vote for practically anything. *What had changed?*

Before she could think more on it, she was drawn back to the meeting upon hearing the word "raiders." Lady Athena was going over relations with Wilderose. Her estate was right along the mountain borders, so she dealt with Wilderose the most out of those on the council.

"There have been rumors of raiders causing trouble on the Wilderose side of the border, but it seems that they are more than just rumors." Ravenna glanced over at Liam, whose body tensed at this report.

"No one from Lyra had previously experienced anything during travel to Wilderose for trade, but within the last month, more of our merchant caravans have been raided. Those who have had to regroup in Wilderose's towns have brought back reports that raiders have been attacking the people of Wilderose for years." At this, everyone looked openly over at Liam.

It is true. We have been focusing on trying to get rid of them, but their numbers seem to keep increasing, and we haven't found their leader yet.

Ravenna told the rest of the council what Liam had said.

"I beg your pardon, Your Highness, but why have we not heard of this before now?" one of the lords asked.

You were aware of the raiders. They were the ones responsible for the deaths of the former queen and king of Lyra. Messages have been sent to Lyra's capital with no response. Part of the reason behind my visit was to mention it to the queen.

"You seem to have been distracted from your goal, Your Highness," Lady Athena said firmly after Ravenna had related Liam's words to the group. Ravenna realized that the raiders must have been why the Lady had voted for the military budget allocations over school funding. Was this what her uncle had known about too? Then why hadn't either one of them mentioned the raiders until after the vote?

"We should meet tomorrow to share everything that we know and come up with possible solutions. I don't know about the rest of you, but I would like to not have a working dinner, and we still have a few more reports to go over. Shall we move on?" Ravenna asked. Everyone other than Lady Athena looked relieved as they voiced their agreements. "Very well then. Do you have anything else to add or may we proceed?" Ravenna said, looking over at Lady Athena.

"No, Your Majesty."

And with that, the next Lord proceeded to give his report.

CHAPTER 18

"Are you all right, Your Majesty?" Liam asked, breaking the silence during dinner.

"Hmm?" Ravenna looked up from her plate where she had spent the last several minutes using her fork to push her food around.

"You have barely eaten and haven't said a word," he pointed out.

Ravenna sighed and pushed her plate away as she slumped into her chair. "There's just a lot to think about."

"Would you like a listening ear?" She bit her lip. Cress had told her to ask Liam for help with all of the accidents. Even though the raiders weren't related, it was something that she could talk to him about. However, someone must have been lying to her about how severe the raider problem had become because of the conflicting reports she had been given. It struck her as a possibility that Liam might even be the one deceiving her.

"Why did Wildrose lead Lyra to believe that the raiders were a contained problem after they killed my parents?"

Liam froze when he heard the icy tone in Ravenna's words. After a few moments of silence, he looked down, not meeting her stare. "I initially thought it was a smaller issue than it turned out to be."

"Well, you were wrong."

Liam flinched. "Let me make it up to you now though." He looked directly into Ravenna's eyes. She saw his sincerity in the way he held her gaze.

Ravenna sighed and leaned back into her chair. "Tell me what you know."

Liam nodded. "Raiders pillaging trade routes isn't something new. I was," he paused, rubbing the back of his neck, "put in charge of protecting my subjects as best as I could before Sophia was crowned queen. At first, everything seemed routine. Once every other month, the same group of thugs would attack a trade wagon, or some lone travelers, and then my men would investigate and imprison the ones we could catch."

"Then what happened?" Ravenna prodded.

"Slowly, the amount of attacks increased. Not enough to notice at first, but then it seemed to happen at least once a week. The way they attacked also changed: they became more organized and used military tactics."

Liam paused and took a sip of water. "Before I could go to the border myself to see if I could find something, my father died." He looked down again, and Ravenna thought he must be reliving the grief of his father's passing. Before she could say anything though, he continued, "Life was a blur after that. The funeral. Planning for Sophia's coronation. The investigation became a lower priority. It wasn't until they attacked your parents that it became my main focus again."

"But why didn't you let Lyra know that the problem was no longer contained?"

Liam made eye contact with Ravenna again. "I sent missives, but no one answered. It didn't make any sense, so I came here myself." He sighed. "But then..." He grinned sheepishly. "I made a promise."

Ravenna looked away. "You don't have to keep it, you know."

"Promises aren't meant to be broken. I promised that I would break the curse. Just like I promised to handle the raiders."

"But you haven't," Ravenna whispered. "You haven't taken care of them." She stood up to leave the table.

"Your Majesty, wait." She stopped moving and was startled by the hard look of determination on Liam's face. "I haven't given up on that. I will help you tomorrow in front of the council. You will not look as misinformed as you did today." She winced at the reminder of how caught off-guard she had been.

"Thank you. And my name is Ravenna," she said, too stressed by the council meetings to consider right now why he still insisted on not calling her by her name.

Before she could leave, he reached for her hand to start their after-dinner routine. When she declined his offer of marriage, they headed toward their separate bed chambers. One still a human. The other a dog.

Ravenna waited until she couldn't hear anyone outside of her room. She opened the door as quietly as possible to peek out and make sure that the hallway had indeed cleared. Everything was dark as she silently walked through the castle with only an occasional fireplace's dying embers or a single lit candle to guide her.

Finally, she made it through the kitchen to the adjoining vegetable garden door and stepped through it into the night. The full moon shone enough light for her to make her way into the forest, and she could hear the rustling of small animals in the bushes beside the path. A lone owl called out a warning hoot to let the intruder know that he owned this forest.

Ravenna made it eventually to a stump next to a small pond. She had found the spot a month after her parents' funeral while searching for a place to escape from all of the people who were looking at her to become queen at seventeen. The flower gardens used to be where she would go to hide, but they were no longer an option for her after everything that happened there with *him*.

"Oh, Hoseenu, I don't know if I can trust him," she said, looking up at the night sky. "He could have stopped the raiders before they killed my parents." Her voice started to waver. "If he had, I wouldn't have to worry about finding a king so soon, and I wouldn't have to navigate the court's political games, or stress about raiders attacking my people." The tears that she tried to hold back spilled out, and she started sobbing, folding in on herself.

"Hoseenu, I feel so alone right now, and tired of always being strong in front of people."

Ravenna couldn't remember the last time she had cried without worrying about being overheard. She had been so busy during the past year - from her parents' funeral to her coronation to forming the alliance treaty - that she had not had many opportunities to let her guard down completely.

After she had cried to the point that she had no more tears, she sat back up, closed her eyes, and took a deep breath. A gentle breeze blew through the forest, and for a brief moment, it felt like a hand caressing her face. She got up feeling less burdened than before and headed back toward the castle.

CHAPTER 19

The council met again soon after breakfast the next morning. Liam hoped that the meeting wouldn't go as long as it had the day before. He reflected on his conversation with Ravenna the previous night. It was clear she was upset with him about the lack of information, and to some extent, he could understand why. However, he *had* sent messages to the Lyrian court. For some reason, they hadn't reached her.

He still felt guilty though. He knew that she wouldn't be in the mess she found herself in today if he had gotten the job done a year ago. He hadn't been able to fall asleep the night before, and when he heard her leave her rooms through the connecting door, he followed her into the forest. He wasn't completely sure why he did. Ever since his father had had him train with the military, a sense of duty to protect was thoroughly drilled into him. However, it seemed like more than that now. He owed her. It was only fair that he should be the one to give her back some stability after being semi-responsible for taking it away. And part of that was to make sure that she would be safe. He hadn't been able to bring himself to comfort her when she cried though.

He looked over at Ravenna at the head of the table. She had told the council what he shared with her during dinner and was currently listening to the concerns of the council members about the raiders starting to attack Lyrian subjects.

"Word should be sent to Queen Sophia that we wish to honor our alliance with Wilderose and offer to help on her side of the border in any way we can," Ravenna said.

Murmurs of agreement came from the rest of the nobility in the room.

"But we don't have the budget for it, Your Majesty."

The room instantly fell silent. Damien had been quiet during the whole meeting and chose now to finally speak up. Liam had a hard time not letting a growl escape. He did not appreciate how Damien treated his own queen and niece.

"This would fall under the contingency plan of the budget," Ravenna calmly replied. "As I said yesterday, during times of emergencies, the money would be put back toward the military."

Damien frowned and tipped his head in acknowledgement but added, "Should I continue to be responsible for the military?" He eyed Liam pointedly.

"Yes, you should," Ravenna replied, and she adjourned the meeting.

Do you not trust me? Liam asked when it was finally just the two of them.

Ravenna sighed. "It's not that I don't trust you per se."

But?

"But it hasn't even been a week yet. There's still time for you to change your mind."

I guess the only way for you to see that I am here to stay is by showing you, Liam said with conviction, daring her to contradict him.

"I guess you're right."

CHAPTER 20

A messenger was sent to Wilderose to let Queen Sophia know that Lyra would offer assistance, and a couple of weeks went by. Ravenna also noted that it had now been three weeks since Liam had first entered her life. They had started a routine of meeting at breakfast, attending any meetings and seeing to other official business, and then taking a walk through the forest or in the market. Dinner was the only part of the day she did not thoroughly enjoy. Not because Liam wasn't pleasant company, but because she felt guilty that she couldn't break the curse. She didn't flatter herself to think that Liam loved her in such a short amount of time, and logically she knew that even if she did say yes to his proposal, neither one of them loved each other enough to break the spell. But still, it was hard for her to witness daily how her past actions caused someone as kind as Liam to struggle living life as a dog.

They were currently walking side by side in the forest, each lost in their own thoughts. It wasn't until she reached her private pond that she finally took in her surroundings. When she looked over and saw Liam sitting, she followed suit and sat on her stump. They sat quietly like this for a while.

Why do you avoid the flower gardens?

Ravenna nearly fell off her stump, having forgotten Liam was even there while she thought about their relationship and how it had kept her up most of the night.

"Huh?" she asked as she turned to look at the red dog.

The gardens. You always avoid them, and anytime Tatiana asks you to join her, you're always busy at that moment.

Liam continued to stare out at the pond while Ravenna tried to think of a reasonable answer.

"I love the gardens. I used to spend all of my time there."

But?

She sighed. "But a couple of years ago, it just became too painful to visit." At this, Liam turned and looked at her. He held eye contact with her as if he could find the truth within her eyes. She knew that her answer wasn't very satisfactory, and if she had asked the question, she wouldn't have settled for her own answer. She closed her eyes and turned her head away, not willing to let him learn the full reason quite yet. She knew it was childish to avoid the gardens, and she was ashamed of herself for letting those memories dictate her present.

After a few moments, Liam quietly said, *I'm sorry for intruding on your privacy.*

She blinked and glanced sideways at him, surprised that he wasn't demanding a better answer from her. She nodded her head in acknowledgement. Her stomach twisted with anxiety. How were they supposed to break the curse if she couldn't even tell him what had happened? She made a promise to herself that she'd be more open at dinner.

After sitting together for a little while longer, they got up and walked back to the castle.

Upon arriving at the castle, Ravenna headed to her room, leaving Liam to wander around until dinner. They had entered through the kitchen, and he watched as Ravenna walked up the small servant stairway to avoid running into people. It was midafternoon and he could see Tatiana and Cook chatting over a cup of tea.

When he first moved into Lyra's castle, he quickly realized that he could usually find Tatiana either in the kitchen or in the gardens. He decided that it had been a while since he had visited with the two ladies, so he trotted over to them. He could hear them chuckling over a story about the kitchen's mouser getting covered in flour while chasing after a rodent. Liam had never minded cats before, but ever since he had become a dog, he seemed to now loathe them, so he felt oddly satisfied at hearing the cat had messed up its one job.

They called out a greeting to him that he answered with a bark and then lay down near the fire and watched as Cook and Tatiana continued to talk. It was frustrating not being able to join in, especially after today's conversation with Ravenna - or at least the attempt at conversation.

Ravenna was a puzzle he couldn't solve. One moment she acted carefree; the next, she put up walls higher than the ones surrounding the castle. He let out a small sigh. Tatiana and Cook must have noticed; they stopped talking and observed him closely.

"Are you all right, Your Highness?" Tatiana asked him. His tail gave one little thump. "Would you like to go out into the gardens with me?" She got off her stool, called out a farewell to Cook, and walked toward the exit without even checking to see if Liam was following. He decided that going to the gardens with the fairy was better than moping around inside.

They walked through the gardens until they reached an area with rows and rows of rose bushes. Tatiana leaned over one of them, checking the leaves for pests.

"Ravenna's favorite flower is the rose."

Liam sat and tilted his head at the fairy, waiting for her to continue.

"They don't bloom until they feel warm enough. Not a moment before." Tatiana looked over at the dog prince. "She is warming up to you."

Liam snorted in response.

"It's true. No one else has lasted this long before. It scares her to hope, so she will use her thorns as a way to protect herself, but she'll bloom in front of you. You'll see." Tatiana continued walking down the garden path. Liam stayed behind, looking again at the budless rose bushes.

CHAPTER 21

Dinner that night was a simple lamb stew. It hadn't snowed again, but the nights were still cold, and Ravenna gave thanks to Hoseenu that Cook was the best cook in all of the realm. While Ravenna and Liam ate, they played with a deck of cards. She had insisted that they play a card game after he kept beating her in chess.

She chose one of her favorite games that she used to play with her family. In the game, all players began with a hand of thirteen cards. When everyone got their hand, they would place a bid at guessing how many tricks, or rounds of play, they could win based on the cards they had. For every play, each person went around in a circle trying to play the highest card to win the round. Whoever won would take that group of cards and set the pile aside as a trick toward their bid. After all thirteen cards are used up in the hand, each person would count the number of tricks they won to see if they were able to meet their personal bid set at the top of the game. Despite it being a four person game, Ravenna and Liam were able to figure out how to modify it for two people.

Ravenna smiled as she took another trick pile, causing him to miss his bid.

He groaned, "You must be cheating."

"Are you accusing a queen of cheating?" Ravenna put her hand over her chest with a mock gasp. Liam simply sat back in his chair and smiled at her. Beginning to feel self-conscious, she put down a card to start the round.

"You seem to be more at ease tonight." Liam played a card.

Ravenna hesitated, one hand hovering over the cards she held in her other hand. "I didn't sleep well last night and decided to take a nap." She placed a card down. It was more like she had been *forced* to take a nap. After returning from their walk, Ravenna started going over the reports of the accident. Cress topped by, took all of Ravenna's papers away from her, and pointed toward the bed.

Liam frowned and asked, "Is everything all right?" Ravenna bit her lip. Should she tell him now about the accidents? Right before she could answer, a messenger arrived. She saw Liam's look of disappointment at being interrupted.

"Your Majesty. Your Highness." The messenger bowed to each in turn. "I have a letter from Queen Sophia of Wilderose." Ravenna saw Liam perk up in his chair.

"Thank you. You may go." Ravenna reached for the letter that had been placed before her, and she opened it as the messenger walked out of the room.

"What does it say?" Liam asked impatiently. Ravenna scanned the letter, then looked up at him. "What is it?" he asked again.

"She says that she would like to visit in a month." Ravenna tried to hide a smile. She was sure that if Liam were currently a dog, his tail would be wagging aggressively. As it was, he was giving the biggest grin she had ever seen.

She continued, "And check on her 'dear puppy brother.'" Ravenna didn't even bother covering her smirk.

Liam looked dejected. "She's never going to let me live this down." He sighed, but then smiled at the thought of reuniting with his sister. "But it would be nice to see her again, and I can't wait for you to meet her! A month is also a long enough time to plan on how to retaliate."

"Retaliate? But she hasn't even done anything to you," Ravenna frowned.

"Your Majesty doesn't know my sister like I do. If she's around, then she will perform some sort of prank."

"But she's a dignified queen."

"Who is also an older sister. Just wait and see." Ravenna found this hard to believe, but she figured that Sophia's own brother would know her better than she would. She started to feel a little guilty. Liam was so excited to see his sister, but the only time that he would actually be able to communicate with her was either through Ravenna or in front of her at dinner. There must be some way for them to have a private conversation without her in the room. Ravenna made a promise to herself that she'd start testing the boundaries of the curse.

She started to pick up her hand of cards to play another round when Liam said, "You didn't answer my question."

Ravenna raised an eyebrow. "You allowed me to get away with not answering earlier."

"Ah, but you had answered. As vague as it was." His eyes twinkled.

Ravenna chuckled. "Alright, you win. No, not everything is alright, but it's something that I just have to get over." She held a hand up when he opened his mouth. "I promise I'll tell you more, but I'm not ready yet." He stayed quiet but didn't look satisfied. "What about you?" She turned on him. "You seemed lost in your own thoughts at the pond. It wasn't just me."

His cheeks turned red. "I was distracted by all of the different smells in the forest when I picked up on something I had previously smelled in the gardens." He ducked his head and focused on his own cards. Ravenna didn't know how to reply.

Tentatively she asked, "What did you smell?" She wouldn't have believed that his face would ever be able to match his brilliant red hair, but there it was.

"A rabbit," he mumbled.

"Oh." There was an awkward pause as each one of them tried to figure out what to say next.

Liam recovered before she did. "I'm sorry again for asking you something private. I did not intend to remind you of something painful."

Ravenna took a deep breath and told him, "Liam, I understand that you want to get to know me. I do want you to get to know me, and I want to get to know you too. I..." She looked awkwardly around the room while she searched for the right words. "I just need some more time. But don't feel like you have to censor your questions. Still ask me, even if I can't give you a full answer."

Her eyes pleaded for him to understand. He exhaled as if he had been holding his breath.

"Alright." He grinned. "I'll let you hold on to your

thoughts as long as you let me keep to myself when I smell rabbits and not tell my sister when she comes."

Ravenna burst out laughing. "That's a hard bargain, but I accept your terms!"

Liam grinned. "I believe it's your turn, Your Majesty."

"Why don't you call me by my name?"

Liam looked up from his hand. "I beg your pardon?"

"My name. We've been spending time together for a month now, and you still don't call me by my name."

He flashed her a mischievous grin. "Well, Your Majesty, it seems like your education on Wilderosian culture is lacking."

"Are you not going to fill me in?"

Liam turned back to the game. "No."

After a moment, he looked up at her and laughed at her expression. "I take it from your open mouth, people don't say no to you all that often?"

She blushed. "People say no to me. Just not when I'm asking for more information." She lifted her chin up.

He smiled. "Tomorrow. I'll tell you tomorrow."

"I suppose I can wait that long." She let out a loud sigh but then took the remaining trick pile to win again. It seemed like a trip to the library was in order.

CHAPTER 22

Liam woke up from a deep sleep. Groggily, he looked around, trying to figure out what had woken him up. He tilted his head to try to hear better. That's when he picked up the soft sound of footsteps in the hallway, heading away from Ravenna's room. He groaned as he jumped out of bed. *Does she have some sort of hatred toward sleeping?*

He gripped the special handle in his mouth and pulled the door open as quietly as he could. When he got out of his room, he took a moment to sniff out where she had gone. She seemed to have a weekly routine of taking a walk in the middle of the night, and her scent had always led toward the outdoors on previous nights. Tonight, it went deeper into the castle.

He followed her trail as close as he dared to remain undiscovered, but not far enough away that he would lose her scent. Eventually, he found himself standing in front of the castle library's doors. He hadn't been inside the library since Cori and the rest of the children had given him the tour of the castle, and it was one of the few places that did not yet have the special dog-friendly door handles.

He pressed his ear against the door and could hear what sounded like Ravenna walking around. Satisfied that she was actually inside, he found a spot out of sight of the door to lie down and wait for her to go back to bed.

He wondered, not for the first time, if she would be mad at him for following her during her night walks. After the first time, he made sure to keep enough distance so as to not overhear her to give her privacy as she prayed to Hoseenu out loud. During those moments, he would also pray, asking Hoseenu for wisdom. He was thankful that he didn't need to speak out loud to pray.

While he fought with himself to stay awake, the library doors opened. He watched as Ravenna walked out with a big smile on her face. After she had gone a little ways in front of him, he followed her, thankful that she went straight to her room instead of going anywhere else. Following suit, he went inside his own bedroom and quickly hopped onto the bed and fell back asleep.

The next morning included another rude awakening. Liam looked up and moaned as the door between his and Ravenna's room burst open and Ravenna shouted, "I figured it out!"

Figured what out? He turned over and closed his eyes. *How bad would it be to give up breaking the curse if it meant he could sleep just five more minutes?* he thought to himself.

"How to get you to call me by my name. I know that you're not a morning person, but I couldn't wait until you showed up at breakfast. Besides, it's around the time you would usually wake up."

Liam opened one eye to look at her. When she was this giddy and excited, she truly let her guard down. He decided that he could give up a few more minutes of sleep if it meant he got to see this side of her.

Ravenna produced a handkerchief with her name embroidered on it. "With this token of my name, I grant you permission to court me until I request it back." She looked so pleased with herself as she laid the handkerchief on the chest at the foot of his bed.

For some reason, his heart felt lighter despite it beating faster. His tail wagged uncontrollably, and he panted with a doggy grin on his face.

Ravenna, you are too kind to entrust your name to me. How did you learn about this Wilderosian custom?

"Lyra isn't as formal with our names as Wilderose is, so I had forgotten about only calling people by name after being given permission. However, I remembered a book from my studies on foreign customs and thought I would look there. Not calling people by their names in formal settings isn't quite as noticeable as it is during personal interactions. Why is that?" She tilted her head as she asked.

Names are given by Hoseenu and are to be cherished. It is an honor to be allowed to use another's name outside of family. However, it is not a custom we hold foreigners to, so no one outside of Wilderose really remembers the practice.

Ravenna looked deep in thought. "Why didn't you just tell me earlier?"

Liam turned his head away. He knew that if he were human, his face would have been red with embarrassment.

It can be used as part of Wilderosian courtships. I've been trained since I was a child to follow it, and I was worried that if I were to tell you about it, it would make you feel like you had to do this for me.

Ravenna didn't say anything for a while. Liam started to panic. Maybe this was too much for her. He should have told her upfront.

At last, Ravenna spoke. "That custom as a part of courtship was mentioned in the book. Even though I do not fully understand the implications of your custom, I am privileged that you wanted to honor me the greatest way that you know how. Even though it was frustrating to have to find out through a book, I can sort of understand your reason for not telling me." His tail began wagging again, and he could feel his dog instincts wanting to jump up and lick her face. He focused on controlling himself.

Ravenna leaned against the doorway and smiled. "Now, are you ready for breakfast?" Liam jumped off the bed and followed her through her rooms and out into the hallway. His tail wagged the whole way to the breakfast room.

CHAPTER 23

It was the morning of Queen Sophia's visit and Liam couldn't sit still. Ravenna tried to keep a serious and regal expression on her face, but the excited dog next to her made it difficult. His whole body was constantly wiggling, thanks to his swishing tail. She couldn't really blame him. He hadn't seen his sister in months, and her carriage had just arrived. She had also noticed it was harder for him to keep his canine instincts under control when he was feeling strong emotions.

They sat in the throne room where Lyrian royalty greeted foreign ambassadors or visiting monarchs. It was a grand room with vaulted ceilings and a giant golden chandelier, and the thrones of the king and queen of Lyra sat on the top of a flight of steps overlooking the rest of the people who assembled there.

It was Ravenna's least favorite room in the whole castle.

She hated sitting up higher than everyone else. She already felt distant from the people of Lyra, and it was as if she had to physically live it out here as well. When she was younger, she had asked her parents why their throne room was set up the way it was. They had just made some sort of vague reference to a past ancestor who had had it built as a present for his new queen. After they told her, she had done some research in the library and discovered that 200 years prior, her ancestor's new queen was not happy with her surprise, but no one agreed to remove it, so it stayed. Ravenna had vowed that when she became queen, she would have it leveled. It was just a matter of waiting until her uncle was no longer her regent king. For reasons unknown to the new queen, Damien liked the show of status. She could always have the council vote on it, but she had learned quickly it was best to pick her battles when dealing with her uncle.

"Her Majesty, Queen Sophia of Wilderose!"

Ravenna had to restrain herself from jumping out of her seat in surprise when the herald finally announced their visitor's arrival. She glanced again at Liam whose rump had started to lift off the floor as if his tail were propelling him upward. He kept bouncing from one front paw to the next in excitement. She tried to hide her smile as she watched Queen Sophia walk in.

Ravenna could immediately tell that Sophia and Liam could be nothing less than siblings. They shared the same red hair and light green eyes. They both had a smattering of freckles across their faces. However, while Liam was a foot taller than Ravenna, Sophia was only a couple of inches taller than her. Sophia was dressed in a green gown that matched her eyes, and her face held a serious expression. Liam had insisted that Sophia was a prankster, but looking at the woman in front of her, Ravenna had her doubts.

Queen Sophia had been in the room for only a moment before Liam lost any semblance of self-control. In horror, Ravenna reached out to grab him as soon as he bolted down the stairs, but he was too quick for her. She cringed as she watched the red blur run all the way up to his sister and jump up on her, licking her face and wagging his tail.

"Ugh, Liam! Stop! That's gross!" Sophia shrieked. He ignored her, wiggling and jumping around until she plopped herself onto the floor and laughed as tears ran down her face.

"Okay, fine. I've missed you too! Now will you stop?" Immediately, Liam seemed to regain control over himself. As Ravenna walked down the stairs, she heard him try to speak to his older sister.

I'm sorry! I didn't mean to. Only it came out as a small whimper. Despite not being able to hear her own brother's voice, Sophia reached out and petted him and said something that was too quiet for Ravenna to hear.

"Your Majesty..." Ravenna addressed her.

Sophia looked up from the floor at Ravenna, who stood awkwardly in front of her. Ravenna wasn't sure what else she should say. She had never been taught what to do when a foreign monarch was accosted by their own sibling who had been turned into a dog.

"Ah, yes, you must be the Queen of Lyra. I do apologize for my brother's poor manners." Sophia shot a quick glare at Liam. "But I hope that while he's been here, he's treated you with the utmost respect." At that, Ravenna caught Liam rolling his eyes. Again she had to try to stifle a laugh.

"I can assure you that His Highness has not disgraced the royal line of Wilderose."

Until I lose my human wits, you mean. This time Ravenna was the one that shot him a look. *You know it's true. This wasn't the first time, and I'm guessing it won't be the last time that I won't be able to think like a human,* Liam growled.

Ravenna winced.

"Would it be too much to ask to be part of this conversation, or is this a lover's quarrel that I should let be?" Both Ravenna and Liam turned and gawked at Sophia with wide eyes. Sophia appeared rather smug. Ravenna finally started to believe Liam that Sophia wasn't as serious as rumors had led her to think.

"I am sorry, Your Majesty. We were—"

Discussing dinner plans! Liam shouted as she stalled to think of something to say.

"Discussing dinner plans," Ravenna said for him.

Sophia smirked and looked over at the dog who had moved to sit next to Ravenna.

"Really? Dinner plans? That's all you could come up with?" Sophia chuckled. Liam stared down at the floor when Ravenna glared at him.

"Oh, don't worry. If you don't want to tell me, then you don't have to. Now that dinner has been brought up, I hope that it will be soon. It was quite the journey over the mountains to get here, and something to eat sounds delightful!"

"We will have dinner within the hour. While you are waiting, the servants will show you to your rooms where you can refresh yourself if you would like."

"Brilliant. Thank you, Your Majesty! I will see you within the hour." Sophia bent down and kissed her brother-turned-dog on the forehead and said, "I'll see you then, too." Then she quickly got up and left the room.

Ravenna and Liam just stood there for a moment. "We should probably start getting ready for dinner ourselves," Ravenna said to finally break the silence, and they walked out of the throne room together.

While Ravenna got ready in her room, Liam paced back and forth in his. He hadn't realized just how much he had missed Sophia. Of course he had missed her! Growing up, she had been the only one who understood how much he didn't like being cooped up inside with the nobles' children. She indulged his need to have "adventures" in the Elven Wood. She was his best friend and the only one who could convince him that joining the military was the ideal way for him to help their country. When their father put him in charge of rounding up the raiders only for him to fail when the Lyrian king and queen were murdered, Sophia had told him that she still trusted him enough to go after them. What bothered him, though, was that he had expressed how much he missed her by reacting as a dog would react when it hadn't seen its owner for a long time. It was not how a brother would greet a sister.

As the curse remained unbroken, the brief moments when he didn't remember that he had ever been human were becoming more frequent. Even during dinner when he was human, he now noticed small changes. He could hear servants moving in rooms down the hall. Not only could he smell better as a human than he ever could before, he could still sense other humans' emotions like he was able to when he was a dog. He was glad that Ravenna hadn't heard him growling at the kitchen's cat, which had wandered into the dining hall during dinner. He wasn't completely sure, but he suspected that his hair was getting thicker on his arms and legs.

Liam sighed and collapsed onto the floor in front of the fireplace. Ravenna didn't know how much the curse was affecting him. He couldn't hide the obvious moments, like when he chased squirrels on their walks...or when he tackled his sister in front of the whole Lyrian court. He winced at the memories. It was bad enough that he felt embarrassed at making himself look like a fool as an untrained puppy, but every time something like that happened - where he acted more like a dog than a man - he could tell that Ravenna felt guilty, which made it that much worse. She closed herself off after she apologized for every incident.

He knew that they didn't love each other enough yet to break the curse, but he at least could tell that he was starting to care about her. He hated that she had to deal with her uncle trying to undermine her authority and that she felt like she had to carry the whole weight of Lyra alone.

When he followed her on her nightly walks, he could sometimes hear her praying to Hoseenu. Because he stayed back to give her privacy, Liam couldn't always make out what she said, but sometimes she would laugh. Other times, she would cry. She was vulnerable with Hoseenu in a way that she was not with anyone else. He had noticed that, besides Cress and Tatiana, she didn't allow herself to truly relax around anyone. She always put on a show for everyone else's benefit.

He didn't mean to intrude on her privacy, but he could smell predators that hunted at night, and he was not going to leave the queen unprotected. Despite what she had said about Lyra being safer than Wilderose, she didn't seem concerned by the bears, wolves, and cougars wandering the woods. So he would continue to follow her and let her have these moments for herself as best as he could. Even though she didn't know that he made sure she was safe while she prayed, it was another way to show how much he did care for her.

When he realized that he had started to hope she would trust him enough to be vulnerable with him, he understood that she had become more than just a duty to him. She was not just a means to having a fairy godmother protect Wilderose. He wanted her to feel safe around him and not always be on guard about how he was handling the curse. The less she knew about the side effects, the better. It would be one less thing for her to worry about.

Liam lifted his head when he heard the knock on the door between his and Ravenna's room. *Come in.*

Ravenna peeked her head around the open door. "I'm ready."

Liam got off the floor and walked to dinner with her.

When they got to the door leading to the dining hall, Liam could hear Sophia inside waiting for them. He started walking forward when he realized that Ravenna wasn't walking with him. He looked back and saw Ravenna fidgeting with her skirt. It was something he noticed that she did to prepare herself before putting on her queen persona.

You don't have to worry about Sophia. She seemed to be comfortable with you.

Ravenna jerked still at his words. Liam padded up to her and nuzzled his head underneath one of her hands. His tail wagged as she unconsciously petted his head.

She gave him a small smile. "So turning her brother into a dog makes her warm up to me? I can't imagine what you've done to her that she would be so pleased with this turn of events."

He huffed, voice filled with mock indignation, *I treated her as best as a little brother could treat his older sister.* Ravenna let out a little chuckle and slowly opened the door. Liam felt the familiar sensation of magic as his form changed.

"Liam!" a voice cried out from behind the door.

He was caught off-guard as he was knocked down to the ground, struggling to breathe, as his sister squeezed the air out of his lungs with a bone-crushing hug. The only thing he was aware of was Ravenna hiding another smile behind her hand despite it shining through her eyes.

"Get off of me!" He gulped in air as soon as Sophia let go of him and glared at her when she snickered.

"I've been waiting to pay you back the favor for nearly half an hour!" she cried. Liam gave Ravenna a look that said, "See what I have to put up with?" Although he would never admit it out loud, he loved that he and his sister could still act like children with each other.

After they had picked themselves up off the floor, Sophia bowed her head toward Ravenna. "Thank you again for hosting my brother and for allowing me to visit him."

Ravenna smiled and nodded back, "You are more than welcome to visit as often as your duties allow."

Liam followed the two queens to the table and sat himself next to Ravenna, across from Sophia. After filling their plates with food, Liam and Sophia started to catch up on everything happening in Wilderose. It wasn't until dessert was served that Liam realized Ravenna hadn't said a word. Looking over at her, he noticed that she was staring at her plate of food, swirling her fork around to make designs in her potatoes.

"Are you okay?" he abruptly asked her.

Ravenna's head shot right up. "Yeah, I'm fine." Her answer was rushed, but before he could comment any further, she added, "I'll be right back."

He knew that she must either be asking Cook something

about their meal or refreshing herself with the intention of coming right back. She had been leaving in short bursts during dinner the last couple of weeks, but he almost always remained human during those absences. There had been one time when he turned back into a dog while he had been in the middle of drinking some wine. The goblet had fallen onto the table, spilling wine everywhere. Ravenna had returned shortly afterwards and was extremely apologetic for indirectly getting wine in his fur.

After a moment of staring at the door once it had closed behind her, he heard Sophia clear her throat.

"So, do you love her?" Sophia asked.

He turned to look at his sister. "No," He sighed.

Sophia frowned. "Are you sure?"

He took a moment to answer her, "I don't *not* love her." Sophia remained silent. He leaned his head back against the chair's headrest and closed his eyes. "I care about her. I just don't love her."

"You know Hoseenu says that love is an action and not just a feeling, right?" Sophia reminded him.

Liam opened his eyes, looked at his older sister, and sighed, "Yes, I know."

"But?"

"But for the curse to break, this has to be true love between both of us. Even if I choose to love her enough to sacrifice my life for her, that love cannot truly flourish unless we both commit to it. You should know that better than anyone." He saw her wince as she turned away from him and immediately regretted bringing up her past heartbreak so callously. "Soph, I'm sorry. I shouldn't have said that."

"No, you're right. I do know that, and I'm sorry for implying that you're not thinking this through." She smiled up at him with her eyes twinkling. "However, I'm not going to forgive you for slacking off on all of your duties!"

He barked out a laugh. "You got me. I thought that being cursed would be better than filling out paperwork." Sophia joined his laughter. It was good to be with his sister again.

After Ravenna left the dining hall, she went to one of the nearby window nooks that were scattered throughout the castle. As a little girl, she would play hide-and-seek with her father and always preferred hiding underneath the tables with long tablecloths that sat under the windows. On rainy days, she would find a nook that had a bench instead of a table and read a book there.

The window nook closest to her had a bench, so she sat down and pulled her legs up onto it. She rested her head on her knees as she watched the scene outside the window. It overlooked the stables, and she could watch all of the horses being taken care of while she thought.

She knew she couldn't be away from dinner for long. Ever since Sophia's letter came announcing her impending visit, Ravenna had wanted to be able to give Liam time with his sister as a human and had started experimenting with the curse during dinner. After a lot of trial and error, she discovered that as long as she intended to come back within fifteen minutes, he would stay as a human in the room. If she stayed away any longer, the curse forced him to turn back into a dog. On the nights she took her experiment too far and he changed before she could make it back, she supposed the curse just assumed that her answer for the night was 'no.'

She caught movement out of the corner of her eye. The mare that had given birth to twins a few days ago was being led out from the stables to the nearby field. Her foals followed closely behind. When they got into the field, Ravenna watched the tiny foals play and run around together, and she smiled at the sight. She had always wanted a sibling. Cress came close, but it wasn't the same as what the foals had. Or what Liam and Sophia shared.

It was obvious, even within the last couple of hours, how close they were. Liam was always formal around her, and he never got excited at seeing her like he did with Sophia. He was never filled with enough anticipation to lose control over himself. Then she saw that Sophia, a queen that had a reputation of being level headed and collected, lost all formality around her brother. Ravenna would be lying if she said she wasn't jealous of how open and carefree they were around each other. She and Liam tended to walk on eggshells around each other.

Taking one last look at the foals, Ravenna got up from the bench and went back into the dining hall. Before she entered, she put her ear to the door and heard the two siblings laughing together. Taking a deep breath, she pushed the door open.

Sophia, who was facing the door, cried out to her. "Your Majesty! I'm so glad that you're back! Before I head off to bed, I wanted to see if you were free for lunch tomorrow." She cast a sly look toward her brother. "Without male company, if you are willing."

Ravenna looked over at Liam who just raised his eyebrows in acknowledgement. "I would love to, Your Majesty."

"Good! Thank you, Your Majesty, for allowing me to

join you both for dinner. However, I think I must call it a night." Sophia got up and nodded her head toward Ravenna. She tousled Liam's hair as she walked past him and left the room.

Neither one of them moved after the door closed behind Sophia. Then Liam leaned back in his chair and closed his eyes, resigned to the fact that his time as a human was up for the night. "Are you finished with dinner?" he asked. Ravenna bit her lower lip. She was tired, but Liam didn't look ready to leave. "I haven't had dessert yet." Cook had made miniature custard tarts, and there were still a couple left for her. They didn't talk as she started eating them. Ravenna didn't know what to say. Was it too personal to ask about his conversation with his sister? Should she ask him how he was doing? Had he realized that he could go home with Sophia when she left?

That last question gave her pause. It was the one that worried her the most, and despite herself, she had really begun to hope that Liam would be the one to break the curse. That hope frightened her.

"Where did you go during dinner?"

Ravenna jumped a little when Liam broke the silence and looked at her with a puzzled expression. She shifted back and forth on her chair. She wasn't sure whether to lie or not.

"I wanted to let you have time alone to talk with your sister. To be human with her." She looked down at her hands.

"How did you know that the curse wouldn't turn me into a dog the moment you left?" His tone didn't sound surprised. It was almost expectant.

"I have been testing the limits of the curse ever since I

heard that Sophia was coming." She could feel how red her face was turning due to getting caught.

"Ravenna."

She looked up at Liam. Her breath caught her in her throat when she saw his genuine smile.

"Thank you."

She couldn't help but smile in return.

CHAPTER 24

The next day, Ravenna woke up slowly to the sound of bird song. She briefly contemplated staying in bed, but realized that she still had several things to do before lunch with Sophia. Sighing, she pulled off the covers and started getting ready. When she was done, she thought about seeing if Liam wanted to join her for breakfast, but he'd probably want to sleep in after she had woken him up early the day before to get ready for Sophia's arrival.

As she quietly closed her bedroom door and walked into the hallway, she admired how the rising sunlight shined in through the tall windows. The sky was clear of any clouds and it promised to be a beautiful day. Maybe she would be able to fit in a walk in the woods after breakfast and before her dress fitting with Cress.

By the time she got to the breakfast room, no one else had arrived yet. She went to the buffet to get some bread and cheese and a cup of tea. Instead of sitting at the table, she went over to sit at the window bench where she could see the gardens down below. Even though she hadn't walked through them in over a year, she still enjoyed watching the growth of spring.

"Good morning."

Ravenna almost dropped her teacup as she slightly jumped in her seat. "Tatiana! You scared me!" She put a hand to her chest as if that would calm her racing heart. Her fairy godmother smiled in amusement and sat down next to Ravenna on the bench.

"You were lost in thought." Tatiana tilted her head. "Care to tell me why?"

Ravenna snorted, "It's not like you don't already know."

"True, but it's better to talk out loud about it."

Ravenna sighed, "Did mother and father ever try to have another child?" She looked into Tatiana's eyes.

Tatiana didn't answer right away. "Does seeing Liam and Sophia together make you feel alone, child?"

Ravenna's face felt hot from the effort to hold back tears. Tatiana hadn't called Ravenna "child" since she became queen.

"A little." She turned to look out the window again.

"Ravenna, look at me," the fairy gently demanded. Ravenna obeyed. "The past cannot be altered. You can only change the future. Hoseenu knows you because He made you, and He will not leave you truly alone."

Ravenna nodded, feeling like a little girl again.

"You will also always have me, and even though humans will come and go, it is still worth letting them into your life. No matter how long or short that time may be." Tatiana reached over and pulled Ravenna into a hug. The young queen let herself relax in the warm embrace of her godmother. After allowing herself a few minutes of comfort, Ravenna pulled back.

"Thank you. I should go now and get fitted before Cress chews my ear off for making her wait."

Tatiana laughed, "Best not keep her waiting, especially because she's another person who will always love you and be there for you." Ravenna smiled and left the breakfast room.

When she entered the sewing workroom, she stood for a moment watching the blonde seamstress clean up what looked to be an explosion of fabric. "Need any help?"

Cress jumped up and dropped the fabric she had just picked up.

"Oh, it's just you! I thought the head seamstress had arrived," Cress said as she put her hands on her hips, glaring at her queen.

Ravenna hid her grin behind her hand. "Nope, just me. But really though, do you need any help?"

Cress dropped her glare with a look of relief. "Yes! Several of the merchants we purchase fabric from decided that they should drop off all the orders this morning. I thought it would be easier to just open all the packages at once to sort like-fabric with like. Now I see that it would have been better to open them one at a time." Cress gave a sheepish smile.

"Tell me what to do," Ravenna said.

Cress explained that the fabrics were first organized by type, like silk, satin, and wool. Each type would be stored on their designated racks by the walls and then sorted by color.

"I've been able to at least get all of the different materials separated. I just need the bolts to be placed near their racks and then I'll separate them by color after your fitting," Cress finished.

While they were moving bolts of fabric around the workroom, Cress spoke up, "So, have you told Liam about the accidents yet?" Ravenna looked up from the pink silk that she was holding. Cress continued moving a pile of gray wool with her back to Ravenna.

Setting down the silk, Ravenna answered, "There hasn't been time."

Cress turned around. "What do you mean 'there hasn't been time?' It's been almost three months!"

Ravenna winced. "There also haven't been any recently to tell him about."

Cress crossed her arms and stared pointedly at Ravenna.

"I know I could have mentioned that they *have* happened, but I don't see the point if they've stopped."

Cress only raised her eyebrows in response. Ravenna sighed, "It's only been a little over two months. Besides, we've been getting ready for Queen Sophia's arrival." All of a sudden, Ravenna sat up straight. "Oh, that reminds me, do you have the handkerchief?"

"Yes, I do, but don't try to change the subject. What do you even talk about on your daily walks and dinners?"

Ravenna looked away. "We don't really talk. I mean, we play games during dinner and talk about what we're playing, and we might mention fun childhood memories or discuss our different cultures, but we say nothing extremely personal."

"How are you supposed to fall in love with him if you don't open up to him about things that matter to you right now? How is he supposed to fall in love with a stranger?" Cress said gently.

"I don't know," Ravenna said as she picked up the pink silk and put it with the rest of the silk. Cress sighed and went back to work as well. While they finished up organizing the fabric, Ravenna thought about what Cress had asked her. She felt comfortable around Liam. She enjoyed the time they spent together, but she still felt just a fondness rather than love for him. How could they really love each other if they kept things at a surface level? Wasn't love built on life shared together during good times and bad rather than simply checking in on each other's days? She still couldn't talk with Liam like she could with Tatiana and Cress about what was happening in Lyra. Sure, he'd gone to the meetings with her and had agreed to tour the surrounding area to get things ready for the summer festival. But she'd never asked him what he thought about how Lyra was run. When he asked her questions, she kept her answers as professional as possible without getting her personal feelings involved.

"If there's another accident, I'll tell him as soon as I learn about it."

Cress looked back at Ravenna. "Promise?"

"I promise."

Cress squealed and ran over to give her friend a hug. "I'm sorry for constantly bringing this up, but I think it's important."

Ravenna gave a small smile. "I know. It's part of my duty to marry a king."

Cress stepped back, cocking her head. "It's more than that, and you know it! I just want to see you happy, and from what I've seen and heard, I really do think he could make you happy." Ravenna only nodded in return. "And I think that you will make him happy too," Cress finished.

Before Ravenna could ask Cress what she meant, the clock in the room struck noon.

"Oh, no! I'm supposed to meet Queen Sophia for lunch now! Can I have the handkerchief?"

Cress quickly went toward a small desk on the far side of

the room. Pulling open a drawer, she got the handkerchief and quickly gave it to Ravenna. "Here you go."

"Thank you so much," Ravenna said as she grasped it in her hands.

"No, thank you! You helped me so much with the fabric. I guess we'll have to reschedule your fitting for another time."

"It just means that I get to spend more time with my favorite seamstress before she becomes too famous to stay in Lyra."

Cress responded playfully, "I'll be sure to visit you. Now go, before you start a war by being late to meet a foreign monarch." Ravenna rushed out of the room, laughing as she went.

When she arrived at the small dining room, she discovered that despite being a few minutes late, she was still the first to arrive. She played with her skirts, picking them up and smoothing them back down. She was unsure if she should wait for Sophia outside or stay at the table. The staff had already placed the food out.

Before she could decide one way or the other, the doors opened and Queen Sophia walked in. The Queen of Wilderose seemed less hyper than she had the previous evening. It was a glimpse of what, Ravenna assumed, was Sophia's queen persona: reserved and dignified.

"Good afternoon, Your Majesty." Ravenna bowed her head.

"Good afternoon, Your Majesty," Sophia replied. They made their way toward the table in the middle of the room. Despite the length of the table, only the head had place settings for the two queens.

After they sat down and placed the roast lamb and potatoes on their plates, they gave thanks to Hoseenu for the food and started to eat. After a couple of bites and some shared pleasantries over the quality of the food, Ravenna pulled out the handkerchief.

"Your Majesty, I would like to give you a token of my name as a sign of trust between us."

Sophia beamed as she accepted the gift. "Thank you, Ravenna, for this honor. I hope that you will also accept a token of my name as a sign of friendship between us." Sophia pulled out a small glass bottle of rose water with her name etched on the glass and gave it to Ravenna.

"I gladly accept, Sophia."

"Good! Now that we have moved toward trust and friendship, I would like to discuss your and my brother's courtship." Sophia leaned forward, rested her elbows on the table, and steepled her hands. Ravenna grinned. Here was the no-nonsense Queen of Wilderose.

She leaned back in her chair. "What do you wish to know?"

"I know my brother. Once he's committed to something, he sees it through. For whatever reason, he has decided that he will be the one to break this curse, and I believe that he will."

Ravenna raised an eyebrow.

"Oh, I know you don't believe it yet, which is fair. All of the neighboring courts have lost count of how many suitors you have had, but again, none of them have been Liam." Sophia straightened up in her chair. "Even with your doubts about the matter, I am fairly certain there will be a marriage alliance between our countries. So I would like to start working out the details of how we can benefit each other now, rather than wait until you both finish falling in love."

"I see that you're quite the opportunist."

"I have to be. You and I are the youngest monarchs

around, and even with the peace alliance you have managed to set up in your first year of rule, there's only so much trust that we have with some of our fellow monarchs. It doesn't hurt to strengthen bonds between friends. Don't you agree?" Sophia took a dainty sip of tea and looked over her cup at Ravenna.

"What conditions would you like to include in this possible marriage alliance?"

Sophia grinned at the word "possible." Though Ravenna still could not bring herself to say that it was a done deal that she would marry Liam, she did see the logic behind Sophia's words. Despite the peace alliance, countries like Silvermeadow and Ironedge had been known in the past to break trust if it meant better advantages for themselves.

"First off, none of your descendants will have any claim to the Wilderose's throne. Secondly, during trade arrangements, Wilderose will take precedence over any other country trying to make the same bid."

"The first one is fair, but the second might not be in Lyra's interest. Why should I accept?"

"Since Wilderose borders the Elven Wood, it is the only country that is friendly with the elves. We're the only ones that trade with them, and until today, we have not offered to trade elven goods with other nations."

Ravenna stopped herself from gasping. The only way that anyone else was allowed passage through the Elven Wood was if they had a Wilderosian guide, but trading with the elves was impossible.

"That is a bold claim. I assume that you have some sort of proof."

Sophia's smile grew wider. Ravenna watched as she pulled out a necklace that had been hidden underneath her bodice. Sophia unclasped it and handed it over to Ravenna.

Ravenna took it and saw that the chain was made of silver with a lily pendant of moonstones. No human could make a chain as delicate as this one that could also never break. Not to mention that moonstones could only be found in the Elven Wood; even then, it was rare to come across them as a stranger of the wood.

Passing the necklace back to a smug Sophia, Ravenna said, "This does change my perspective. I accept your conditions with a couple of my own." Sophia waited for Ravenna to continue. "Lyra is the only country that Wilderose will trade elven goods with. And I would like to open a foreign exchange program and have Wilderose be the first country we partner with."

Sophia frowned in confusion. "Could you explain more about this exchange program?"

"Wilderose is known for having a good education system. I want that for Lyra. I believe that for a country to truly become great, everyone needs, at the very least, to know how to read, write, and do basic mathematics. Though I'm currently trying to improve the Lyrian schools, I still want our students to have a chance at learning more about the world through an exchange program. If Liam and I were to marry, our countries would have the most trust between us to send our children to study in each other's countries."

"What about Faircoast? Your cousin, Lady Irena, is going to be the queen when Crown Prince Titus takes over his parents' throne. Surely Lyra has more trust with them than they do with Wilderose?"

Ravenna shook her head. "We do, but Faircoast...how should I put this?" Ravenna hesitated before continuing. She didn't want to tell another nation's queen outright that she hated Faircoast's education system even more than Lyra's. Nor that she did not fully trust her own cousin. "Faircoast has more pressing concerns than the state of their nation's education system. Wilderose has one of the best methodologies and would be the ideal one to start with."

Sophia raised a brow but said nothing about Ravenna's evasiveness. Instead she said, "I accept your conditions," and reached out her hand toward Ravenna who shook on their verbal agreement. Ravenna let out a quiet sigh of relief as Sophia continued, "Once the curse is officially broken, we can begin having papers drawn up."

Ravenna nodded her head as she swallowed some tea.

"Where is Liam anyway?" Sophia asked.

"He's probably playing with the castle children."

Sophia quirked an eyebrow as Ravenna chuckled.

"Apparently, they found him on his first day in Lyra a few months ago and have taken a liking to him ever since. I personally think they are happier that he's a dog than a 'boring human prince.'"

Sophia burst out laughing. "If that's true, then he's probably the only prince who would take that as a compliment!"

"What do you mean?" Ravenna cocked her head, unsure why Sophia would think that Liam would like to be valued as a dog rather than a prince. Sophia's laughter died down quickly as she took in Ravenna's confusion.

"Liam doesn't like being a prince. He's always been thankful to have been second born so that I would be the next ruler of Wilderose. Our father didn't know what to do with him as a child. He'd always escape his tutoring sessions and would only allow himself to be found after coming home from riding his horse on some sort of 'adventure,' as he would call his excursions. Honestly, if it weren't for the military, I'm not sure what Liam would have ended up doing."

"But he always seems so serious when he's not a dog. There's only a hint of what you say is his wild side."

"When Father had him join the military and then eventually take it over, his wild side died down some. But it's always there, ready to burst forth."

Ravenna immediately thought of his greeting to his sister, as well as how he had played in the snow with the children. "I guess you're right."

Sophia leaned over the table and took Ravenna's hand. "Ravenna, I know that we've just met, but you and I have both had to take over a country at a young age while still mourning the deaths of our parents. I've seen how reserved you are, and I think you could use a bit more time out of your head. Let Liam do that for you. He's loyal to you and will always protect you, but he will also make your life so much more joyful if you let him."

Ravenna wasn't sure how to respond. On one hand, she admired how the siblings were able to relax around each other, but on the other hand, they were both practically strangers to her. She wasn't sure how much she could drop her guard around them. Sensing Ravenna's tentativeness, Sophia squeezed her hand and let go.

Deciding to be a little vulnerable with the other queen, Ravenna asked, "How do you show strength to your people as a new ruler but also mourn the death of your father?"

Sophia's mouth opened a little in the shape of an O. She then took a moment to think over her answer.

"I pray. Hoseenu knows I can't do this otherwise. However, it also helps to try to think of what my father's advice would be. It makes me feel like he's not gone, but with me." After a pause, she asked, "What about you?"

Ravenna gave a small smile. "I try to not really think about it when I'm with people. The peace treaty was my parents' idea, so I had to do something for them as a way of saying goodbye. Other than that, I go somewhere private and talk to Hoseenu. I didn't really know how much I needed Him until after I took the throne."

Sophia gave a self-deprecating laugh. "He never lets me forget that."

"Liam mentioned something about how Hoseenu takes care of Wilderose by directly communicating with the current ruler. Is this true?"

Sophia nodded. "Yes, but as much as I know He loves me, I know that He also holds me responsible for Wilderose's wellbeing. If I make a decision that would cause harm to my people, He lets me know in a dream. I've been lucky so far in only needing to receive one dream."

Ravenna bit her lip before asking, "Would it be alright if I asked what happened?"

Sophia looked away and toyed with her necklace, and for a moment, Ravenna wondered if she had gone too far. But Sophia answered, "I wasn't even queen yet, so I didn't expect it. It's rare for an heir to receive a dream, but I suppose it was because I was thinking of abdicating the throne."

Ravenna was surprised. She never would have suspected that Sophia would give up her birthright. Sophia gave her a tight smile. "It was when Liam was still in training, and I had sent him a letter to think about becoming king, when Hoseenu made it very clear that I was supposed to become queen." She shook her head. "I understand now His reasoning for it, but it was still a hard lesson for a young princess to learn that she can't always get her way."

Ravenna was debating whether or not she should ask for more details when Sophia said, "Well, enough about that. How about we go and find Liam now?" Her smile was obviously forced, so Ravenna decided that she wasn't going to press it. Instead, she agreed, and they both got up from the table and went looking for the dog prince.

CHAPTER 25

Sophia's visit went by so quickly that it was over before Liam knew it. Even though most of the time he wasn't able to talk with his sister without Ravenna translating for him, he was thankful that he could see her. He was also thankful that Ravenna had the foresight to figure out a way to give him some time alone with Sophia as a human.

During one of those times alone with Sophia, she had confided in him that she liked Ravenna and told him to not screw it up. His tail wagged at the memory of his smaller older sister pointing a butter knife at him to make sure she got her point across, trying to give a threatening glare without dissolving into laughter.

He watched Ravenna and Sophia give each other a hug goodbye, and he was frustrated that he couldn't even give a verbal farewell to his own sister.

"I'll send a messenger as soon as I arrive back home,"

Sophia told Ravenna. Liam walked over to Sophia and licked her hand to remind her that he would want to know, too. "Liam!" Sophia shrieked. He gave a small bark and wagged his tail in reply. He noticed that Ravenna was again trying to stifle her smile. A warm feeling filled his chest at being the reason for her amusement.

Be safe! he told Sophia through Ravenna.

"Of course I'll be safe. You've put the fear of Hoseenu into my bodyguards so that they aren't willing to let me go anywhere without them." Sophia rolled her eyes as she pointed to the group of soldiers near her carriage. Liam sat and gave as proud of an expression as a dog could muster.

Right before Sophia got into her carriage, she pulled Ravenna into a hug and whispered something that even Liam's improved hearing couldn't pick up. Ravenna nodded, and then they both watched as Sophia and her company left the castle's courtyard.

After they were out of sight, Liam and Ravenna headed inside.

What did my sister tell you?

He watched as Ravenna's face turned red. "If she wanted you to know, she wouldn't have whispered it, now would she?"

Liam sulked in response. He told himself it was a good thing he hadn't been turned into a cat; otherwise, he'd be dead from curiosity.

Ravenna jokingly reprimanded him, saying, "You shouldn't pout." He looked sideways at her but didn't reply. "It's not dignified for a prince." He saw her grin when he unintentionally let out a low growl.

He knew he was being petty, but it felt like another brick added to the wall between them. Ravenna was full of secrets that she kept to herself. Not that he needed to know all of them - he had a few of his own that he kept from her - but to be trusted with at least one would be encouraging.

She was the only one who could understand him for most of the day. He wasn't used to having to rely on someone else to communicate some of his basic needs. Despite the specially designed handles on the doors that were common entrances and exits for him, there were still plenty of doors he needed to go through less regularly that he would either have to ask for her help or act like a buffoon trying to get someone nearby to understand what he needed.

Sophia's obvious approval of Ravenna added to his desire to see the side of the Lyrian Queen that she saved for her closest confidantes. However, he also understood that such a position wasn't something he could force himself into. Ravenna had to freely give that to him, and despite months of spending time with each other, she had not. The fire of hope he had felt after she gave him her name was now just a mere ember that barely survived on fleeting moments where he saw her attempt to relax around him - mostly when she teased him or while they played their games during dinner. She was only open around him then because she was so focused on what she was doing that she ignored the world around her. However, if this was all she was willing to give to him, they would never break the curse together like he had promised. He would never be human again, and he wondered if the side effects would continue until he no longer even remembered he had ever been human.

He shook his head as if he could shake away his thoughts. "Are you alright?"

Liam stopped and turned around when he realized that Ravenna had stopped walking.

I'm alright.

She didn't seem satisfied with his answer as she pursed her lips. She started to open her mouth in protest.

Really, I am, he interjected before she could say anything. *It's been a long day already, and I think I shall retire in my room with the latest reports on the raiders.*

"But it's just now an hour past noon."

He gave her a look as if to say, "What does that have to do with anything?" She continued, "Perhaps we could go for a walk after dinner now that it's still light out later in the day?"

My apologies, Your Majesty, but I'm going to go to bed early. Liam bowed his head and trotted away from Ravenna. Seeing her wince at the use of her title instead of her name caused him to regret his words, but not enough to apologize for it. He didn't want to see her right now, and he knew she got annoyed whenever people didn't call her by her name. Hopefully it would bother her enough to leave him alone.

When he got to his room, he finally gave in to his inner dog and let himself droop. The tip of his tail dragged on the floor, and he let out a little whine after he plopped himself onto his bed. Before he fell asleep, he allowed himself to grieve a little for the loss of his humanity.

CHAPTER 26

Ravenna tossed and turned in her bed. Liam hadn't just declined her invitation to a walk after dinner, he hadn't even come down for dinner. Something was wrong with him, but she wasn't sure what it was. She had thought that it was just because Sophia had left, but when he didn't call her by her name, it felt like he had a problem with her. Was he going to give up on her?

Sophia was right when she had whispered that she wasn't trying hard enough, but how was she supposed to force herself to love him? Wasn't being in love supposed to mean butterflies and nerves? Clandestine rendezvouses and stolen kisses?

She shook her head to remind herself that that wasn't what true love was like as she used to think; but then what *was* it?

She cared about Liam: his well-being mattered to her, and she liked his company. She was even close enough to him to understand his dog-human hybrid body language. She just couldn't allow herself to trust him.

Giving up on sleep, Ravenna got out of her bed and looked out the window. The full moon shone silver light onto the forest. There was not a cloud in the sky. She quietly put on a dressing gown and left her bedroom.

The castle was quiet as she roamed the halls. It was the magical time of night when the last people awake finally went to sleep, and there were still a few hours left before the early risers awakened. It truly was her favorite time; there was no one around to notice who she was or what she was doing.

As she slipped out of the kitchen and into the night, she took a moment to exhale. She could feel her body start to relax after being uptight from all the tension she had been feeling. This was the first time she had truly had time to herself since Sophia's arrival.

She slowly made her way to the forest entrance, taking the time to admire the stars glittering through the tree's branches. Despite the full moon's light, she still found some of her favorite constellations.

While she was walking toward one of the lakes she liked to visit, she thought she heard the bushes near her rustling. But every time she looked over her shoulder, nothing was there. She felt the hair on the back of her neck stand up. Resolutely, she continued walking, only stopping to pick some dewberries for a midnight snack.

The lake reflected the moon, and its mirror image was the only thing that Ravenna could see on the water. Before sitting down on what she now considered "her rock" that sat at the edge of the lake, she took a moment to look around to make sure that she was truly alone. The only things she could hear were the waves lapping at the lake's shore and a lone owl crying out a hunter's call. She hadn't realized how tense she was until she let her shoulders relax. Pulling her knees up under her chin, she stared out at the lake.

"It's been three months, and I still have a hard time trusting Liam." Ravenna looked up at the sky as if she could make out Hoseenu's throne. "Everyone wants me to trust him and fall in love." A gentle breeze brushed her face as tears threatened to spill over. "I was fooled once before. *He* fooled almost everyone. I can't make that same mistake again. I know that I'm not making it easy for myself, and I keep trying to tell myself that it's for the good of Lyra. We would have a marriage alliance with Wilderose and would have access to more goods to trade, as well as a chance to increase education in Lyra." Ravenna twisted the fabric on her skirt. Hoseenu knew all of this; it wasn't new to Him. She felt frustrated that she was the one holding her own country back.

"Could you at least help me somehow?!" she practically shouted into the night air. "You are Hoseenu of everything! Can't you just make me fall in love with him?"

Before she could continue yelling at her maker, a low growl came from behind her. Ravenna held her breath as she slowly turned around and made eye contact with a creature whose eyes reflected the moonlight. She couldn't really say she blamed Hoseenu for sending a hungry cougar to attack her after her blatant display of disrespect. She would have been tempted to do the same if the roles had been reversed.

The cougar crouched down, ready to attack its prey. Ravenna slowly looked around to see if she could find something to fend it off while making sure she kept the cougar in her line of sight. A stick that looked like it could be used as a baton lay a few feet behind her near the water's edge. It was too far away for her to get to before the cougar lunged at her.

She closed her eyes as the cougar lept. She waited to feel its teeth and claws tear into her. However, nothing came. She opened her eyes and saw a red blur wrestling with the cougar, holding on to the cougar's shoulder with its teeth.

Liam.

Ravenna raced toward the stick. She grabbed it and rushed back to the two animals fighting each other. By now, the cougar had removed Liam from its shoulder and was biting into Liam's neck. Liam kept growling and snapping his teeth, but he could not escape the cougar's jaw.

Ravenna raised her baton and whacked the cougar over its head. It immediately let go of its hold on Liam and staggered away. Before the cougar could come to its senses, Liam sunk his teeth into the cougar's neck and shook the large cat until an audible crack came from its neck.

Liam dropped the dead cougar from his mouth, panting heavily. Before Ravenna could even speak, Liam collapsed onto the ground next to the cougar's body.

"Liam!" Ravenna started running to him. Tripping over a root, she fell and scrambled on her hands and knees the rest of the way. To her relief, he was still breathing, and he let out a little whimper when he saw her. "Can you get up?"

Liam slowly rolled over from his side onto his stomach. His legs trembled as he tried to stand. Before he could get all the way up, he fell back to the ground and let out another pitiful whine.

Ravenna was terrified. They were a mile away from the forest's entrance where the closest guard was, and she wasn't strong enough to carry a big dog by herself. While she tried to think of some way to get him back to the castle, she tore at the hem of her dress and dipped some of the cloth pieces into the lake water to clean Liam's wounds. She ripped some more and wrapped his neck and his shoulder where the cougar had bitten him.

"Liam, I need you to stay awake for me, please. Don't fall asleep." Liam's only reply was a small huff. "Hoseenu, please tell Tatiana where to find us. Please don't let him die." Ravenna choked back a sob. She couldn't lose her head yet.

"I need you to try standing up one more time. I'm going to try to get us home." Again, Liam slowly hoisted himself up. Before he could fall, Ravenna reached underneath him and clasped her hands together right behind his front legs. She raised him up so he was standing on his hind feet, and she gradually started walking onto the path.

"Look, you're walking on two legs outside of the dining hall!" She tried to laugh, but this time, the sob she was holding back came out. Liam scoffed at her attempt at a joke, but then he whimpered again.

"It's okay. We're going to make it. You're probably going to need stitches, but after that, you'll be able to go to bed and not wake up until way past noon." Ravenna continued talking to Liam as they made their way down the forest path. He was heavy, and she had to take several breaks to catch her breath, but she needed to ensure that he didn't fall unconscious.

When they were three quarters of the way to the forest entrance, she heard movement on the path ahead. She froze. *Please don't be another cougar*, she prayed. Liam started panting heavily. He hadn't spoken a single human sentence to her, and that frightened her almost as much as his bleeding.

Before she could decide whether or not she should hide

them, a group of guards with horses, led by Tatiana on her gray stallion, rounded the bend in front of them.

"We're here!" she called out to them.

Tatiana looked straight at her and shouted something to the people behind her. Ravenna gently lowered Liam to the ground. When the guards reached them, a few picked him up and started to lay him on a horse. However, before one of the guards could mount up behind him, Liam squirmed frantically and looked around with wild eyes. Anytime someone tried to calm him down and have him be still, he would growl and snap at them. It wasn't until he made eye contact with Ravenna that he stopped moving. He still wouldn't let anyone near him though.

"Ravenna, ride with him!" Tatiana cried out to her. When Ravenna walked up to the horse Liam was on, he visibly relaxed. Liam nuzzled his face into her hand, and she scratched behind his ear right before she mounted on the horse behind him.

CHAPTER 27

When they arrived at the castle, they were quickly escorted to the king's chambers. Ravenna watched as the guards lowered Liam onto the bed while the veterinarian ran around the room getting his supplies ready. She felt like she would just get in the way, so she headed toward the door to her own room.

Stay.

Ravenna spun around and saw Liam looking right at her.

Please.

He had finally spoken. How could she not do what he had asked? She sat on a chair near the bed, still out of the way of the veterinarian sewing the stitches.

She could hear him mumbling to himself, "He shouldn't be alive. It's near impossible for dogs to kill cougars."

When he was finished, he shooed everyone out from the room except for the queen. Liam lay still on the bed.

"Your Majesty?"

"Yes?"

"Your prince should recover. However, I need him to stay as still as possible. He's lost a lot of blood and needs to regain his strength. After three days, he should be able to move around some. But not to the dining hall until after his stitches have been removed." Ravenna nodded while she tried not to cry at the doctor's implications. Liam wasn't strong enough to turn into a human. She wanted to argue with him. Surely magic would allow him to transform unharmed? However, she accepted what he had to say. Tatiana would know more about this sort of thing than a human would, so she didn't waste her breath.

When the doctor left, she looked over at Liam. He seemed to be asleep, so she made for the door between their rooms again only to hear him shuffle on the bed. Liam looked directly at her and let out a low painful whine. Immediately, she went right to him.

"You shouldn't be moving!" she said when Liam tried to make room on the bed for her. He looked at her with mournful puppy eyes. Her own eyes filled with tears, and she got onto the bed next to him.

"I'm so sorry," she cried. Liam just licked the tears off of her cheeks and fell asleep.

Liam woke up feeling like his body had been run over by a horse and then set on fire. He cracked his eyes open, but he closed them quickly when the flood of light almost caused him to throw up. He could hear a whimpering sound and wondered where it was coming from when he realized it came from his own body.

"Are you alright?" a groggy voice asked. Before Liam tried opening his eyes again, he took a deep breath and picked up Ravenna's smell. Her scent lingered right next to him, so he wasn't surprised as much as he was confused to open his eyes and see her worried face lying right next to his head.

You're in my bed?

She looked puzzled. "Do you not want me to be?"

It's not appropriate for a queen.

She gave a small chuckle. "Don't worry about it." Frowning, she added, "But really though, how are you doing?"

Liam took a moment to remember what had happened. He had followed Ravenna out through the woods to the lake as usual, but last night, he had caught the scent of a cougar. The next thing he remembered was Ravenna trying to get them back to the castle.

I think I'm alright. Are you hurt? He looked her up and down. The only thing that looked wrong was how tired she seemed. If he was correct, she had woken up right after him, and the pale lighting from the window showed that it was afternoon - way too late for her to still be asleep.

"I'm fine. Thanks to you." Her smile looked sad as she started to get up. "I need to take a bath, and you need more rest. The doctor is going to check in on you soon."

Wait! She paused and turned to look at him. *I'm sorry about yesterday, Ravenna.*

A wistful smile appeared on her face as she leaned back

over the bed and scratched behind his ear, making his tail wag slightly.

"It's alright, Liam." And she stood back up and walked through the door separating their rooms.

CHAPTER 28

It had been a couple of weeks before the doctor finally allowed Ravenna and Liam to eat dinner together. Ravenna had asked Tatiana if the curse would delay Liam's healing, and sadly the answer was yes.

They sat in the dining room, playing another game of chess. It was Liam's turn, and Ravenna watched as he ran his hand through his red hair and squinted at the board.

"You know that I'm just going to win on my next turn regardless of what move you take." She smiled proudly, full of satisfaction. He didn't even bother acknowledging that he had heard her. She continued watching him. She saw the angry, red scars from the cougar's claws where it had scratched the left side of his face. If the collar of his shirt was lower, she would have been able to also see the matching scars on his neck and shoulders. The only reason she knew they were still there was that when he was a dog, the fur hadn't grown back where he had been hurt.

Guilt continued to haunt her. Liam kept reassuring her that he was going to be alright, but it was just one more way she had needlessly disrupted his life. She had stopped going out at night and kept to her window seat whenever she really needed to get out of her head and pray to Hoseenu.

Liam's growl pulled her out of her thoughts. "I admit defeat," he said as he knocked over his king. Ravenna smiled widely.

"Finally! I was beginning to think that you were going to hold us hostage here while you stalled the inevitable." She gave him a self-satisfied smile. He just shook his head.

"If that's what you want to believe." He smiled warmly at her. She felt her cheeks grow hot and tucked a loose hair behind her ear.

"How long have you been following me at night?" she blurted out. That question had been haunting her since the night of the attack. His eyes widened right before he looked away.

"Since the first week that I've been here," he said. She inhaled sharply and he turned to her. "After the first night when I realized that you were praying to Hoseenu, I've made sure that I'm far enough away to give you privacy."

"Why?"

He frowned. "Because you like your privacy."

She barked out a laugh. "No. Why have you been following me?"

"I know that you've said that Lyra is different than Wilderose, but the queen is too important to be left unguarded."

It was her turn to frown. "So being queen is the only thing that's important about me?"

Liam shuffled uncomfortably in his seat. "No, of course

not. You're worth protecting for just being you." She cocked an eyebrow at him, waiting for him to continue. He ran both of his hands through his hair.

"Ravenna, you're worthy of being loved. Your whole kingdom loves you! Your soldiers are willing to die for you as a sign of Hoseenu's unconditional love."

"My soldiers are not willing to die for me because they love me." Liam tried to speak up, but she kept talking. "They die for me because they love Lyra. They do not love me," she said as tears pooled in her eyes. Abruptly, she stood up from the table and before Liam could call after her, she rushed out of the room.

Liam pawed at Ravenna's door. He knew that what he had said during dinner had upset her, but he didn't know why.

Ravenna? It's me. He tried to project his thoughts to her through the door. With his stronger sense of hearing, he could hear her getting off her bed and slowly walking across the room to open the door. Her bloodshot eyes showed that she had obviously been crying. He tried to look as pitiful as possible. Lying down on the floor with his ears laid back, he let out a small whine.

"That's not a very dignified look for a prince." She laughed halfheartedly. He perked right back up and wagged his tail.

Can I come in?

She backed away from the door to allow him room to enter. He walked past her and headed toward the fireplace and took his spot in front of the fire near her chair, waiting expectantly for her to come over.

She sighed and let herself be silently persuaded to tell her dog prince what was wrong. "I'm sorry for leaving dinner early." He waited for her to continue.

"No one knows why I am cursed, other than my parents and Tatiana. Others have been able to correctly piece together that it was my fault." She held up her hand to stop him from his obvious desire to protest. "No, it really was my fault." Ravenna smiled slightly to herself as disbelief crossed over Liam's face. She had gotten good at reading the red setter's expressions.

"I trust you enough to tell you." Nervously she added, "If you would like?"

I would be honored.

"His name was Garrett."

CHAPTER 29

Two Years Ago

Ravenna sat on one of the garden benches near the rose bushes. It was a clear night, and the moon and stars cast a pale silver glow. She was getting nervous. What if he didn't show up? What if he already had, but he had left because they hadn't clarified when exactly "tomorrow night" was? The Lyrian Castle Gardens weren't the biggest gardens in the world, but they were still quite large. Would they even be able to find each other?

She was thinking she'd wait another five minutes when she saw a figure walking down the path toward her. She stilled for a moment. The gardens had always felt safe to her no matter what time of day, but she was alone and had snuck out of her room so no one knew where she was. The only one who even knew that she planned to meet a man tonight was Cress, but it's not like she would know if anything happened to her while she waited.

As soon as she realized it was Garrett, she relaxed. He had come.

"Hello, Ravenna."

"Hello, Garrett."

They smiled at each other for a moment. Again, Ravenna started to feel unsure of herself. At only fifteen, she had lived a sheltered life in the castle. She had never done anything like this before and didn't know what to do next.

"Shall we take a stroll?" Garrett offered her his arm. She gladly took it and relaxed by his side. After a couple of minutes, she gathered her thoughts enough to actually have a conversation with this incredibly handsome man.

"So you're a soldier?"

"Aye. I joined the military a year ago and was recently stationed at the castle."

That's why I haven't seen him before. As future queen, Ravenna always went with her parents to the military stronghold near the castle for royal inspections. It was just a formality for her and her mother to go; between her father and mother, her father knew the ins and outs of the military and was the one in charge of it. He and her uncle had been soldiers before her father had married her mother, who was the princess at the time. Since it was the Crown's duty to make the final calls for military action, the current king or queen could decide which one between them would look over it. As a former soldier, her father was naturally inclined toward the role. Her mother had always joked that the only reason she married her father was because if Lyra ever went to war during her reign, they would be doomed with her in charge of war strategies.

Even if my parents find out that I've snuck out to meet a soldier, they couldn't possibly get upset. I'm a lot safer being with him than a minstrel. She smiled to herself at the thought.

"What made you decide to enlist?" she asked, continuing their conversation.

"My mother was a soldier and always spoke highly of her time in the military. Since I didn't really have my father's disposition toward farming, I thought it'd be best to pursue my mother's career."

He led them past the rose bushes. The buds were only just beginning to show their petals.

"But tell me more about you. What were you doing at the marketplace?" He quickly cut her off from asking more about his background.

"I went with my friend Cress to look at different fabrics that she had wanted to get her hands on. She's training to be a dressmaker while working as a mender."

"I was right to think that you are a kind friend. Beautiful inside and out!"

Ravenna ducked her head at the compliment. "You haven't seen my cousin, Irena. She's the one that's beautiful. I'm just pretty."

While Ravenna had near-black hair and dark green eyes like her mother, Irena took after her father and his twin with blonde hair and blue eyes. Irena had also inherited her height from their fathers' side of the family. Ravenna knew her short stature just didn't stand a chance compared to the radiant goddess that was her cousin. She wondered again why Hoseenu made her the way she was.

Garrett stopped walking immediately, causing her to do the same. Turning her to face him, he said, "Look at me, Ravenna."

She raised her eyes to meet his.

"I have seen your cousin, and while yes, she is beautiful, she does not hold a candle to you. You are far more than just 'pretty.' I've only just met you, but I can tell that you are a good woman, and that shines through to your features. Do you know what the other soldiers have said about you?"

She shook her head as she tried to fight off tears.

"They say that we have the most beautiful princess in all of the lands. You may share the same blood as your cousin, but you have your own unique personality. Don't ever forget it."

And with that, he took her hand and kissed the top of it. Ravenna stilled. It was the most intimate touch she had ever experienced. She looked into his eyes and saw a spark of adoration for her.

"I will never forget. Thank you," she whispered.

"It's getting late, and we both should be getting to bed." He paused. "But I will come back tomorrow night and the night after that. I will continue until you are good and tired of me."

She giggled shyly, "I don't think that will ever be possible!"

"Good. Now let me walk you back to the castle." Instead of offering her his arm, he took her by the hand and led her out of the gardens. She had never been so happy in her life.

They continued to meet for weeks. She never tired of him, and he always came back. Night after night. They learned more about each other. He was four years older than her and had a lot of survival skills that he had learned from his mother, but Ravenna was more equipped for political discussion.

He didn't talk much about his family. She only knew what he had said their first night together. He, however, learned about how much she loved her parents and her fairy godmother.

She became extremely tired during daytime hours as the time spent with Garrett at night grew longer and longer. Eventually, her mother caught on to Ravenna's unusual fatigue and stopped by her rooms one afternoon.

"Ravenna, I couldn't help but notice that you seem…less awake than usual," Katherina gently pried.

"I haven't felt any more tired than usual." Ravenna felt bad about lying to her mother, but if her mother knew that she was sneaking off at night to meet a man, she would put a stop to it.

Her mother raised a brow. "Darling, you fell asleep in the middle of eating breakfast. You can't fool your own mother."

Ravenna groaned at her own failed attempt at lying. "I'm sorry, Mother. I just haven't been getting to sleep at a decent hour."

"And why is that?"

The princess bit her lip. She tried to figure out how to word it. "I've been seeing a friend in the gardens."

"A male friend, isn't it?"

Ravenna widened her eyes in surprise. "How did you know?"

"Have you forgotten that you have bodyguards?"

Ravenna looked at her bed and grumbled, "I thought that sneaking out the window meant that they wouldn't know I left the room."

Katherina snickered, "Your window has been guarded since you were born. We don't take your safety lightly!"

"Then how come it's only now that you've told me you know about my sneaking out to meet Garrett?"

"Because it wasn't disrupting your duties as Crown Princess of Lyra until today." Her mother's gentle tone reassured Ravenna when she added, "Plus, I remember what it was like sneaking out to meet my very own suitor, and he turned out to be the best husband I could have hoped for. If this Garrett is of the same cloth, how could I interfere?"

"Thank you, Mother," Ravenna said as she threw her arms around her.

"However, now that it is getting in the way of your life, you need to bring him into the light for a formal introduction to your father, me, and the rest of the court. Otherwise, you can no longer see him on a regular basis."

"I'll ask him tonight about it."

"Good. Now that you know that we know, please stop climbing out the window. It has been causing Sir Gawain's hair to turn gray."

Ravenna laughed and promised that she would.

That evening, she met Garrett in the gardens as usual.

"You're awfully quiet tonight," he remarked. "Is everything all right?"

Ravenna could hear the concern in his voice. "Yes, I was just wondering..." Ravenna paused as she tried to figure out how to phrase the question that would either make their relationship more serious or end it completely. Garrett saw a bench and walked over to it so they could sit, and he waited for Ravenna to collect her thoughts.

"I mean, would you be alright meeting my parents?"

Then she very quickly added, "And the rest of the Lyrian court?" She couldn't bring herself to look at him.

"Did you just ask me to be formally introduced as someone who is courting you?"

"Yes?"

She hesitated. He stilled as though if he were to move, he would answer her question prematurely.

"I will gladly make it known that I am courting you."

"You will?" She looked up in amazement. Did this mean that he loved her? That he was willing to publicly announce their relationship, not just to her family, but the entire country of Lyra?

"I will," he affirmed and leaned his head closer to hers. She could see that he wanted to kiss her so she closed her eyes to let him. It was soft and tender, and even though it was brief, she knew without a doubt that it meant that he loved her.

Garrett won her parents and the court over. He had a charm about him that made him popular among everyone. Ravenna was extremely happy that everyone approved. Well, almost everyone.

"Why don't you like him, Tatiana?" Ravenna was out in the gardens watching her fairy godmother get dirty as she planted flowers in the sunshine.

"I don't dislike him. I just think you can do better than Garrett." Tatiana didn't even look up from her work as she replied.

"Is it because he's not a prince? My father was a soldier when he met my mother."

"It's not because he's not a prince. He's virtually unknown. He's only been a soldier for a year, and you haven't even met any of his family. He's too perfect."

Ravenna scoffed, "How can someone being too perfect be a problem? I think that's a desirable quality!"

At this, Tatiana finally stopped planting flowers and sat back up on her knees. Looking directly at Ravenna, she told the young princess, "No one is perfect, Ravenna. Every person you meet is going to be good or bad, but even then, it's not black and white. Good people have flaws, and even bad people have good intentions. Someone who pretends that nothing is wrong with them is someone who is lying about themselves. How can you build trust with someone who you don't even know?"

Tears welled up in Ravenna's eyes. "I do know him! You just need to spend more time with him." And she ran off before Tatiana could say anything more to her.

It had been three months since they had first met in the gardens at night. Garrett had been busy learning politics with Ravenna while still being involved in the military. Ravenna was entrusted with more and more royal duties and had to attend more meetings with her parents. So when Garrett suggested they sneak away to the gardens, just the two of them, Ravenna gladly accepted.

They were silently walking the garden path, enjoying one another's company, when Garrett spoke. "I've been thinking."

"That sounds dreadfully dangerous," Ravenna teased before he could finish.

"Hey!" He gave a playfully hurt look toward the princess, making her laugh.

"My apologies for interrupting. Please continue, oh, great thinker."

Garrett gave her another jesting glare but let the remark slide. "As I was saying, I've been thinking over the last month, and I don't know anyone else I would rather spend my life with than you." At this, he stopped walking. Ravenna's heart started to pound harder in her chest as she watched Garrett get on his knee in front of her. "Ravenna, would you do me the honor of becoming my queen and making me your king?"

"Yes! Yes! A thousand times yes!" she cried as he stood and kissed her so passionately that she forgot about how he had asked her to make him king instead of her husband.

Cress was the most excited of anyone at the news of Ravenna's engagement. She jumped up and down after Ravenna told her.

"Does this mean that you'd be willing to make my wedding dress?" Ravenna grinned and started laughing as Cress stopped jumping and her eyes grew wide.

"Wait. You mean, I could, you know. Oh my goodness, yes!" Her friend rushed over to Ravenna and gave her an enormous hug.

"When do you need it by?"

"Well, we were hoping to get married in two weeks."

"Two weeks?" Cress shouted.

"Is that too soon for you?"

"No, of course not, but why the rush? You're not, you know..." She gestured toward her stomach, making a rounding motion.

"No, of course not!" Ravenna shrieked in embarrassed horror. "We just don't want to wait."

Cress looked unconvinced but shrugged it off. Ravenna knew that Cress was finally getting her dream of making a gown that would get public attention.

"So, what do you want your dress to look like?" Cress asked.

Ravenna's parents were a little more vocal than Cress about the timeline.

"Darling, isn't that a little soon to plan a wedding?" her mother asked.

"Invitations need to be sent out tonight if we want any of our neighbors to attend," her father added.

Ravenna supplied a solution. "We could just have the ambassadors represent their respective countries' monarchs. It doesn't have to be extravagant. We just want to start married life together as soon as possible."

Her parents exchanged a look. King Tristan sighed, "If this is what you want, I see no reason to stop the wedding. Garrett seems to be a good man, and he makes you happy."

"Thank you, Father!" Ravenna skipped out of the room in delight. She couldn't wait to tell Garrett the good news of her parents' blessing.

The night before the wedding came faster than anyone expected. All the guests who were able to make the trip were settled into their rooms. Cress was finishing up the final fitting for Ravenna's wedding dress, and the groom was out with his friends at one of the taverns near the marketplace outside the castle.

"Maybe we should surprise Garrett," Ravenna told Cress.

"And do what?" her friend replied incredulously as she tried to finish another stitch in the hem. "Would you stop moving?"

"Sorry, but I'm just so excited!" Ravenna stopped her fidgeting. "Anyway, we could just sneak over and pay for the drinks. Nothing extravagant."

"'Nothing extravagant' says the wealthy princess," Cress mumbled through the needle and thread in her mouth.

"Okay, I'll pay for the drinks, and you can keep me company."

"Oh, alright. I'll go with you. But if you are yawning through your own wedding tomorrow, you can't blame me."

"Thanks, Cress. This will be fun!" Ravenna bounced. "Ouch!"

"I said stop moving!"

Cress and Ravenna walked down the road. They pulled the hoods of their coats up as rain started to pour down unexpectedly. It took them a couple of tries to find the right tavern, but they finally spotted Garrett when they looked through the window of The Boorish Pig Tavern. He and his friends had obviously been there for a while. They were getting louder and louder with every drink they downed. The owner looked less than thrilled at the rowdy bunch.

"Ravenna, have you ever met Garrett's friends before?" Cress asked, narrowing her eyes at the group of men.

Ravenna hesitated. "Well, no..." She had never seen such behavior inside the castle before.

"Bartender! Another round of drinks for the future king!" one of the men shouted while the rest of them roared with laughter.

"How on earth did you convince the princess to marry a lout like you?" another shouted into Garrett's ear, oblivious to how physically close he was to his friend. An annoyed look flashed across Garrett's face, but he quickly shrugged it off and shouted right back, "Because she actually believes that I love her and not her throne!" He roared with laughter and then drunkenly kissed one of the barmaids.

"My good sir," he then addressed the bartender. "Don't forget that all of this is being charged to the Crown."

"Yeah, because this good-for-nothing can't afford even half a pint of the rottenest ale!" another cracked.

Ravenna gasped.

Cress muttered, "Well, seems like he had the same idea as you did to have you pay for all of his drinks."

Before she could even think twice about it, Ravenna barged in and walked up to Garrett. He was laughing at something the man next to him had said, but as soon as he caught sight of Ravenna heading toward him, he stopped.

"Hello, darling." Garrett's words were slightly slurred.

"Do you love me?" Ravenna asked bluntly. Garrett blinked at her. "Do you love me?" she asked again. Tears pricked her eyes.

Looking down, Garrett sighed and said, "No. I don't."

Before she could say anything else, she felt Cress put a hand on her shoulder. "Come on, Ravenna. Let's go home." Her friend guided Ravenna out the door and back to the castle, leaving Garrett behind and hoping to never see him again.

It was late at night when Ravenna knocked on her mother's door. She opened it slowly when she heard the queen say, "Come in." Tatiana and Katherina sat in the window seat, drinking tea.

When Katherina saw her daughter, she said, "Oh, Ravenna, come here, child." She opened her arms wide when she saw the tears running down her daughter's face. Ravenna fell into her mother's loving embrace and openly wept. She tried to feel the comfort of her mother stroking her hair while her fairy godmother got up to make another cup of chamomile tea.

When Ravenna had started to calm down a little, her mother asked, "What's wrong, Ravenna?"

"He doesn't love me!" Ravenna wailed as more tears trickled down her face.

"How do you know Garrett doesn't love you?" Katherina gently pulled away to look into her daughter's eyes.

"He told me he didn't."

"Why would he do such a thing like that?" Tatiana had a hard time keeping the anger out of her voice.

Ravenna sniffled through her explanation of what had happened at the tavern and then started crying again as she declared, "I hurt so much. I feel sick every time I think about it. I don't ever want to feel this way again!"

"Oh, honey, I'm so sorry you have to go through this." Ravenna's mother hugged her again and prayed to Hoseenu to help comfort her daughter.

"What about the wedding?" Ravenna whispered.

"We can cancel the wedding. All you need to do is take some time to heal. I know you're hurt now, but it won't feel this way for forever. You can sleep in my room with me tonight if you would like."

Ravenna nodded into her mother's shoulder. Tatiana gave her a kiss on the forehead and headed out to leave mother and daughter alone.

Days turned to weeks, which turned into months, and Ravenna still felt like her broken heart would never heal. As much as her mother and father had tried to cancel the wedding with as little fanfare as possible, rumors had spread about what could have happened. She could see the nobles whispering amongst themselves in the dining hall, and servants became quiet as soon as she walked by. No one knew what had happened to the soldier who was supposed to become king. The official report stated that the king had had Garrett stationed to guard the border between Lyra and Wilderose. The popular rumor, however, said that he had been exiled. Only Queen Katherina, King Tristan, and Tatiana knew that Garrett had taken the border post on his own, instead of sticking around in the face of a scandal.

Cress visited Ravenna as often as she could, bringing sweets from the kitchen to share, but Ravenna just said that she was sorry that no one would see the beautiful wedding dress that Cress had made.

"Don't worry about it! I'll make another gown for you for some major event in your life that will jumpstart my career. This is about how *you* are doing." Cress gave her friend a hug. "And you're not doing well, but your family and friends are still here for you." Ravenna felt thankful that she had their love, but it didn't feel like it could take the place of the love she had lost.

"Thank you, Cress. I'm the luckiest person alive to have you for a friend."

"Yeah, you are!" Both girls laughed at Cress's lack of humility. "I need to get back to work, but it's good to hear your laugh." Ravenna watched Cress leave her room, waiting for a bit until Cress had walked down the hall, and then she headed out of her room to find Tatiana in the gardens.

CHAPTER 30

*L*iam was silent as Ravenna shared her past with him. She didn't know what he was thinking and couldn't bear to look at him. She wouldn't blame him for thinking she was immature. She had been a spoiled child that had acted out dramatically and, consequently, had ruined his life.

"And then I asked Tatiana for a curse to prevent my heart from ever breaking again," she finished, as she fiddled with her skirt.

No one should have to go through something like that. Especially you. Liam moved in front of her and put his paw on her knee. Ravenna stared at it emotionlessly.

"No, but I've learned my lesson. A queen is not a person. She represents power and nothing more."

You are *your own person who feels and thinks just like everyone else. Yes, you have greater responsibilities than most people will ever know, but you are still human.*

Ravenna finally brought herself to look up and meet his soft gaze with her hard stare. She could see the sincerity on his face. He *was* different than Garrett. Everyone who knew him well mentioned that it was never his desire to become king. Tatiana liked him, which should have allowed her to let her guard down around him. But now he had seen all of her and accepted it.

"Thank you," she whispered. He nuzzled his head against the back of her hand that still grasped her skirt. Suddenly, he stopped and looked up at her.

What happened to your personal guards who watched you sneak out? he demanded.

Her face turned red and, with a sheepish grin, she said, "I had them reassigned to just guarding the castle and not me specifically."

His eyes narrowed, and she could hear his low growl.

"I'll have them stationed at their old post," she sighed in defeat. Liam's tail gave a small wag, and he licked her hand. It was a testament to how tired she was that she didn't even protest it. Liam yawned as a sign that she wasn't the only one who was tired.

"We should get to sleep."

He nodded and stood up. She followed suit and opened the door between the king's and queen's chambers.

Thank you, Ravenna, for trusting me. Goodnight, Liam said as he walked through the door.

"Goodnight, Liam," Ravenna softly called out before closing the door behind him. When the door shut with a click, she leaned her back and closed her eyes.

I'll break this curse as a way to thank you, she silently promised to Liam and to herself.

CHAPTER 31

Liam noticed a difference in Ravenna in the weeks after she told him more about the curse. She was more relaxed around him, as if she was no longer constantly weighing her words before speaking. She laughed more readily, and as usual, it was one of his favorite sounds.

There were still a few moments of hesitation, like during council meetings whenever anything was brought up involving raiders or past mishaps some of the nobles had run into. It was fine with him, though. She was willing to trust him with other things. Maybe it was time to be vulnerable with her.

"What's wrong?" Ravenna asked.

Liam looked up at Ravenna from his spot by the fireplace. After dinner, they had gone to her rooms where she sat at her desk, going over notes for tomorrow's visit to the nearby school. It was the one that Cori went to, and she had already told him that all her friends knew she was his favorite. He had just barked playfully and started a game of tug-of-war with some rope.

What do you mean?

Ravenna quirked a brow at him. "You sighed as if you had resigned yourself to a horrible fate."

He didn't know if he should be thrilled or concerned that she could read him so well. *It's nothing. Do you need any help for tomorrow?*

He could tell she didn't believe him based on how her lips were drawn into a thin line, but she let it slide. She did surprise him by agreeing to let him help her. It was another small difference in their relationship now. She wasn't just telling him about her life; she was letting him share in it.

He walked over to her and sat next to her desk. *What do you need help with exactly?*

Ravenna frowned at some papers, biting her lip. "For starters, I want to make sure that I don't miss anything." Her mouth formed a tight line before she added, "I had tutors growing up, so I've never actually gone to school. I know that Wilderose has a great education system and that you and Sophia were required to go, as well as the rest of your court's children. I wonder if you could tell me more about it and what makes your schools superior."

Liam took some time to think. Sophia was probably the better of the two royal siblings to answer this question. He had always tried to skip classes to ride his horse and hunt.

From what I remember, the class sizes were small enough that the teachers knew all of their students well. Which made it extremely difficult to sneak out or get away with anything, he huffed.

Ravenna's eyes widened, and she laughed. "Sophia was right! You were a difficult child!" Liam did his best to glare at her, but his tail started to wag and gave him away.

I still managed to get good marks. He raised his head indignantly.

Ravenna scoffed.

It's true! I would get everything done before I decided I didn't need to be there.

Ravenna shook her head. "Whatever you say." But then she scratched him behind his ears. Liam pressed up against her leg so she would get the hint to keep going. Sadly for him, she pulled her hand back and shuffled through the papers on her desk. Liam lay down on the floor.

"What did Wilderose teach their students?" Ravenna tried to get them back on track.

Science, arithmetic, language arts, history, and foreign languages. Those were the foundations, but there were other subjects you could study if you wanted to. He looked up and saw Ravenna scribbling down what he had said. She wrote with such concentration that he was positive that if someone else would have walked in at that moment, she would never have known.

"What else?" she asked when she finally looked at him again. Ravenna continued questioning Liam about Wilderose's schools for a couple more hours before Liam looked out the window. When had it become so dark?

Ravenna, you're going to be too exhausted to do anything tomorrow if you don't go to sleep now.

Ravenna followed his gaze to the window. Her mouth dropped into a large O. "You're right. Thank you for staying up with me." Her smile warmed his heart. He found that he couldn't form any words and just nuzzled her hand with his head. She obliged him and scratched behind his ears again before she stood up from her desk.

"Goodnight, Liam."

Goodnight, Ravenna.

CHAPTER 32

Ravenna couldn't sit still on the ride to the school. She wiggled in her seat as she looked out the window, watching the landscape move past the carriage. Liam was taking a nap on the seat across from her, so she was alone with her thoughts.

Despite having been queen for a year, this was the first time she was able to start working on something she felt personally invested in. The peace treaty was a fulfillment of the work that her parents had begun, and even though she had wanted it too and had seen her parents' dream to fruition, it hadn't been *her* project. She wanted her initial visit to the highest ranked school in Lyra to go well.

Even though Lyrian schools were not the worst in the realm, it was still common knowledge that they were far from the best. She wanted to change that. From what she had learned from her parents, tutors, and participation in council meetings, Lyra itself was very wealthy, but the general population was poor. Cress had been lucky to get a job in the castle and was now in a position to make a name for herself, but for others who wanted to rise above their station, joining the military was their only option.

She had noticed from historical studies of other countries, like Wilderose, that good education was part of a long-term solution to improve things for all people, not just the upper class.

Liam woke up right before the carriage stopped. Ravenna snickered as she watched him try to reorient himself. He had not been happy this morning when she got him up. It had slipped her mind to tell him they were going to get there an hour before the children even arrived, which meant an earlier wake up call. She felt bad for keeping him up late, but she knew by now that he would have had the same reaction even if he had slept for over a day, so she didn't feel too bad.

A footman opened the carriage door. Liam jumped out first to give her more room to maneuver her long skirt. Cress had insisted that since she was there on official royal business, she must wear a dress that would suit a queen. The dark green dress did complement her almost black hair and pale skin, but the heavy material left her worried that she wouldn't be able to kick out the long skirt properly to take steps, ruining the "queenly impression" that Cress had worked so hard to give her.

Hoseenu, help me walk, she silently prayed.

Headmistress Schooner was at the top of the school stairs waiting for Ravenna. Liam had waited beside the carriage and followed right behind her as they made their way up the steps. Her reestablished body guards walked behind him. The elderly woman gave a low bow. Ravenna nodded her head for the other woman to rise.

"Welcome, Your Majesty." She glanced over at the dog sitting beside the queen. "And Your Highness." She nodded to the dog. Liam nodded his head back.

"Thank you for allowing us to visit your school, Headmistress Schooner."

"Please call me Edna, Your Majesty. It's less of a mouthful." Her eyes twinkled at the queen and Ravenna's polite smile grew into a genuine one.

"As long as you call me Ravenna." She didn't dare speak for Liam. Formalities with names and titles were something she didn't want to mess up with him, despite the fact that he had reassured her that Wilderosians didn't expect the custom to be honored by foreigners.

Liam hadn't said anything to her, so she stayed quiet as Edna led them inside the school. She gave the school's history and shared that summer break was a week away so the children could help their families with the summer harvest.

The school's large, three-story, square building had a hollowed-out middle for a courtyard. A school bell hung at the top of the third story, parallel to the entryway. Edna's office on the first floor looked directly across the courtyard at the entrance. Ravenna's bodyguards stood outside the office doors while she and Liam walked in after Edna. As Edna moved behind her desk to sit, she gestured to the chair sitting in front of the desk. Ravenna sat in it while Liam sat next to her on the floor.

"I'll give it to you straight," Edna said as she leaned forward to rest her elbows on her desk and brought her hands together. "I know that you are here to learn what needs to be improved in the Lyrian schools, and there are two major problems that you will see for yourself."

Ravenna raised an eyebrow, impressed with the older woman's bluntness.

"We are understaffed, and our students' families can't always afford for them to come to school. Whether it's because of a lack of money or a lack of help at home, students are not able to go to school for the whole school year." Edna looked over her glasses at Ravenna and continued. "Schools are expensive, and while that leads to us being able to provide quality supplies and curriculum, our students can only come for a few months out of the school year. The current system is set up on daily payments because we understand that families won't be able to pay for a school year upfront. But we want to at least give our students the chance to feel like they can come every day."

Edna sat back in her chair and took off her glasses. "Of course, this policy is only allowed for lower-class families. Those who can afford monthly or yearly payments are not allowed a daily payment." She chuckled to herself. "We do need to have enough funds for our own immediate expenses."

"Of course," Ravenna agreed. Edna took a moment to look the young queen up and down, assessing her for what, Ravenna didn't know. She seemed to pass the test because Edna gave a firm nod.

"You will be in Mistress Ana's classroom first. She teaches the five-year-olds."

They made their way out of Edna's office. While Edna had been talking, the courtyard had filled with children of all ages. Some were playing games together while others stood in groups talking and giggling.

"Liam!" Ravenna recognized the mop of brown curls running toward them as Cori. A few of the other children from the castle followed right behind her. Liam's tail wagged nonstop while he licked the children's faces, causing them to squeal in delight.

"Miss Cordelia! Manners!" Edna firmly said to the little girl currently rubbing Liam's belly after he had tumbled down under the weight of all the children. Cori stood up and looked down at her feet. The other children stood up as well.

"Sorry, Headmistress," they said together.

Cori looked up at her and said, "But Liam plays with us at home." While they were being scolded, Liam had moved to sit next to Ravenna.

"But are you at home now?" Edna said, looking at the dog prince with her eyebrows raised. Liam lowered his head and gave a soft whine of apology.

"No, Headmistress," Cori said.

"Well, as long as you ask His Highness if he wants to play with you lot before classes start and he says yes, then you can."

Cori turned to look at Liam, who stood up immediately, his tail wagging as he danced on his front paws. The children shouted and chased Liam, who had run toward the middle of the courtyard, allowing some of the other students to join in their game of chase.

Ravenna had watched Cori and the other children play with Liam before, and they always looked like they were having fun.

"Do they remember that he's actually a human prince?" Ravenna turned and looked at Edna, who was watching Liam chase after a little boy who giggled as he ran.

"Apparently they all met him his first day in Lyra before he set off the curse. As to whether or not they remember he's a prince is a different story."

Edna continued to watch them play for a while before turning and looking at Ravenna. "Does *he* remember that he's actually a human prince?"

Startled, Ravenna looked over at Liam. He jumped and barked at Cori, who held a stick above his head for him to try to get. When she threw it, he took off after it and returned it to her.

Ravenna chewed her lower lip. When was the last time he had spoken to her using human words? It was so easy to know what he was trying to convey with body language that she hadn't noticed that he hadn't actually spoken with her recently. The realization made her nervous.

Before she could answer Edna's question, the bell rang, and the children quickly gathered their things and scrambled to get to their respective classrooms. Liam trotted over to the two women, panting heavily but with a huge doggy grin.

"Right this way please," Edna said as she led them to a flight of outdoor stairs.

"You looked like you were having fun," Ravenna whispered to Liam. His only reply was a small woof. Ravenna tensed a little.

When they arrived at Mistress Ana's classroom, she tried to think of something to ask Liam that he would have to answer with words. However, Edna interrupted her thoughts by leading them to a woman that Ravenna had to tilt her head almost all the way back to make eye contact with. She assumed this must be Mistress Ana.

The young woman smiled and bowed. "It's an honor to have you in our classroom, Your Majesty." Her students stood up and bowed as well. Ravenna saw that Cori's younger brother, James, was in this classroom. He was one out of what seemed like fifty. Edna was right about being understaffed if this was the normal class size.

Ravenna nodded to them and said, "It's an honor to be

here." The students sat back down at their desks, and Mistress Ana started teaching the lesson. Ravenna and Liam moved toward the back of the classroom to sit and watch.

She smiled at the students who tried to sneak glances at her before quickly looking away, giggling with their friends. When Mistress Ana gave them a small break as she rearranged the room, a few of the children walked up to her, including James.

"Hello." She smiled at them, hoping that she came off as warm and friendly instead of how shy she was feeling inside. James said hello and then went straight over to Liam, who was lying down in front of Ravenna, to give him a big hug. Liam sat up to make it easier for James to wrap his little arms around him.

"Is he your dog?" a little girl asked Ravenna from behind her straight brown hair.

Ravenna ruffled the top of Liam's head. "He's my prince."

The girl's eyes widened. "You mean *he's* the dog prince?"

"He is."

The other students nearby whispered among themselves in excitement. It was the first time they had met anyone under a curse.

"Alright, class, our break is over." The children slowly made their way back to their desks. Liam plopped back down on the floor and closed his eyes to take a nap. Ravenna still wanted to talk to him, but she never got the chance.

Before Ravenna knew it, it was time for the students to have their lunch. Because it was warm today, all of the students could eat outside in the courtyard instead of in their individual classrooms.

Ravenna watched as all of the children rushed outside and down to the first floor. Mistress Ana stood next to her.

"They were all so invested in what you had to teach them," the queen commented.

Mistress Ana smiled to herself. "Yes, but even though I have the smallest number of students, it's still so hard to keep track of all of them."

Ravenna frowned. "This is the smallest class?"

Mistress Ana nodded, "We're the only school left near the capital city after the other schools closed down. We take in the students from the city and the countryside that borders it. It makes for a large population."

Suddenly, Ravenna realized that Liam wasn't by her side. She looked around and spotted him in the courtyard playing with the children again. She sighed in relief but then furrowed her brow as she understood how used to his presence she had gotten.

Mistress Ana followed her students outside. Lost in thought, Ravenna found herself alone in the classroom. She hurried to catch up and tried not to trip over her skirt.

When she got to the bottom of the stairs, Liam rushed over to her, took her skirt in his mouth, and tugged her to come out into the middle of the yard.

"Liam!" Ravenna tried to pull her skirt back, but his grip was tight, and she worried that the skirt would tear. The students giggled at the spectacle of a dog pulling their queen. *So much for looking regal*, she mused. After reaching their supposed destination beside Cori, Liam picked up some nearby rope and placed one end into Cori's hands. He nudged Ravenna to step behind Cori. She and Cori looked at each other, confused.

"What are you trying to do?" She tried to keep the exasperation out of her voice.

Tug-of-war, he replied as he went over to the other end of the rope and picked it up with his mouth. Ravenna was so relieved to hear him speak. She immediately told Cori what Liam wanted to play, and the girl shouted for some of the others to join.

It didn't take long for the children to pick sides, and Ravenna wondered if she should be concerned that Lyra's future generations preferred a dog prince over herself. Her focus shifted to the rope and to trying to pull the other side toward her own. The remaining students had circled around to watch and cheer.

Ravenna could feel herself starting to sweat as Cori shouted for everyone to pull harder. The next thing she knew, Liam's team landed on the ground after a huge lunge on her team's part. Cori jumped up and down in excitement along with the rest of her teammates. She quickly reached for Ravenna's hands so that the queen could jump in victory with her, but before she could grasp them, Liam knocked Ravenna down and assaulted her with slobbery dog kisses. She laughed hysterically and tried to form the words to tell Liam to stop. The children nearby shrieked in laughter. Some tried to pry Liam off of Ravenna, but he was too determined to stay by his queen.

"Alright, alright. Off!" she finally gasped out. Liam backed away with his tail wagging and his tongue hanging out of his mouth. He seemed pleased with himself for wrinkling her dress. Ravenna winced at the thought of Cress seeing the state of her gown when they got back home.

The school bell rang, and just like in the morning, everyone rushed to their classrooms. Ravenna headed toward Edna's office with Liam trailing behind her.

Edna stood in front of her door with a bemused smile on her face. Ravenna could feel a blush blooming on her face, but she pretended it was normal for the Queen of Lyra to be so disheveled.

Edna bowed and said, "Thank you again for visiting our school."

"It has been a pleasure. Thank you for opening up your school to me."

Edna followed them out.

Liam walked down the stairs and into the waiting carriage. Before Ravenna could join him, Edna stopped her. "He will make a great king for you." Ravenna beamed and nodded her head in acknowledgment and walked away.

CHAPTER 33

Liam followed Ravenna out to a clearing in the forest. Servants had set up a picnic dinner for them since Ravenna had previously mentioned that because the weather was good, it would be nice to have dinner outside. If he didn't turn into a human, they'd just pack up and go back inside.

Just like crossing the doorway into the dining hall, as soon as he stepped into the meadow, he turned back into a human. He felt relief, partially because he wanted to enjoy the sun without a fur coat. He smiled at Ravenna, who looked like she was feeling the same relief as him, perhaps for different reasons.

When they had loaded their plates and settled onto the picnic blanket, Ravenna immediately started in on her questions. "What did you think of today's visit?"

The tone of her question confused him a little. It sounded like she was trying to be nonchalant, but she failed miserably.

They hadn't talked on the way back to the castle. He had immediately fallen asleep in the carriage, and when they arrived, Ravenna's uncle whisked her away to talk privately, leaving him alone.

"Headmistress Schooner was right that they are understaffed. What did you think?" He popped some grapes into his mouth, waiting to see where Ravenna would take the conversation. She seemed to relax a little when he mentioned what the headmistress had said. *Interesting...*

"I was wondering what happened to the nearby schools that made this one the only school in the area. When I talked with my uncle, he just said they couldn't afford to stay open. Despite schools being private, they still get stipends from the Crown when they hit hard times." She frowned. "It's not like we can't afford to keep schools open, or even make them free for everyone, especially after we updated the budget to move funds from the military to education."

Liam loved seeing her so passionate. This topic really enraptured her, and she practically glowed as she thought up ways to make it possible for Lyrians to have better opportunities. "What if you made them free for everyone?"

Ravenna looked up at him, remembering he was still there. "Say that again?"

"You said that you could afford to make schools free for everyone. Why don't you?"

Ravenna gasped, and her eyes widened. "You're brilliant!" But she deflated slightly, adding, "That'll only solve part of the problem. The other part is that some families need the extra help for their own daily lives. It'll also increase classroom sizes even more."

They were silent for a while, lost in thought. Liam reached over to grab some cheese for his bread when Ravenna jolted upright and startled him enough to make him drop the loaf.

"We could open up some sort of government funded facility for those in need of jobs to help find people part-time work. People in need of work can apply to them, and families who have children can hire from those facilities instead of employing their children during school hours!" Ravenna wiggled where she sat. "Then we could open up a college to help increase the number of teachers. That's probably where we would have to draw the line on free education, but we could have a scholarship program for it!"

Liam sat back with a wide smile and listened to Ravenna ramble on about her ideas to help Lyra. He found himself wanting to watch her put all of her plans into action. He wanted to support her dream so badly that the desire physically hurt.

He froze. When had he started wanting to spend his future with her? Hope bloomed in his chest. He had truly fallen in love with her. Now he had to wait for Ravenna to fall in love with him.

"Liam!" Ravenna was waving her hand in front of his face.

He shook his head. "I'm sorry. Did you ask me something?"

She bit her lip. "I wanted to ask you why you didn't talk to me today."

He frowned, trying to remember when he hadn't. "I didn't?"

She tensed up again. "Well...I mean...I understood you most of the time, but you only said one word to me, and that was 'tug-of-war' because neither Cori nor I knew what you wanted us to do with the rope."

Liam felt the blood drain from his face. That wasn't like him at all. He remembered everything that people had said throughout the day, but he couldn't remember what he had said in return. He was aware that he had been communicating with Ravenna and everyone else as best as he could. The only time that he remembered losing complete control of himself was when he saw Ravenna let her guard down around the students when her team had won.

"Liam? What is going on? You can tell me."

He saw the concern etched on Ravenna's face. He had tried so hard to not make her worry about the curse and to help her forget how much it was changing him. But now he realized he couldn't hide it anymore. He released a long breath.

"I think that part of the curse is to strip away my humanity. I'm having a harder time remembering that I am human during the day," he said slowly, trying to gauge her reaction. She still looked concerned.

"No one else has mentioned this before." She frowned.

He smiled. "No one else has stuck around this long either."

"You're right. No one else has." Her gaze filled with questions as she looked at him. He wasn't sure what puzzle she was trying to figure out now. "Why haven't you given up? You seemed to have known about this part of the curse for a while, yet you're still here."

"I made a promise, and I keep my promises."

She rolled her eyes at his response. "Yes, you keep reminding me that you made a promise, but you never told me why you made it in the first place."

At this he looked away, trying to figure out how to tell

her this piece of information that he would be ashamed of her finding out. He closed his eyes. "I made it because Tatiana said that being part of the Lyrian royal family meant that my sister and the rest of Wilderose would also fall under her protection." He could hear her inhale sharply, but he continued.

"I was undisciplined growing up. I snuck out of class, ran around the edge of the Elven Wood, played pranks on Sophia, and disappointed my father." When he opened his eyes again, he couldn't see the meadow they were sitting in. He was back in Wilderose, remembering the look on his father's face after another lecture about how he was a prince and needed to act like one.

"At some point, someone suggested to my father that I enlist in the military. My father was at his wit's end trying to get me to behave, so he agreed to it. Turns out the structure was what I needed, and I loved it."

He snorted, "Everyone was surprised, including myself. So my father gave me more responsibilities over the military and the guard while Sophia was given more diplomatic authority. We didn't know it then, but he was sick and he knew he was dying."

Liam started to choke on his words, thinking about when his father had called him and Sophia into his study and broke the news to them. "He was so powerful and full of strength that it was impossible to believe that he was weakening. Then one day, he asked me to be completely in charge of capturing the raiders. It was the last task that he allowed himself to work on. Everything else was given to Sophia to handle. I wanted to make him proud of his delinquent son. After he died, I got so caught up with the funeral and getting Sophia ready for her coronation that capturing the raiders became secondary." He gave a mirthless laugh.

"If I had focused on them, your parents would still be alive. My sister's reign would not have started with the fear of war against Lyra. I had to make it right."

He finally made eye contact with Ravenna. He saw tears welling up in her eyes, but he pressed on. "At first, it was like I said before. I came to sign the peace treaty so that we could share resources to fight off the raiders. But then Tatiana picked me out of everyone present to ask if I would try to break the curse. I thought that it must be Hoseenu showing grace."

"I see," was all that Ravenna seemed able to say.

Liam grabbed her hand with both of his, and Ravenna stared at their hands in shock.

"But then I got to know you and see what a caring and wonderful person you are. Ravenna, I am not going to give up on you. I love you." Her eyes flew to his, searching his face to see if there were any insincerity there.

"Will you marry me?" He held his breath. He hadn't planned on telling her that he loved her. He hadn't even really known that he loved her until after they had started eating dinner, but now it was out there for her to know as well.

The tears that she had held back spilled over. It was the first time she had let him see her cry. He wanted to kiss the tears away and hold her in his arms, but he held still.

"I'm sorry. I can't." He let go of her hands as she quickly got up and walked away from him. He watched her go, no longer as a human but as a dog, and felt for the first time the pain of rejection.

CHAPTER 34

Cook was the only one in the kitchens when Ravenna went looking for Tatiana. She wasn't in her rooms, nor the small breakfast room. There was only one place left to find the fairy.

Ravenna stood in front of the gate leading to the flower gardens. She hadn't stepped foot in them since she had asked Tatiana to curse her. The collection of memories of midnight rendezvouses with Garrett made it too painful to walk through, but right now she had to know more about the curse for Liam's sake. She might not love him like he apparently loved her, but she would not be the reason for him to permanently stay as a dog. She walked through the gate.

"Hello, Ravenna."

She found Tatiana sitting on a bench facing west. It was still daylight out, but not for much longer. The sky had already darkened slightly, and its hues had changed from the bright blue of daytime to the pinkish hues of sunset.

Ravenna shook her head. "You knew I would be looking for you today, didn't you?"

Tatiana nodded in silent admission.

"Then why couldn't you have been anywhere except the gardens?"

Instead of answering Ravenna, Tatiana moved down the bench and patted the seat next to her. Ravenna sat down and pulled her legs up so her chin could rest on her knees. Tatiana put an arm around her in a gentle hug and let Ravenna lean into her side.

"You used to love the gardens growing up. You'd follow your mother and me out here to help as much as you possibly could." Tatiana's gaze softened as she remembered years past. "You shouldn't let one man take more from you than he already has."

Ravenna let Tatiana's words sink in. Garrett had stolen so much from her: not only her ability to trust in men, but also her ability to trust herself to love. Liam was helping her to regain those parts of herself, but ultimately, it was for her to decide when to no longer let her past define her.

"Liam told me today that he loves me," she whispered. She was sure that Tatiana would already know. Tatiana always seemed to know when important events happened, despite not being around during their occurrence.

"That's not a surprise. You are very lovable." Tatiana looked down at Ravenna and smiled. Ravenna snorted. Trust her fairy godmother to be biased.

"What? It's true!" Tatiana said before she sighed, "And yet, you do not love him."

Ravenna shook her head. "I am fond of him, but I

thought someone loved me before. I thought he was telling the truth when he said that he loved me, but I was wrong."

Tatiana shifted so she could look straight at Ravenna. "Look at me, child." She reached out to tilt Ravenna's head toward her. "Love isn't without its risks, whether it's with Liam or someone else. The man you marry is going to hurt you even while he loves you. Hoseenu is the only one that can love you without unintentionally hurting you. But you know this already." She smiled at the young queen who nodded in reply.

"And you are going to hurt your husband and king even though you will love him. That's just how life is. But true love will ask for forgiveness, and it will forgive without holding on to the past."

Again, Ravenna's thoughts turned to Garrett. Could she forgive him if he were to ask? Would she want him back in her life again? But instead of remembering his blue eyes, a pair of green eyes flashed through her mind. Garrett wasn't here, but Liam was. That brought her back to the other reason why she had sought out Tatiana. She sat back up and put her feet on the ground.

"What is going to happen to Liam if I can't let myself love him back?" She watched Tatiana's face closely and saw a sadness sweep over her features. Ravenna braced herself.

"He'll talk less to you as a dog. Then, when he is human during your dinners, he'll keep more of his dog appearances until he can no longer turn fully human. Eventually, he will not remember anymore that he was ever human."

"Why would you have that be part of the curse?" Ravenna cried out.

Tatiana held no remorse in her voice as she shrugged, "If he didn't truly love you, that would be reason enough for him to stop wasting his and your time."

Ravenna slumped back against the bench. She saw the logic of it, but that didn't mean she liked it. Either she would end up loving Liam or he would stubbornly keep his promise to never give up and would stay a dog for the rest of his life.

Hoseenu, help me to let the past go. Please. I don't want this to happen to him.

CHAPTER 35

*L*iam slowly made his way back to the castle after dinner. His head and tail drooped. He felt so stupid. Of course she would tell him no. She didn't love him. Even if for some reason she had said yes, the curse would still not be broken, and it would have proven that fact. From here on out, his reason for wishing that he weren't compelled to ask her every night wasn't only because it was embarrassing. It would now be painful, too.

"You sound pathetic."

He looked around for where the voice had come from. He hadn't realized he had wandered near the mending rooms until he spotted Cress leaning against a doorway. He cocked his head at her.

"You've been making pitiful whines since you entered this hallway. Probably even long beforehand, by the looks of it."

He didn't know how to respond. It wasn't like he could talk to her, so he just fell on his haunches and let out a miserable breath.

Cress gave him a small smile. "Come in and help me. It'd be good for you to not be alone."

He did as he was told, not knowing what else to do. He didn't really want to go to his room where he could hear Ravenna on the other side of the wall, but he also didn't have the heart to play with Cori and the other castle children. Helping Cress was his only other option besides moping around, which he had already been doing since dinner ended.

"Can you see color?" she asked.

He shook his head. Color was something he didn't realize he would miss until it had been taken away from him. He had almost gone crazy when one night during dinner he couldn't see color anymore even as a human.

Cress pursed her lips while she tapped her chin with her forefinger. Suddenly, she lit up and said, "But you can still see different items of clothing. I'm going to need you to bring the different items to my workstation when I ask. You can bring any one of the dresses over first. I'll work on it as soon as I finish patching up these work pants." She pointed to several different dresses and shirts hanging on a rack on the far side of the room. Then she went over to her workstation and started gathering hangers.

He was stunned. No one had ever told him what to do before, outside of the military. People tended to not be so bold toward him or any other person of nobility. So this was Ravenna's best friend. Cress had been too busy for him to truly interact with her before this moment, and he was glad to finally get to know her more.

She looked back at him and saw that he hadn't moved. She seemed to know what he was thinking. "Look, I don't care about stations. I care about who you are as a person. You are a good human being, and since you are helping me and I'm the one that knows what I need help with, I'm not going to bother groveling to royalty. It's a waste of time." She smirked, "Ravenna's used to it, and since I'm guessing that you're going to stick around, you might as well get used to it too." Cress turned around and continued the project she had been working on.

Liam went over to the rack of clothes, and with his mouth, tugged one of the dresses off of its hanger and walked back with his head as high as he could so as to not trip on it. He put it on the table next to where Cress was sitting. Unsure of what to do, he lay down by her feet.

"Thank you for saving Ravenna's life. I know it was a while ago, but I haven't had a chance to tell you since then." Cress didn't look at him while she spoke. Instead, she continued pulling a needle and thread through the pants. "We're all rooting for you, you know? No one else has stuck around this long, and that has made Ravenna even more jaded."

Liam could see that Cress was sewing only by muscle memory rather than by focusing on it. She was too wrapped up in her thoughts.

"Sometimes I blame myself. I was too excited for Ravenna when Garrett started pursuing her. When she told me that they were engaged, all I could think of, besides being happy for them of course, was that it would finally give me a chance to show off my skills as a dress designer instead of just a mender."

Cress finally put down her sewing and truly looked at Liam. "I've been talking you up as much as I possibly can to make up for it, though. You really are good for her, and deep down, she knows it too. Please don't give up on her."

Liam felt a little unsettled by this. Did she already know that he had told Ravenna that he loved her? Was she worried that he would leave like everyone before him? He didn't waver from her gaze though. He stared straight back and nodded. She released a long breath, and her shoulders relaxed.

Cress smiled at him. "Good. Now let's get back to work."

CHAPTER 36

Dinner the following night was awkward. Ravenna had seriously considered skipping it by claiming to be too tired, but she didn't know how much longer Liam would be able to enjoy a fully human body, and she couldn't bring herself to take the opportunity away from him.

"It's alright. Nothing has to change between us. You know this, right?"

"But it already has. Liam, you love me and I—"

"And you don't. Okay, so, you're right. That has to change," he said with a rueful smile. "But I would like to think that we are, at the very least, still friends?" He cocked his head at her like he did when he was a dog.

That made her happy. They had become friends. Two people sharing this much life together without hating one another couldn't be anything less than that.

"And now *you're* right. We are still friends."

Before either one of them could say anything else, there was a knock on the door. They looked at each other, confused. Usually no one disturbed them during dinner. Everyone knew that this was time spent for just the two of them.

Without waiting for an answer, Damien opened the door. Ravenna saw Liam narrow his eyes at her uncle. Liam had never warmed up to her father's twin brother. Not that she could really blame him...Damien wasn't an easy man to warm up to. But he was still her family.

"Ah, you're still here. Good," Damien said as if it were perfectly natural for him to make an appearance in the dining hall at this hour.

"Why would we not be here? Dinner has just started." Liam's voice took on a formal manner, but there was a slight undertone of a growl. She had never heard that sound come out of his human mouth before.

"But of course. How foolish of me," Damien said. "I just wanted to announce that Ravenna has been assigned a new bodyguard, effective next week." Ravenna tried hard to keep her expression neutral. This was hardly the proper time to give them such news.

"I see. Thank you for letting us know," she said quickly, to cut off whatever Liam was going to say.

Damien bowed. "You're most certainly welcome." Then he opened the door. But before stepping out, he looked over his shoulder and added, "I didn't want you to be caught off guard when Garrett reported for duty." And with that, he swept out of the room.

Ravenna froze. Garrett was going to be her bodyguard? Liam started growling in earnest this time, a sound that no human could possibly master. Surprised, she looked at him.

His lips were pulled back in a snarl, and he stood in front of his seat looking as if he wanted to run after Damien.

"Liam." When he heard her call his name, he pulled himself together. Dazed, he sat back down in his chair.

"Is he the one who appoints your bodyguards?"

She was relieved to hear that his voice sounded more human this time. Even if he was obviously upset. She sighed. "Yes, he is. Until I marry, he is the ruling half that oversees anything related to national security, including my bodyguards."

She heard Liam mumble angrily to himself. She grinned, "We could always get rid of my bodyguards."

He stopped. "No," he said with a firm tone. "Your safety is what's important. If Garrett has been appointed to be your bodyguard, then he must have come highly recommended." This time, she could hear what he muttered to himself, "Or at least he better be."

Regardless of whether or not she currently loved Liam, she felt warm at the thought of how much he loved her. He made her feel safe, and she knew that she could trust him to put her safety above anything else. She could still see the scars that the cougar had left on his neck.

"Come on. Let's actually eat, and then I'll beat you in a game of chess." Ravenna said.

"I think you mean that I'll let you beat me in a game of chess." She laughed in delight to see him come out of his gloom.

She'd worry about seeing Garrett again later. For now, she just wanted to enjoy time spent with her friend.

CHAPTER 37

Ravenna refused to pace the floor of her study. This was the room where she privately met with foreign dignitaries and any courtiers that had personal business with her. It was also where she met any new members of her own personal guard. But she was queen here. This was a part of her domain, and she would not show any signs of weakness. No matter how anxious she was about seeing Garrett for the first time in two years, she would show him that she was not the naïve princess he once knew.

For a moment, she wished that she hadn't told Liam not to be here with her. He had protested, but there were some things that she needed to do for herself.

A knock sounded at the door. She took a deep breath from her chair behind her desk and then called, "Enter."

A young man with dark hair and startling blue eyes walked in. He bowed low to her. Ravenna's breath hitched.

Garrett had somehow become even more handsome since she had last seen him. She desperately tried to stop the blush from growing on her face because seeing him took her back to the garden where they had shared her first of many kisses.

"Your Majesty," he said, rising from his bow.

"Garrett," she replied.

For a brief moment, all they could do was stare at each other, but then she broke the silence.

"So you have joined my personal guard," she said with a brow raised.

"Aye. I wanted a break from the mountain pass, and this was the only assignment close to home."

She nodded. She had already known this. As soon as her uncle told her about his upcoming arrival, she had immediately requested all reports about Garrett and why he was about to come back into her life. She still found it hard to believe that this was truly the *only* available spot in the capital for a soldier.

"The regent king seems to favor you. He said you were highly recommended for the post and would serve honorably despite our past history."

Garrett shifted slightly where he stood. It was the only sign he let show that indicated he was slightly uncomfortable with her bringing up their previous engagement. "It is my duty to serve Lyra and her queen to the best of my abilities." He hesitated briefly. "And Ravenna, I have also come to ask for your forgiveness."

Ravenna kept her expression neutral despite the shock. He wanted to apologize? For being unfaithful to her? For using her as a means to the throne? It was all she could do to not leap across the desk and slap him.

But Tatiana's words came back to her about how true

love asks for forgiveness. Did this mean that Garrett truly loved her? It was so tempting to go back to those nights in the garden when she could believe a man who said he loved her. He was familiar. He thought she was beautiful.

Images of Garrett kissing another woman in the pub filled her mind.

"Forgiveness for which part exactly?" Her voice was filled with steel, making him wince.

"For leading you on and trying to take advantage of you." Despite his obvious discomfort, he kept eye contact with her. "We didn't meet by chance. It was my horse that I saved you from. I paid one of my friends to let him loose when I saw you and Cress in the marketplace. I did it for the sole purpose of finding favor in your eyes. For all of this, I wish to apologize."

She felt her heart shattering all over again. Everything she had known and felt about him was a lie. She wanted to cry right there in her study but kept control over herself.

"You never loved me?" She watched as he looked heavenward as if Hoseenu himself would appear and take him away.

"I was fond of you." It was the only thing that he seemed to be able to say.

"I see." She took a moment to compose herself. "Thank you for your honesty. I will accept your apology, and I will accept your position in my personal guard."

She held up her hand when he opened his mouth to speak. "You may give thanks to Hoseenu for this second chance. However, if I find any hint of a secondary motive for you coming here, there are worse assignments than serving at the mountain pass. Understood?"

"Yes, Your Majesty."

"You are dismissed."

Garrett bowed again and left, leaving her alone once again.

Ravenna wasn't sure where to go now. She wanted to confide in someone about her heartache at learning that she had never been loved, not even slightly. It felt too much to bear alone. It was the kind of news that she would usually take to the lake and cry out with Hoseenu, but now she couldn't go unless she had at least one member of her personal guard with her.

Or Liam.

She bit her lip. Could she ask this of Liam? Could she really ask the man who said he loved her to accompany her to watch as she poured out her heart to Hoseenu about a man who had previously said he loved her?

Then again, she mused, he had been secretly watching her pray for months about several things that must have made him uncomfortable.

Hoseenu, help me.

A knock on her door startled her out of her thoughts.

"Enter."

A boy popped his head around the door. He was scrawny with a mop of dirty blond hair and wore a messenger's uniform and bag. He couldn't possibly be older than eleven.

"Come in," she commanded him gently. The boy stumbled in, searching around his bag for an envelope.

"This is for you, Your Majesty," the boy stuttered, handing over the envelope with a shaky hand.

"Thank you. What is your name?" she asked as she took the message.

The boy straightened up and said, "It's Benji, Your Majesty."

"It's good to meet you, Benji. My name is Ravenna."

Benji frowned and cocked his head at her. She started to

worry about his confusion - was there dirt on her face?. It would be just her luck to have gone through a whole conversation with Garrett and find out afterward that she looked like a mess.

"Is something wrong?"

He immediately turned bashful. "It's just that everyone knows your name, Your Majesty." He shrugged his shoulders as if that were all the explanation needed.

Ravenna let out a little chuckle. "It seems to me that everyone keeps thinking that my name is 'Your Majesty,' so I thought it would be appropriate to remind you otherwise."

"Does this mean that you want people to call you by your name?" His eyes were as big as saucers.

"It does."

Benji smiled wide, and Ravenna could see a gap where one of his lower teeth had fallen out.

"The others aren't going to believe this," he whispered to himself.

Ravenna couldn't help but smile at his amazement. "Thank you again for the letter, Benji. It was nice meeting you."

"It was nice meeting you, Your, er, Ravenna," he corrected himself.

Ravenna waited until he left her study before opening the message he had delivered. It had come from Lord Rivers's estate. He was one of the closer relatives to the Crown. Frowning, she started reading it.

Her frown deepened as she continued the letter. Lord Rivers's steward had written to inform her of his master's death. He had fallen through a broken stair. That alone shouldn't have killed him, but apparently the shock had caused his heart to give out.

Ravenna tossed the letter onto her desk and massaged her temples. As much as she wished she could believe that these were all just a string of bad accidents, someone had actually died this time. And it continued to not be lost on her that everyone who had had the misfortune of experiencing something of this caliber were all related, no matter how distantly, to her.

She had hoped that the possibility of producing an heir would end any thoughts of a civil war to win claim over the throne. Whoever the perpetrator was hadn't been as active since Liam had activated the curse. Every so often, someone would have some sort of mishap, but that had included nobles who weren't possible candidates, so she had thought that maybe those seemingly normal accidents were just a part of life.

However, Lord Rivers's death made her decide that she would need to become involved herself. And to her own chagrin, she would need to keep her promise to Cress and ask for Liam's help.

She felt like banging her head on her desk at the thought of first wanting to ask him to be her guard to the lake, and now getting him involved in the underbelly of Lyrian politics. It felt wrong to take advantage of him so shortly after he had told her he loved her.

Accepting the inevitable, she rose from her chair and headed out of her study to look for her dog prince. This day was turning out to be only slightly better than the one where she had been attacked by a cougar.

CHAPTER 38

"Wearing a path in my carpet isn't going to make Ravenna's meeting go by any quicker."

Liam looked over at Cress, mending at her workstation, her eyes never leaving her sewing. He continued his pacing.

When Damien had told them that Garrett would be put on Ravenna's personal guard, he had wanted to protest immediately. However, he knew just how little power he held in the Lyrian court.

Damien let Ravenna remain unguarded for the past year, he growled to himself. *How can he be trusted to pick the best soldiers?*

He stopped his pacing when his ears picked up Ravenna's familiar footsteps rushing down the hall toward Cress's workroom. Immediately, he rushed over to the door to greet her as she came in. Cress put down her mending when she noticed Liam heading to the door and went to open it for her friend. She saw that Ravenna was still a few paces away.

"Your guard dog heard you coming," she called out.

Liam didn't even acknowledge the comment and went straight to Ravenna, sniffing around to try to pick up her mood. She was definitely worried and concerned, but before he could ask her what was wrong, she scratched behind his ear and said, "It's not what you think." She slipped inside the workroom, closing the door behind Liam.

"Lord Rivers is dead," Ravenna announced. Cress's mouth dropped open. Liam cocked his head, looking between the two girls.

Who is Lord Rivers? he asked.

Ravenna turned and looked at him. "He was my mother's cousin."

Liam caught Ravenna's gaze flick over to Cress, who gave the queen a deadly glare in return.

"And the latest victim in a long list of suspicious accidents," Ravenna finished quickly.

What do you mean a long list of suspicious accidents? he asked slowly.

Ravenna's hand gripped the skirt of her dress, and she wrapped part of the fabric around her finger. She looked over at Cress again with a silent plea for help.

"This is between the two of you," Cress said as she raised her hands up. Liam tried to wait patiently, but he struggled to contain a small bark of annoyance at not knowing what was going on.

Ravenna let out a sigh heavy enough to her shoulders drop and sat down on a nearby chair. "Since I've become queen, a lot of nobles have had accidents. Which isn't odd in and of itself as accidents can happen to anyone, but they've mostly happened to nobles who have a greater claim on the Crown. I have reason to believe that these so-called accidents are actually sabotage."

Liam walked over to where Ravenna was sitting and sat down next to her chair, hoping to comfort her with his presence. Unconsciously, she reached over and started stroking the top of his head. It was soothing for both of them.

Have others died from these accidents?

Ravenna shook her head. "No, he is the first. Though I don't think anyone would have predicted that Lord Rivers's heart would have gone out by falling through a broken stair."

Cress stood up. "I'm going to head out and let you both continue talking. I can only hear Ravenna so it doesn't make sense for me to stay."

Ravenna reached out her other hand to Cress. "Wait, please stay. I need both of you to help me."

Cress's brows raised skepticism, but she sat back down.

Ravenna looked again at Liam, attempting to explain herself. "I'm sorry that I haven't told you this sooner, but I didn't want Lyra to appear weak."

Liam snorted, and Ravenna shrugged in response.

"So what do you need us to do?" Cress asked. "I'm sorry to ruin whatever moment you two are having, but I don't understand why you don't just tell Damien and everyone else about your suspicions."

Ravenna's face immediately turned red at Cress's insinuation, and she pulled her hand away from Liam. On his part, Liam nearly growled at Cress for interrupting Ravenna's petting of his head.

"Whoever is behind this knows the court personally. Each accident has been tailor-made for each person based on their habits. If I were to let anyone outside of this room know, the culprit might find out and either hide themself or attack with more animosity," Ravenna said as she tried to compose herself.

"What about Tatiania? Shouldn't we tell her?" Cress asked.

"Knowing her, she probably already does know. I'll speak with her later. For now, Cress, you have access to staff and nobles since more ladies of the court are asking you to design their dresses. See if you can overhear anything about their accidents. Liam, you've been able to pick up on things that humans can't notice. I need your help to sniff around when I visit the different families that have been affected. We'll begin with the Rivers Estate."

Liam looked over at Cress to see what she thought of this plan. The seamstress seemed resigned to it.

Do you have any idea what the possible motive could be? he asked.

Ravenna shook her head. "The only idea I have is based on when my uncle has mentioned that there has been a lot of unrest because I'm not married."

How does that translate to accidents?

"I don't have an heir, and as one of the youngest single queens in recent history, the curse has, uh, decreased my chances of continuing the royal line. It makes people nervous. If something were to happen to me before the line could directly continue, chances are good that anyone with some royal blood would fight for the throne."

"So you think that someone is trying to better their odds of becoming future king or queen?" Cress interjected. "But why not just kill them outright?"

"It's all a theory, so I could be completely wrong."

Liam noticed that Ravenna was rubbing her temples, so he nuzzled his head on her knee. She accepted his subtle invitation and started petting him again.

Cress sighed, "Okay, well, I guess I'll start tomorrow. Lady Wentworth has a fitting appointment, and I'll see what I can learn about Lord Wentworth's boating accident."

"Thanks, Cress! You're the best." Ravenna got up from her chair and hugged Cress.

"Yeah, I know," Cress chuckled. "It's getting late. You two better go to dinner so I can finish my work here."

Liam followed Ravenna out of the room. He wasn't sure he liked the idea of Ravenna investigating all of these accidents on her own. He could only console himself with the fact that he'd be with her for future inspections.

He watched her carefully while they walked toward the dining hall. She looked exhausted.

We can skip dinner, you know.

Startled, Ravenna jerked a bit. "No, we can't."

Her voice was firm, but Liam had grown accustomed to challenging her when she wasn't thinking of her own well-being. *Yes, we can. You look like you're going to fall asleep, and your head will land onto your plate if you doze off at the table.*

Ravenna spun around abruptly and stopped. Liam wasn't quick enough to stop himself from bumping into her legs. After a moment, Ravenna whispered, "I haven't told you yet, but I found out from Tatiana that if the curse doesn't break, you'll end up becoming a dog permanently."

Liam stood there and looked at her. It had always been a possibility that this would happen to him if he didn't give up trying to earn her love. *I kind of figured that out on my own.* Liam was quiet when he replied.

"That's why we need to have dinner tonight. I want you to have as much time as possible being human in case we run out of time."

Liam sat and looked up at her with his head tilted to the side. *Don't worry about it, Ravenna. It's going to be okay. You need to rest.*

She crossed her arms in front of her chest and raised a single eyebrow at him in defiance. "I'll rest after dinner."

She turned around and continued walking toward the dining hall. There was no convincing her otherwise, so he went along with her.

Dinner was already laid out when they walked in. Ravenna didn't look directly at him until they both sat down. Liam heard her sharp intake of breath when she did finally glance over at him.

"What's wrong?" he asked.

"Your face. It's, um..." She struggled to find words.

"What's wrong with my face?" Liam asked hesitantly.

"It's your teeth."

Liam slid his tongue along his teeth and could feel that they were longer and sharper than what would be considered acceptable for a human.

He sighed, "It's nothing to worry about, Ravenna. We literally just talked about it." He smiled at her, but then he realized his mistake; she frowned when she got a better look at his teeth.

He dropped his smile, but before he could say anything else, she cut in. "Liam, I am going to worry. This is my fault. I wasn't aware that there was some sort of deadline."

Liam sighed in defeat. He clearly couldn't convince her to not worry about what was happening to him, so he did the next best thing and changed the topic. "How did it go with Garrett?"

She glared at his obvious attempt to get the focus off of him, but she let it slide. "It was fine."

He raised his eyebrows at her.

She sighed, "I've decided to let him be a part of my personal guard." Before he could object, she held up her hand. "He's made it clear how remorseful he is about the past, and he wants to make up for it. He's given up any desire to claim the throne."

She looked exhausted. All he wanted to do was go over to her, hold her in his arms, and try to take some of the load off of her shoulders. Instead, he took a sip from his glass and asked, "Do you want to get away from the castle?" Her brows furrowed as she looked at him. He shrugged, "You haven't left the castle in weeks. You used to go out at least once, if not twice, a week."

Ravenna stared at him. He wasn't sure what she was thinking, and it made him a little nervous. Had he said the wrong thing? Finally, she spoke up with a small smile on her lips. "I would like that."

He grinned in response. "Would you want to go now or in the middle of the night?" His eyes sparkled in amusement.

"I could always just sneak out, you know, and pretend like I don't know you're following me. For the nostalgia," she laughed.

He was happy to see that he could get her mind off of everything else. "Then midnight it is." He raised his glass toward hers and she clinked her glass against his.

Then her face became somber. "You don't actually have to follow me though. We haven't had time to go out for a walk in the woods in a while. I'd rather you walk with me." Her eyes searched his face as though looking to see if he would say no. This time, he *did* reach out to her, taking her hand in his and gently squeezing it.

"I would be honored." Her smile could have put the sun to shame. It warmed up his chest and pulled out a smile from him as well.

CHAPTER 39

The night air felt cool and refreshing. Ravenna and Liam walked with the light of the moon guiding their path. Ravenna had been worried that the cougar attack would ruin the forest for her, but instead she felt even safer with Liam by her side.

They didn't talk as they made their way toward the lake. No matter how much pain seeing Garrett earlier had caused, it had faded when put into perspective of Lord Rivers's death. Liam's quiet presence also helped soothe the ache in her heart.

When they arrived at the lake, Ravenna sat on her rock near the water's edge, pulling her knees up under her chin. Liam sat down next to her, and they both gazed at the moon reflected on the water.

Even though you can pray to Hoseenu at any time and anywhere, why do you come here? Liam said, breaking the silence. Ravenna stayed quiet for a moment to gather her thoughts.

"It's peaceful here, and I can feel His presence better when I'm not surrounded by people and reminders of everything that I need to do," she finally replied. "And being able to see all of the stars reminds me that Hoseenu is indeed Hoseenu."

Liam made a noise of understanding. Ravenna turned and looked at the dog sitting next to her, who still looked over the view in front of them.

"I know you said Sophia has dreams with Hoseenu in them, but have you ever seen Him for yourself?"

Ravenna wondered if she had crossed a line by asking him that since he continued to stare at the lake. He finally responded, *I think so. It was when I was little and wandering around the Elven Woods. I had gotten lost and started crying when I couldn't get back home. That's when a lamb appeared suddenly in front of me. As soon as I saw it, I felt what my father told me he felt when he dreamed of Hoseenu: a powerful and benevolent presence. The lamb started walking away but waited for me to follow it. It led me all the way home.* Liam's tail wagged as he talked. *It was late, and everyone was looking for me. When I was found and taken to my father, I told him about the lamb, and he said that must have been Hoseenu because a lamb is one of the many forms that He takes.*

Ravenna let out a happy hum. She remembered her mother telling her that Hoseenu could physically appear to humans in different ways, but He chose not to appear to everyone. Most of the time He was invisible but always present. She had always longed for Him to appear to her, so she loved hearing the stories of when people met Him face to face.

Have you ever seen Him? Liam asked as he finally looked at her.

She shook her head. "No, but I know that even if I don't while I'm alive, I will see Him when I see my parents again in the hereafter."

Liam nuzzled his head against her foot resting on her rock. She reached over and scratched behind his ear. "Thank you for coming with me tonight. Today was really hard, but being here with you is comforting," she whispered.

I will always be here when you need me, Ravenna. I love you.

Ravenna closed her eyes as she continued to pet Liam's head.

CHAPTER 40

The next morning, Liam woke up to the sound of Ravenna moving around her room on the other side of the door. He groaned and rolled over, trying to fall back to sleep, but his mind kept wandering back to the night before.

Ravenna had finally told him more about her meeting with Garrett, and even though he knew that Garrett said he didn't have feelings for Ravenna, Liam couldn't help but feel slightly jealous. Ravenna had truly loved Garrett, despite him not deserving her love.

Again, he wanted to hold her in his arms and kiss her in a way that would make her forget about her heartbreak. But what he could offer her right now was his companionship and the comfort that only a dog can give to a human.

The door between the king's and queen's chambers opened. Ravenna peeked exuberantly into his room. He didn't understand how anyone could look so lively in the morning, especially after such a late night. A green ribbon that matched her eyes pulled back her dark hair. Or at least he was pretty sure it was the same shade of green as her eyes...it was hard to tell as a colorblind dog.

"Are you ready to go?"

Liam let out a low growl and turned over. He wasn't sure when Ravenna had started acting extra cheerful in the mornings just to annoy him, but she always smiled even more brightly after he gave her some indication of displeasure. He sometimes gave her a hard time in the morning just to make her smile. Not that he would admit that to her. Even on pain of death.

"Come on, sleepy head. We need to talk with Cress before we visit Lord Rivers's family." Ravenna had fully entered the room at this point, and she leaned against the bedframe with her arms crossed. He opened his eyes, but immediately shut them again when he saw her smug grin.

Suddenly, he felt someone trying to shove him off the bed. He looked over at Ravenna's small frame pushing his body. Instead of helping her by getting up himself, Liam flopped on top of her.

"Get off! I see your tail wagging so I know you're not actually still asleep," Ravenna shrieked with laughter.

Stupid tail, giving away all of my secrets, he thought.

Liam huffed and jumped off the bed, his traitorous tail still wagging as he panted in delight. When he reached the door, he turned around to see that Ravenna had gotten stuck on the plush mattress as she tried to get up.

I'm ready to go. Why are you still on my bed?

"Why, you mangy dog!" Ravenna cried out.

Liam took off in fear of what she would do if she caught him.

After breakfast, they went to Cress's private room near the sewing workroom. Liam looked around the small room that held only a bed and a wardrobe. Despite its size, Cress had used leftover fabric scraps to decorate the room and had sewn a patchwork quilt to give the room a homier feel. Cress sat on her bed and Liam lay on the floor while Ravenna paced back and forth.

"To start, we should focus on the latest accidents," Ravenna said. "We can always compare them to the earlier ones, but I think we'll have better luck going to where memories are fresh and anything out of the ordinary could possibly still be there."

Ravenna looked to Cress. "When you go for Lady Wentworth's fitting, I need you to talk with one of my contacts there. He is one of the sources that led me to believe these weren't mere accidents, and he would know how to spread word that if anyone has any more information, they should go to you first. He's one of the gardeners, and he'll approach you if you put a daisy behind your ear."

Do you have spies at all of the courtiers' estates?

"Don't all queens?" Ravenna scoffed.

"Don't all queens, what?" Cress fumed.

"Have spies," Ravenna quickly said. "I haven't had a need to really use them thus far. It wasn't even until a couple of months before the alliance treaty that I found my father's notes about his spy network. I want to build my reign on trust and only use them domestically for emergencies."

Liam decided to not comment on her choice of using the word "domestically." Of course all monarchs had spies within the neighboring countries. Some of Wilderose's spies reported to him. It reminded him that Ravenna never seemed to get access to some of her spies' reports, and that Damien always seemed to bring them up at council meetings. He decided he would look into that more later.

Ravenna's voice pulled his attention back to the matter at hand. "Liam and I will visit the Rivers Estate today, and we'll plan on visiting Lord Rook tomorrow. Cress, is there some way that you can arrange for Lady Elliot, Lady Winter, or Lady Maria to have fittings sometime this week or next?"

Cress tapped her finger on her chin. "Lady Elliot and Lady Maria do have orders with me, so I can arrange something with them. But you know Lady Winter; she doesn't patronize new fashion designers. She only goes to the well-established ones."

Ravenna smiled at Cress. "That's her loss. Besides, within the next year or so, everyone in court will be demanding a custom-order gown from you!"

Liam noticed that Cress immediately sat up straighter.

"I think that's everything?" Ravenna looked between Liam and Cress. The seamstress nodded her head.

We'll figure out what's going on, Liam said to reassure her as he got up and walked toward her.

"Good, we can meet later today to compare notes." As they left Cress's room, Liam tried hard not to show how relieved he was that they wouldn't have to go to another early morning meeting.

CHAPTER 41

The Rivers Estate was at the mouth of the Song River, the largest river in Lyra. It crossed through the capital all the way to the border of Clearford.

Lord Rivers and Ravenna's mother had been cousins. He had almost become her regent king after her parents died and while she remained unmarried, but the council had voted in her uncle's favor. Ravenna wondered how her first year as queen would have been different if the council had voted otherwise.

When she and Liam arrived, the butler escorted them to a small room on the side of the manor reserved for intimate visits with close friends and family. Ravenna had grown up playing with the Rivers children whenever her mother and father wanted to hear the advice of Lord and Lady Rivers. She had looked forward to these visits; they meant that she could get off the castle grounds and skip out on boring tutoring lessons.

While they waited for Lady Rivers, Ravenna whispered to Liam, "Are you ready?"

Liam's tail thumped once on the ground to show her that he was. They had discussed on the way to the estate how he would blend in with the Rivers's family dogs, which were allowed to freely roam around the house and the grounds. While Ravenna talked with the household, he would leave and look for anything out of the ordinary, using the special door flaps that the Rivers had specially installed in the manor's doors for their beloved pets. Liam decided to ask Ravenna later if the castle could be modified to add these doors as well. If the curse kept progressing the way it had been, he might need them…

I think Lady Rivers is coming, Liam said as he cocked his head with an ear facing a side door.

"Go!" Ravenna whispered. Liam got up and went through the flap of the door they had come through that led to the main hall. As soon as his tail slipped through, the side door opened and in walked Lady Lucinda Rivers.

As a tall woman whose brown hair had silver streaks running through it, her presence usually commanded respect. However, Ravenna noticed how much older she seemed since she had last seen her on the previous service day. The brown dress and veil that Lucinda wore to symbolize a loved one had returned to dust only amplified how haggard she looked.

"I'm so sorry for your loss," Ravenna said as she hugged the taller woman. Lady Rivers's eyes filled with tears as she hugged the young queen.

"Thank you, Ravenna. It means so much to me that you have come so soon after William's death. He always tried to keep an eye out for you." Her chin quivered as she tried to stay composed.

When they pulled apart, Lucinda looked around the room. "Where is your companion? I had heard that the dog prince accompanied you."

"Ah, he went to, um, relieve himself," Ravenna answered as the two ladies sat down in the arm chairs. She hoped Lucinda would think that the hesitation in her voice was due to being embarrassed about mentioning a topic that she knew Liam was still sensitive about rather than stalling to form a lie.

Lucinda nodded her head, and Ravenna let out a small breath of relief at the much-needed distraction when a servant brought in a tea tray. After they had poured their cups of tea, Ravenna changed the topic. "I hadn't realized that Lord Rivers had a sensitive heart."

"That's the thing: he never complained about his heart." Lucinda's voice trembled for a moment. "He would moan and cry about the littlest of ailments, mostly I think to get a rise out of me." She smiled fondly. "But the doctor always said that he was as fit as a horse." She leaned back in her chair and a puzzled expression came over her face. "It happened so suddenly and out of the blue that I thought the doctor must have been mistaken. Surely William didn't die due to shock at almost falling through a broken stair."

"That is extremely odd," Ravenna agreed. She sipped her tea to give her a moment to think of how to phrase her next inquiry.

"Do you have someone taking care of getting the stairs fixed so you don't have one more thing to worry about?" She put as much sympathy in her voice as possible, trying to be sensitive to the fact that her husband hadn't even been dead yet for a full day.

"Our housekeeper is looking into it for me. I was originally going to see to it as a way to keep my mind off of... well, you know...but the carpenter that had done some work for us last week was unavailable. So I just decided to let the housekeeper take care of finding another carpenter and focus on making arrangements for the people who are coming to stay for the memorial." Lucinda's voice broke when she said 'memorial,' and all of the tears she had been holding back burst forth from their dam. Ravenna immediately set down her tea cup and went over to comfort the grieving widow.

After several minutes, Lady Rivers's sobs died down. "I'm so sorry for pulling you into my mess," she said as she wiped the last of her tears off her face.

"Don't be sorry," Ravenna said. "Life has dealt you a hard blow, and Hoseenu himself would not ask you to pretend that you are perfectly fine."

"You're right, Your Majesty. My, how have you grown." She looked at Ravenna as though seeing her for the first time. "Your parents would have been so proud of the woman and queen that you have become."

Ravenna blushed and sat back down in her own chair. She prayed that what Lucinda had said was true.

Liam was lost. He had noticed that the Rivers Estate looked massive from the front, but he hadn't realized how far back the manor went, let alone the grounds. He had been able to find the private stairwell the residents used, where Lord Rivers had died, but trying to make his way back to Ravenna proved to be more of a challenge. He blamed the pungent smell of sour sweat all over the stairwell making it hard for him to smell anything else, including his own trail that would lead him back to her.

When he had gone hunting with his hounds what now felt like a lifetime ago, he had never imagined that one day he would be the dog sniffing for prey. He admitted to himself that it did make things more efficient not having to wait for the dogs to let him know what they had found.

As he wandered down a hallway looking for a way back to Ravenna, another dog turned the corner and faced him. Liam immediately stiffened. Oddly enough, this was the first time he had come into close contact with a dog since being cursed. For some reason he never could figure out, he had unintentionally steered clear of dogs at the Lyrian castle. As if he knew somehow not to be in their territory...

The dog in front of him was the same breed as him. Liam felt a need to roll onto his back, belly up, as a way of saying that he wasn't trying to take over this dog's territory. He fought to control that impulse. He wasn't a dog! He was a man.

The dog came up to him and sniffed. Liam stayed as still as possible until the other dog moved to smell his rear end. Then Liam automatically circled and smelled the other dog. He learned that this was one of the betas of the house and thanked Hoseenu he hadn't run into the alpha.

Liam didn't like how he knew his next thought intuitively, or how it felt like he was taking a backseat view of what his body was doing...but somehow, he was able to pick up from this dog that Lord Rivers had smelled different yesterday. It was the sour smell from the stairs.

The dog nudged Liam as he walked past. Liam immediately started to follow, still not sure how he was communicating without actual words. He wondered if he would have done this the first month that he spent as a dog or if this was something new. Liam shuddered at the thought of the curse progressing.

Finally, the dog led him to a bedchamber, which Liam assumed was Lord Rivers's personal room. Liam could smell that same sour smell coming from a wooden box on a table next to the bed. He walked up to it for a closer look. When he got nearer, he couldn't smell anything besides the sour stench, which caused him to sneeze. But he was able to read the label on the box - it was a brand of tea from Faircoast. Liam had tried this one before, but he had never thought it smelled this awful.

He turned around when he heard a whimper, and he saw that the other dog had jumped onto his master's bed. Liam felt sorry for this dog who had lost his human. A picture of Ravenna came to his mind, and without verbal thought, he felt the pain of not being near her. He whimpered back to the dog and went over to lick his muzzle. Then he turned around and left to find his human.

After Liam returned to the private sitting room, Ravenna shared one last bit of condolences with Lady Rivers and left with her prince. She tried asking him if he had found anything, but he didn't say anything to her. He just pressed up against her legs, making it hard for her to walk without tripping over him.

His odd behavior didn't disappear when they got into the carriage. Instead, he sat almost on her lap and wouldn't stop licking her face, so she had to shove him aside. He put his head on her lap and let out several small whimpers. It was starting to frighten her. What had happened to him while he was away from her side? She begged him to tell her what was wrong, but received no response.

When they got back to the castle, he never left her side once, even when she needed some privacy to relieve herself and closed a door to keep him out. She heard him pacing back and forth, whimpering the whole time.

After tending to her needs, Ravenna immediately sought Tatiana and found her in the kitchen, talking to Cook.

"Tatiana! Something is wrong with Liam!"

The fairy looked at the dog following closely behind Ravenna. "He's just suffering from separation anxiety. He'll be fine after dinner." Instead of her soothing voice calming Ravenna down, the queen became more concerned.

"Separation anxiety?"

Tatiana nodded as Cook went and got a cup of chamomile tea for Ravenna and a couple of plain biscuits for Liam.

"Something must have made him worry about being away from you, and it drove him into an instinctual state of existence. It shouldn't happen often."

Instead of sitting at the counter, Ravenna sat on the floor with Liam and petted him. It seemed to calm him down a little. "He needs to give me up. I can't bear this."

Cook and Tatiana exchanged a look that Ravenna couldn't make out. Then Tatiana joined Ravenna on the floor and hugged her goddaughter. "Are you forgetting that there's another way to break the curse?" she quietly asked.

"I can't love him," Ravenna whispered. Liam shifted closer to her, giving her his body warmth.

"My dear child." Tatiana stroked a strand of Ravenna's hair back. "You know, it's past lunch time. If you're hungry, you can have an early dinner."

"Alright," Ravenna said with a shuddering breath. "Can you have someone ask Cress to join us?" Tatiana nodded as they both got up.

Before Ravenna and Liam headed toward the dining hall, she gave Tatiana another hug.

CHAPTER 42

As soon as Ravenna and Liam entered the dining hall and he had turned back into a human, Liam hugged Ravenna tightly. She froze. This was the first time he had made physical contact as a human. Before she could do anything, he pulled back but still kept his grip on her shoulders.

"You're alright. You're still here," he said more to himself than to her.

"I've been right here; but are *you* alright?" She watched as Liam looked around the room realizing where they were for the first time.

"I am now."

"What happened while you were searching the Rivers Estate?" she asked, and then, as they made their way to the table, added, " You weren't yourself after you came back."

There weren't any main dishes available yet, but a basket of bread had been brought out. She guessed it was still too early for the full meal to have finished being prepared.

Liam shut his eyes. "I ran into one of Lord Rivers's dogs who was mourning his death."

She waited for him to expand on this thought.

Instead, he changed the subject and said, "There was a box of tea in his room that didn't smell right. I also found the scent of the tea where he died. I don't know what it was, but I'm sure I'd recognize it if I were to smell it again. Did you learn anything more from Lady Rivers?"

Ravenna's eyes narrowed. Liam was hiding something from her. However, it would have to wait until after dinner. "It seems like there shouldn't have been anything wrong with Lord Rivers's heart. If anything, he was the picture of perfect health."

"I think he may have been poisoned," Liam said.

Before she could ask him to elaborate, Cress walked in.

"I'm starving!" she said as she walked straight to the lone bread basket on the table and took a roll before sitting down next to Ravenna, across from Liam.

"Nice to see you, too," Ravenna said with a dry tone.

"But of course it's nice to see me! I am your best friend, after all." Cress winked at Ravenna.

Liam tried to cover a laugh with a cough.

Ravenna sighed in resignation. "Did you learn anything?"

Cress waited to speak until she finished chewing a bite of her roll. "Lady Wentworth was upset that they had only hired a carpenter to make some repairs on the other side of Lord Wentworth's ship rather than hiring him to look over the whole ship. Her husband had insisted that it wasn't necessary to examine the whole thing."

"That's bad timing," Liam said.

Cress had shoved more bread into her mouth, so she just nodded.

"Wait - did you say they had hired a carpenter beforehand?" Ravenna asked.

"Yeah. Lady Wentworth went on and on about it. You know how much she hates inefficiency."

"Lady Rivers mentioned hiring a carpenter the week before, too," Ravenna mumbled to herself.

"You think there might be a connection?" Liam seemed hesitant.

"They both hired a carpenter, and both of them ended up with their leg stuck in a hole," Ravenna said.

Cress's eyes widened.

"But those are just two of the accidents. The rest don't follow the same pattern. Besides, we don't even know if it was the same carpenter hired for both projects," Ravenna hastily added. "Were you able to talk with our gardener friend?"

"He's going to pass the word along to everyone else to let him know if they remember anything suspicious."

After finishing off her bread, Cress stood up and waved at her royal friends. "Well, I'll be off. Enjoy dinner!"

Liam stared after her as she left. "She's enjoying herself, isn't she?"

Ravenna chuckled, "I think she gets bored working here. It's just a stepping stone for her career as a dressmaker, so anything that gets her out of the castle is a holiday for her."

"Is that why you asked her for help?"

"Partially. Mostly it's because I trust her completely, and her reputation as a dressmaker makes it easy for her to talk with people who would be more reserved around me."

"More reserved?"

Ravenna slumped back in her chair. "It's easy to warm up to people like you, Cress, and Sophia. You're all so approachable. I make people nervous. Before, I would have said it's because I'm a queen, but then I met Sophia," she scoffed.

Liam furrowed his brows. "Ravenna, people like you. They like having you around."

Ravenna raised her eyebrow at him in skepticism.

"I'm not saying you're not shy. You definitely are. And you do have a wall up around most people, but those who love you will wait for it to come down. They just have to be patient."

Ravenna's heart beat faster when she saw the loving gaze he gave her. She didn't know how to respond.

"Would you care to dance before the main meal arrives tonight?" His question surprised her again.

"What?"

"We haven't danced since the first night that we met. Besides, I don't want to be out of practice. Can't have the Wilderosian dance instructor's lessons go to waste." Liam winked at her.

Ravenna threw her head back and laughed heartily. "We wouldn't want that."

His smile stretched across his face as she accepted his hand so he could lead her away from the table. Liam placed his other hand on her waist while she put hers on his shoulder. She could feel his warmth, and it made her heart race even more.

"We don't have any music," she whispered as he started to lead her in a dance.

"Just imagine it."

She looked up at him smiling down at her. "Okay."

Hours past midnight, Liam still couldn't fall asleep. His sensitive ears could pick up the soft breaths of Ravenna sleeping in the queen's chambers, so he knew that she wouldn't likely go on a late-night outing tonight. Otherwise, she would have left a while ago.

He leaped off his bed and made his way toward the lake that Ravenna liked to pray at. It was the first time that he had ever left the castle alone, and he found it freeing.

When he arrived at the lake, he sat on his haunches and looked up at the night sky.

Thank You for tonight, he prayed. *After what happened today, I don't know how much longer I'll have for her to fall in love with me.*

The stars shimmered down on him as he let himself remember how it had felt to hold Ravenna in his human arms. She looked like she would have let him kiss her by the time they stopped dancing, but when he had asked her to marry him after dinner, she had said no again.

After a moment he added, *You are Hoseenu, and You've made me stubbornly loyal. If she never lets herself love me in return, You know that I'll be loyal to her for the rest of my life.* He then added with chagrin, *Even if I forget that I was ever human.*

CHAPTER 43

Ravenna could see the sunlight, still a soft golden yellow of early morning, peeking out from behind the edge of her curtains. The corners of her mouth turned up and she felt a rush of warmth fill her chest again as she remembered dancing with Liam the night before. They had danced during the Alliance Ball, but she had later been so distracted by him declaring that he wanted to break the curse that she didn't remember how well he could dance. Most of her dance partners were hard to follow; she could feel their self-doubt about how to lead a queen on the dance floor. They always hesitated before making a move and lost the rhythm of the music, or they would not pay attention to where they were leading her and run into other couples dancing. She usually struggled to not take over as lead. But Liam knew his steps and was confident on where he wanted to take her. It was freeing to just let go and not worry about what her partner was doing.

After choosing a soft pink dress for the day and braiding her hair, she went to the breakfast room. She had debated on whether or not she should wake Liam up, but seeing as how she had woken him early the day before, she figured he'd appreciate the extra sleep.

Finding the breakfast room empty, Ravenna grabbed a cup of tea and a cheese croissant and headed toward the gardens instead of eating inside by herself. Tatiana wasn't going to be there at this hour, so it would be her first time in the flower gardens alone since her broken engagement with Garrett. Her stomach tied itself into familiar knots of anxiety as she walked toward the garden gate. However, she knew she couldn't avoid the gardens forever. They belonged to *her*. Not to Garrett. She wasn't going to let the memory of him keep her away.

She found the rose bushes and sat among them as she sipped her tea. The soft fragrance of the flowers filled her nose. She closed her eyes and sighed at the warmth of the morning sun on her face. It was as if Hoseenu himself was planting peace in her heart at that moment.

Until she heard the crunch of gravel underneath a boot.

Her eyes snapped open, and she saw Garrett standing in front of the rose bush she sat behind. She briefly thought that maybe he hadn't seen her and he would continue on… but then he said, "I can see you, Ravenna. I wouldn't make a very good personal guard if I didn't know where you were."

She stood up and frowned at him. "Usually personal guards stay in the background and remain unseen."

"Yes, but you are sitting in the exact place where we first kissed." He smirked at her.

Why did he have to bring that up? He had said that none of that had been real for him.

She realized in horror that she had said all of her thoughts out loud because he replied, "I never said it wasn't real for me. I said that I arranged for us to meet so I could become king, but I also said that I was fond of you. That was real."

Ravenna's face flushed, and she twisted the fabric of her skirt. "Oh" was her only reply.

"This is also my second rotation, and I wanted to take advantage of the opportunity to talk to you without your guard dog around."

She frowned when he called Liam her 'guard dog.'

He continued, "I heard that you are trying to solve the mystery of these supposed accidents that your extended family has been experiencing, and I'd like to help."

Her frown deepened. She'd have to figure out later how he had found out about her investigation. "Why?"

He shrugged. "I want to get back in your good graces." He held up his hands and spoke before she could say anything. "I'm not trying to become king anymore, so you don't need to think that this is like before. I just thought that I could be useful."

Ravenna released a long breath and started massaging her temple. "Fine. I'll let you know if I think of any way you can help."

"Thank you." Garrett walked over to where Ravenna was still standing behind the rose bush, handed her a rose she hadn't noticed he was holding, and kissed her cheek.

`"I'll go back to my place in the background, unseen." He winked and left her there, her hand gently touching her cheek.

CHAPTER 44

Liam liked Rook Manor. It was a lot smaller than the Rivers Estate, but it had better land to go hunting and exploring. He also didn't think he could get lost like last time. However, Ravenna was insistent that he stay with her while she talked with Lord Rook. As much as he wanted to protest, he saw how nervous the thought of him coming back as not himself made her, so he relented.

So he sat next to her, listening to Lord Rook talk ceaselessly about hunting. Apparently, he was a champion hunter with several trophies under his belt. He had been hunting when someone shot him in the leg with a crossbow.

"That hunting trip was a complete disaster. First, Lady Winter's saddle broke right after we started riding out, which caused her to slide off her horse. I would never have forgiven myself if something were to have happened to her."

"Lady Winter was *here* when she fell off her horse?"

Ravenna asked. Lord Rook blushed, and Liam could smell him sweating.

"We had been, er, courting for a week at that point. And her parents do not exactly know..."

Liam was starting to enjoy this young lord's discomfort. It made him seem more human compared to hearing about what an excellent hunter he was.

Ravenna assured him, "Your secret is safe with us. Please continue your story. It's quite thrilling."

"Then, before we could even release the hounds..." He gave a sideways glance toward Liam. Liam wondered if he was sizing him up as a potential hunting dog. "...one of the crossbows that a servant had been carrying fired without reason!" Lord Rook rubbed a spot on his leg as if he could scrub away the memory of the pain.

"Your servant hadn't accidentally set it off?" Ravenna inquired. It seemed reasonable that no servant would want to indict themselves for accidentally shooting their master with a crossbow.

"I'm positive. He had been handing it to me, so his hand was nowhere near the trigger. I was lucky he had it pointed down."

"That is extremely odd."

Lord Rook nodded, "Yes, indeed! As much as I wanted to take Lady Winter hunting, she insisted that we turn back so I could see a physician." He had a dopey lovesick look in his eyes, and Liam commented to Ravenna, *I'm pretty sure she did not suggest it just because she loves him, but because that's what any decent person would do...*

Ravenna hid a smile behind her hand.

Liam tuned the young man out and waited for Ravenna to ask for a tour of the stables. Why would someone deliberately cause these accidents? Whoever it was had been rather incompetent at killing anyone until Lord Rivers. That is, if killing these people was actually the intent. Was someone really trying to remove any competition for the throne, or was it something else?

He regretted getting distracted yesterday from the box in Lord Rivers's room. All he could remember now was that it had been some sort of tea from Faircoast, and the outside of the box had smelled like the stench around the broken staircase.

"I would love to see the work that you have done to your stables!" Ravenna's voice pulled him out of his reminiscing.

"Let's be off then!" Lord Rook enthusiastically led them out of the manor and toward the stables located to the right of the main house. When they got there, he explained, "Not only were we able to add extra stalls for new horses, we were also able to add a larger tack room that could include storage for hunting gear. It's easier than having to carry everything from the house to the stables."

The stable was one of the largest that Liam had ever seen. It was almost bigger than Rook Manor itself. Hundreds of horse stalls lined the inside with various breeds of horses, from race horses to draft horses. They weren't just for hunting or pulling carriages.

"The Rook family has been breeding Lyra's horses for decades," Ravenna whispered to Liam when she noticed him staring. "Were you really not paying attention inside?"

Liam hunched over with his tail slightly tucked under him. *Can you blame me?*

Ravenna quietly laughed, "Not really."

Lord Rook guided them toward the newer half of the stable. As they got closer, Liam growled. Thankfully, Lord

Rook didn't notice as he continued pointing out new features.

"What is it?" Ravenna asked.

It's the same smell that I noticed inside the Rivers Estate.

Ravenna's eyes widened for a moment before she put on an interested expression. "When did you say these renovations were completed?" she asked Lord Rook.

"Around a month ago. Right around the time Lady Winter agreed to let me court her." A lovesick expression appeared on his face.

Ravenna looked at Liam and raised a brow. He nodded. This was the third location of the accidents, and so far, it continued the pattern of someone woodworking beforehand.

"Who was your craftsman?" Ravenna asked, trying to sound nonchalant.

Lord Rook stopped and looked over at her. "You know, I don't actually know." He frowned and scratched his head. "I'd have to ask Reginald. He's the one in charge of all that business. I just told him what I wanted, and he told the men who worked on the stables."

They continued their tour, but Liam felt uneasy. The smell was fainter compared to when he had smelled it the day before, but its sourness still clouded his sense of smell. Ravenna seemed to be aware of his discomfort; after she checked on how Liam was doing, she told Lord Rook that they had to end their visit. Liam was extremely grateful to get away from that place.

A few days passed with nothing more to go on other than learning that the main carpenter had been a different person at each location. Ravenna found herself frustrated with the lack of news, but this changed when Cress came back from working on Lady Maria's dress.

"Someone saw something!" she announced to Liam and Ravenna in the dining hall.

Ravenna frowned. "Who saw what?"

Cress sat down at the table and took a slice of bread and buttered it. "One of the servants who works for Lord and Lady Maria came up to me to talk. Apparently, she had heard through the grapevine that I was looking for information." She took a bite from her buttered bread.

Ravenna and Liam shared a glance.

"Go on," Ravenna encouraged.

"As you know, the chandelier in their main hall almost collapsed on top of Lady Maria. Well, this servant saw a man near the rope. She didn't recognize him at first, but then she remembered that she had seen him working on a project in Lady Elliot's kitchen when she dropped off some gifts from Lady Maria."

"How did she recognize him?" Liam interrupted.

"I guess he's a little hunched over with, um," Cress shifted in her seat, "a distinct odor."

"Let me guess. It's a little sour?" Liam asked.

"That's how she described it," Cress shrugged.

"What was he doing at Lady Maria's House?" Ravenna asked.

"He'd been working on the renovation project for their main hall, which is why the servant didn't think too much of his presence there."

Liam turned to Ravenna and said, "It doesn't seem like

he's the main carpenter. Unless he's been switching names for each project."

"I agree. I think we need to ask around the carpenters' guild to see who he is."

"You could say that the castle needs something worked on and then hire someone," Cress suggested as she grabbed another slice of bread.

Ravenna shook her head. "That would require getting more people involved, and too much time." After a moment lost in thought, she looked up at her comrades in this mystery.

"Cress, are you able to make time to visit the guild with Garrett?" Ravenna winced at Cress's glare and the shocked look that Liam quickly hid.

"Why Garrett?" Liam tried to ask calmly.

Ravenna bit her lip. "Because he offered to help," she said, with a little hint of question in her voice.

"But - " Cress started to say before Ravenna interrupted her with a glare.

"And Liam and I can't go to the guild without a whole guard. It would raise too much suspicion. Besides, I'd feel better if you didn't go by yourself."

Cress continued to glare at her.

"He could be useful."

After a long pause, Cress sighed and stopped scowling at Ravenna. "Fine. I'll go look for him now and tell him that he had better be ready early tomorrow morning."

"Thank you, Cress! You're the best!"

"Yeah, yeah," Cress said as she walked out of the room.

The dining room became deathly quiet. Ravenna couldn't bring herself to look at Liam.

After a while, he broke the silence. "Why didn't you mention before that Garrett knew about what we were doing?"

Ravenna wasn't sure if it would have been worse if he had sounded mad rather than defeated. "I don't know. He seemed like he wanted to prove himself, and I thought I'd let him. There hasn't been a good time to bring it up." She finally brought herself to look over at Liam. He looked exhausted. More red fur covered his skin, and his eyes had stayed his canine brown rather than turning back into the green that Ravenna had come to love.

She tried to tell herself that she shouldn't feel guilty about taking Garrett's offer for help. But she thought of the rose currently pressed between the pages of a book in her room, and her cheek could still feel the tingle of Garrett's kiss.

"Okay." Liam smiled at her, but it didn't reach his eyes. He focused on eating the soup and what was left of the bread loaf that Cress had been eating. The guilt Ravenna felt sank even further into the pit of her stomach.

"Do you want to play cards tonight instead of chess?" Ravenna asked after they were done eating. It had been a quiet meal. She wanted to try to make things go back to normal.

Liam shook his head. "It's been a long day. I think I'm going to go to bed early."

"Oh. Alright. If that's what you want to do," Ravenna replied faintly.

He reached over to take her hand in his and with a sad smile asked, "Will you marry me?"

Ravenna fought the tears threatening to fill her eyes. What would happen if she tried to say yes right now? Would the curse break or would Liam end up even more crushed? "I'm sorry, but no."

She could barely hear the hitch in his breath right before he transformed back into a dog. Ravenna waited for him to recompose himself. As soon as he seemed ready, she gave him a small smile and followed him out.

CHAPTER 45

Liam pretended to be asleep when Ravenna peeked into his room to see if he was awake for breakfast. He hadn't slept at all the night before, but he didn't know how to be around her right now. He didn't want to pry too deeply as to why she had hid her conversation with Garrett. She said it wasn't that important, despite her looking like he had caught onto them doing more than just talking.

He hated how jealous he felt; it wasn't fair to her. But that didn't mean he was ready to spend time with her just yet. He waited for some time after hearing her walk down toward the breakfast room, and then he got up and went to the gardens.

After he had finished relieving himself, he hesitated on going back inside. Ravenna tended to avoid the gardens, so he walked away from the castle and further into the gardens. He found Tatiana sitting underneath an apple tree.

"Hello, Your Highness." She patted the ground next to her, silently asking him to sit with her. He hung his head as he resigned himself to having to spend more time with someone who couldn't understand him and walked over.

"Isn't it still too early for you to be out of bed?" Tatiana teased as she tilted her head.

He just flopped onto the ground with a huff.

"Ravenna mentioned at breakfast that you were still asleep," she continued casually, looking out at the gardens in front of her. He tried not to react to Ravenna's name.

"You've gone through a lot this past year, haven't you?"

He raised his head and looked at the fairy.

"It's hard to watch someone you love struggle to trust you."

He sighed. Ravenna not trusting him was just as hard as her not loving him.

"You are one of the best things to ever happen to Ravenna." She smiled at his disbelieving look. "For starters, if you hadn't been around, that cougar would have killed her."

He snorted. If it weren't for Tatiana showing up with a bunch of guards, they'd still be stuck in the woods because Ravenna had been too stubborn to leave him behind.

"Yes, Hoseenu told me to go to the woods to help you, but we wouldn't have made it in time to prevent the cougar from harming Ravenna."

Liam hadn't been able to figure out how Tatiana had known where to find them. He hadn't known that Hoseenu spoke directly to her.

"One of the benefits of being a fairy godmother is that Hoseenu lets me hear Him directly because I won't be able to meet Him in the hereafter until my sister's bloodline is no longer on the throne." Tatiana somehow answered his unspoken question.

No one knew how to become a fairy godmother, except for other fairy godmothers. The only known fact was that unlike the fae, fairy godmothers had been human once. Liam was starting to wonder if she was going to tell him that secret next.

Tatiana continued talking, but she had a faraway look in her eyes as if she no longer saw the garden around her. "My older sister was one of the first queens of Lyra. She was also my best friend. We would do anything for each other, including making sacrifices for one another.

"After she married her king and had their first child, I ended up getting pregnant. My father, who was still alive after my mother's passing, was going to disown me for having the child. He said I was a disgrace to the new royal line and should be cut off."

Liam put his paw on Tatiana's knee to give some small comfort. She smiled, but he could tell her mind was still in the past.

"My sister did not want that for me. She made sure that my father wouldn't have a reason to cast me aside by raising my baby girl as her own. It was one of the best and worst things she could ever do for me. I would be able to watch my daughter grow up, but she would only think of me as her aunt.

"When our children were several years older, she confided in me about how worried she was about the future of Lyra. We were a small nation that was still so young. Our neighbors could have easily taken control over us. She didn't want to have our children grow up constantly worried about war and famine. I didn't want that for them either.

"I went looking for a fairy godmother to tell me the secret to becoming one." At this, Tatiana finally looked at Liam and chuckled. "I won't be telling you that secret, though." She continued her story. "I bound myself to my sister's bloodline, promising her that I would watch over her descendants and their kings and queens. I would guard their rule from outside forces and guide them to become wise leaders like her and her king. As long as the line was never broken.

"That was an age and a half ago. And I have kept my word as I've watched everyone I grew up with pass into the hereafter. I've watched my daughter's children grow up, have children of their own, and die, never knowing that I was their matriarch. Despite befriending them, no matter what station they've ended up in during their lives, I've kept that fact from them."

Liam immediately thought of all the time Tatiana spent in the kitchen with Cook. Everyone knew that if you couldn't find her in the gardens or in her room, she was bound to be drinking tea in the kitchen. It didn't seem beyond the realm of possibility that Cook was one of Tatiana's descendants.

"And after all this time, I've never done anything as drastic as what I've done for Ravenna." She gave a rueful smile. "She needs you. Just as much as you need her. Hoseenu is the reason you're here, but ultimately, we are still given a choice over what happens."

She scratched behind his ear. "But I'm pretty sure that He doesn't want me to leave my sister's bloodline just yet, so go on and talk to your queen. Forgiving her will be more freeing than avoiding her."

She was right; he should stop avoiding Ravenna. Even if he doubted what Tatiana had said about her needing him.

Tatiana scratched his ear harder, to the point where his back right leg started automatically thumping the air. As much as he wanted to complain about being treated like a normal dog, he did admit to himself that it felt amazing.

"Now, go on and leave this old woman in peace!"

He barked at her. No one would ever look at her and think she was old. They'd think she couldn't be a day over twenty. But now he knew exactly how old she was.

She chuckled to herself at his response as he got up and ran off to find Ravenna.

CHAPTER 46

Cress and Garrett waited for Ravenna in her private study. It was one of the few places she knew without a doubt that no one could hear them talk, so she had asked them to meet her there. Ravenna arrived to their eager faces, and Liam came in shortly after she did.

It was the first time that she had seen him all day. That was partially her fault. After she checked to see if he was awake for breakfast and saw that he was obviously awake but pretending to be asleep, she couldn't bring herself to face him when she heard that he seemed to be looking for her later in the day. She even bribed Cori with extra cookies from Cook to not tell him where she was. It was a low moment.

"So, what did you find out?" she asked, making sure she did not meet Liam's gaze.

Cress and Garrett seemed to pick up that there was something going on between them; Cress kept looking between them, and Garrett sat up straight and refused to look at either of them.

"You owe us a lot of money," Cress said as she folded her arms across her chest and narrowed her eyes at Ravenna. That seemed to break Garrett out of his stare because he glanced over at Cress incredulously.

"What do you mean?" Ravenna asked.

Cress glared. "We had to bribe *so* many people to get information and make sure they wouldn't spread around that we were looking for details. It was ridiculous!"

"It was a rather pricey investigation," Garrett added quietly.

"I'll make sure that you are well compensated." Ravenna gave Cress a smug look. "If you can deliver the goods."

Ravenna heard Liam chuff and let herself take a small peek at him. He was slowly shaking his head, and it made her smile that at least he was still able to enjoy her sense of humor.

"I got the goods all right. Our mystery odor man's name is Rugen." Cress flashed a triumphant smile.

Before she could add anything else, Garrett took over. "He's from Harmon and has worked on many projects for multiple head carpenters for years. Then, as of last week, he disappeared. People think he's staying at the White Bear Inn."

"Thank you both for your help in this. I'll make sure you are paid back." She winked at Cress, who grumbled, "You better," then added, "So now what do you want us to do?"

"I want you two to go get dinner," Ravenna said. Cress again looked between Ravenna and Liam. After apparently coming to some sort of conclusion, she said to

Garrett, "Come on, Garrett. You owe me an explanation as to how you know about my mother's old shop."

Ravenna and Liam stayed behind as Cress and Garrett left.

As soon as the door closed behind them, Ravenna said to Liam, "I'm sorry for not telling you about Garrett's offer to help. I should have let you know, especially because kings and queens of Lyra are supposed to share that sort of information with each other." Ravenna still couldn't bring herself to make eye contact with him. She didn't want to see what he must be thinking of her.

She heard him get up and walk over to her. He nuzzled her knee and then said, *Ravenna, look at me, please.*

His eyes were full of warmth and understanding when she finally brought herself to look at his face.

I forgive you. You are going to make mistakes. I'm going to make mistakes. It's just part of the process of life. He pressed closer to comfort her.

She rubbed both of his ears with her hands. "Thank you," she said, and got a mischievous look in her eyes. "Do you want to go on an adventure with me after dinner?"

What do you have in mind?

"Let's pay Rugen a visit, shall we?"

His tail wagged in response. *We shall.*

CHAPTER 47

They waited until after dinner, during sunset, to sneak out. If anyone should ask where they were going, Ravenna would simply say they were hoping to explore the marketplace before it closed for the night.

During dinner, they discussed how they would sneak away from her personal guards. Liam had told her that he should be able to track where her guards' scents were coming from so he could guide the two of them away. He wasn't amused when Ravenna said, "Having personal guards is such a hassle, isn't it?"

The White Bear Inn was of average quality. It wasn't where some of the wealthier merchants would go to stay overnight, but its prices were too high for the lowest class.

While Ravenna paused to look at a marketplace stall that sold some handwoven baskets, she pulled up her cloak's hood and whispered to Liam, "Have we lost them yet?" She watched as he lifted his nose in the air to take a sniff. After a moment, he replied, *We have, but we have to move quickly.*

Ravenna bought one of the baskets from the stall and followed Liam toward the White Bear Inn. She looked around at the thinning crowd of animals and people while those who ran the different stalls started packing up their wares. What was one more girl and her dog?

They arrived in front of a dull red building with a hanging sign featuring a picture of a white bear. When Ravenna started heading toward the door, Liam tugged her skirt back with his mouth and said, *Wait!*

Ravenna stopped moving, but she looked down at Liam to ask him why he had stopped her.

You're the queen. Somebody is bound to notice you inside. We should go in through the back.

"How are we supposed to know which room Rugen is in if we don't ask?"

Trust me. We'll be able to smell it out. Liam's whole body gave a shudder of disgust. He started walking toward the inn's back entrance from the alley. Ravenna followed closely behind. When they got to the back door that led into the kitchen, Liam again pulled her to the side by her skirt.

"If you keep that up, you might end up ripping my dress," she muttered to him, but he just ignored her as he cocked his ear toward the door. Ravenna also tilted her head to see if she could hear anything, but the only noise she could pick up was the foot traffic at the end of the alleyway. Whatever Liam could hear didn't seem to be much of a problem; he led her back to the door and gestured with his head to open it.

She gave a small tug on the door to see if it was locked. Thankfully, it wasn't, and they were able to peer inside a bustling kitchen. Ravenna pulled her hood closer to her face as she and Liam skirted by all of the activity.

The kitchen, slightly smaller than the one back at the castle, was run by a young, ruddy man with a thick belly. He shouted orders at all of his sous chefs as he walked around personally checking every dish.

For a moment, Ravenna thought he had spotted her, but then the sound of dishes crashing to the floor drew his attention away from her. She rushed toward the door leading out of the kitchen when she heard shouts about a dog. She spun around and saw Liam running from the area where the broken dishes were.

Get out of here now! she heard him cry out to her. So she quickly slipped out of the kitchen into a hallway with a stairwell that was likely used for servants to carry dinners to patrons' rooms.

She waited by the door for Liam to push through. Once he made it out, she grabbed the scruff of his neck and dragged him toward the stairs. They had just made it up enough of the stairs to be out of sight when they heard the kitchen doors open.

"Do you know where it went?" a girl's voice shouted.

"No, but it's out of the kitchen, which is all that matters, right?" what sounded like an older boy answered.

Ravenna held her breath as she listened to where their footsteps would go. It wasn't until she felt Liam relax in her grip and he told her that he had heard them go back inside the kitchen that she finally exhaled in relief as she slid down onto the step.

This really is turning out to be an adventure.

She looked up to see Liam standing on the step above her, wagging his tail and happily panting. She flashed him a wide grin. "Yes, it is, but it's not over yet."

They both got up and continued following the stairway to the second floor. As soon as they reached it, Liam sniffed the area and scrunched up his nose.

This is his floor. He headed down the hallway. At room 216, he stopped and snarled.

"That bad?"

He just nodded his head. Ravenna knocked on the door.

"Go away!" a slurred voice shouted from the other side of the door. Ravenna frantically thought through any possible excuses to get him to open the door.

"Delivery, sir!" she called back. A slow shuffling sound could be heard before a gruff looking man opened the door.

"Well, where is it?" The man looked her up and down and then looked over at Liam, who was trying hard to not look bothered by the odor that Ravenna could now smell for herself.

"Actually, Rugen, we have some questions that we need to ask you."

Rugen's eyes widened and he tried to quickly shut the door, but Liam pushed with his right shoulder to keep it open while Ravenna walked in. Liam then bumped the door closed.

"Who are you?" Rugen whispered as he sat down on an unmade bed. He looked close to tears. Ravenna surveyed the room before answering. It was obviously one of the smaller rooms in the inn, and there were several empty bottles of ale all over it.

"Does it matter? I know that you were involved with the accidents on the projects you've been working on."

Liam gave her a look that she read as either he thought she was crazy or he was proud of her response. She had never before seen that look on him, or any dog, so it was hard to tell which it was.

As soon as she mentioned the accidents, Rugen broke down sobbing. "I never meant to kill anybody!" he wailed, covering his face with his hands.

Out of all the potential outcomes of their confrontation, it had never crossed her mind that they'd have to console the man behind Lord Rivers's death. She looked to Liam, asking for help. He kept tilting his head and seemed just as confused as she was.

"Of course not. No one believes that you did." Sympathy seemed like a good approach. "We just want to know what went wrong." She sat next to him on the bed and placed her hand on his shoulder. Liam stepped closer, right in front of the two humans' knees.

Rugen took a few shaky breaths as he tried to collect himself enough to answer. "I've been trying to raise money to send to my wife and daughter back in Harmon. There was no work there, but in Lyra, there are jobs all over the place. When my daughter got sick, we needed extra money to pay for medicine. I started looking around for small woodcraft jobs on the side. That's when I was approached by him. All he wanted me to do was cause a little havoc for some of the nobles whose names were on his list. They all had projects that I was able to get hired for, and some of the names on this list had ideas written next to them about what could be done.

"I didn't question it. I just needed the extra money. This last job, though, was different. I was given a box to place in the lord's room in addition to what I had already planned on doing."

That must have been the box of tea I saw. It could have possibly contained poison.

Ravenna agreed with Liam. It seemed odd that whoever

was behind these accidents would want to give a cup of regular tea to one of their victims.

Rugen began sobbing again. Ravenna gently rubbed the top of his back in a soothing circle.

"It's okay. You didn't want anyone to die," she consoled. "But, who's 'him?'"

After Rugen had calmed back down a little bit more, he looked up at her with big, tear-rimmed, bloodshot eyes. "I don't know."

Ravenna frowned in disbelief. "What do you mean?"

"He never said. He would just show up at my door randomly with money and the name of the next person off this list that he wanted me to mess around with. I didn't want to question it. I've also made sure to not answer the door anymore to anyone who has a male voice because I don't want his blood money anymore."

Ask him what the man looked like, Liam said.

Ravenna repeated his question out loud.

"He was a short and skinny fellow. The only way you he might stand out is that he has an ugly scar from a gash on the right side of his face," Rugen told Ravenna.

Ravenna, I know him. He's involved with the raiders.

Ravenna could hear the worry in Liam's voice, but she didn't dare talk to him about it in front of Rugen. She just gave a small nod of acknowledgment.

"Thank you, Rugen, for telling us. We'll make sure that he won't bother you anymore."

Rugen started crying again and said, "Thank you, miss! You're an angel!"

Ravenna got off the bed and headed out of the room with Liam, leaving Rugen behind to cry himself into a drunken sleep.

It wasn't until after they had snuck back out onto the

road again that Ravenna felt like she could ask Liam what he knew of this man. However, as soon as they turned off the road where the White Bear Inn was and got onto the main road, they were met by Garrett and another one of her personal guards named Samuel. They were not happy.

"Your Majesty, it is our job to keep you safe. We can't do that if you deliberately hide from us," Samuel said.

Ravenna stood as tall as she could, and with her chin held high, said in a low voice, "Then maybe I need new guards if they lose track of me so easily."

Samuel looked down, ashamed. Garrett continued to look at her.

"Let me remind you that I am your queen, and this," she pointed at Liam, "is your possible future king. We shall not be chastised for your sloppy work."

Now Garrett looked as abashed as Samuel.

"Since this is a first-time offense, there shall be no consequences. Now, you may follow us back to the castle." She strode forward, leaving the two guards behind.

Liam walked beside her. *You really are the queen, aren't you?*

Ravenna smiled at the awe in his voice. "Yes. Yes, I am."

CHAPTER 48

Liam lay by the fire in Ravenna's room, waiting for her to return from talking with Cress. Despite Ravenna reprimanding her guards, they had still given her disapproving glances on the way home. Cress wasn't any happier about the situation. Apparently, Garrett had gone back to the castle at some point to check if they had returned. Cress had known Garrett was supposed to be on his shift guarding the queen and got worried when he wasn't with her, so he had to confess that they had lost the queen and dog prince. Liam wasn't envious of the tongue lashing he was sure Garrett had received from the queen's best friend.

Ravenna walked into the queen's chambers and fell onto her chair next to the fireplace. "So much for being the queen where Cress is concerned."

Liam snorted. He was just happy to be alone with Ravenna. She had promised Cress and Garrett that they would tell them tomorrow what they had learned on their little adventure.

Ravenna took some time to decompress before she brought up the man that Rugen had mentioned. "Who is he exactly?"

He's a messenger for the raiders, but he isn't exactly one of them.

She frowned. "What do you mean?"

He's more of a freelancer. He's discreet about who his current employer is, and he's one of the few people who is willing to do business with people who have an, er, illegal agenda.

"So what you're saying is that the raiders could be behind this, or it could be anyone who doesn't like these certain courtiers?"

Correct.

"Well, I guess we'll have to find him and figure out who he's sending messages for."

After tonight, I'd believe that you can do pretty much anything, including prying the secrets from a man who's known for keeping them hidden, Liam chuckled.

Her eyebrows rose. "Hey! I couldn't have done it without you tonight. I would have been caught by my guards right away. And I never would have found Rugen's room so quickly."

Liam felt his chest warm from her praise. Tonight had been the most fun he had had in a long time, and he wanted to continue having adventures with Ravenna. He took a moment to soak in her beauty and the joy that she radiated.

We make a good team, he finally said.

She smiled. "Yeah, we do."

CHAPTER 49

*I*t was after lunch, and again three humans and one dog met in the queen's private study. Cress still seemed upset with Ravenna for making her worry. Ravenna would have to somehow make it up to her later.

"We learned that Rugen purposefully caused the accidents, but he didn't come up with the idea in the first place," Ravenna started.

"Then why did he do it?" Cress interjected.

"Because he was offered much needed money to send back home to his family."

Cress looked down at Ravenna's desk in front of her. "Oh."

"More importantly, we learned who he'd been receiving instructions from. Or at least who the messenger is."

"Who?" Garrett asked.

Ravenna looked over at Liam. He wagged his tail to let her know it was going to be okay. "We don't know his name. We just know that he has done some work with the raiders as a messenger." Garrett seemed to go pale at the mention of the raiders, so Ravenna asked, "Are you alright?"

"Just bad memories of them from the border."

Ravenna nodded and continued, "There must be some way to track him. Cress, I need you to go back to our," she paused as she glanced over at Garrett, "friends. And ask them for any information about a short, skinny man with a giant scar on the right side of his face."

When Cress agreed, Ravenna looked at Garrett. "Is there some way you might be able to get more information about this man from your comrades?"

Garrett rubbed his chin in thought. "It might take a few days to hear back from them, but it's possible."

"Good. We'll see you both tomorrow."

Cress and Garrett got up and left the study together.

Liam looked up at Ravenna. *Would you like to have a picnic dinner tonight? It's still a little warm today.*

Ravenna narrowed her gaze at him. "What are you up to?"

He shook his head. *Nothing. I just thought it would be a good idea. We don't have to if you don't want to.*

"No, it's fine. I'll go let Cook know."

As she got up to leave, Liam pressed against her legs. She reached down and petted his head. "Are you alright?" she asked.

I just wish that I had more information on him. He's well known by everyone who's been tracking the raiders, but no one actually knows his name or how to get in contact with him.

Ravenna bent down so she could look Liam in the eyes.

"It's okay. You haven't failed because you don't know everything related to the raiders. Show yourself some grace."

Liam's tail wagged in earnest as she spoke to him. It pleased Ravenna that she was able to cheer him up like this, and she wondered for the first time if she would be able to read him just as well if they ever broke the curse.

Garrett's shift to watch Ravenna landed during dinner, and Liam knew that if they ate outside, the guards would have to watch them. After Liam made an excuse of needing to grab something inside, his human nose - stronger than ever thanks to the curse's lasting effects - sniffed out where Garrett had positioned himself behind some trees.

"Your Highness," Garrett bowed to Liam when he saw Liam head toward him, out of sight of Ravenna.

"You're hiding something," Liam said. He could hear a canine growl in his voice despite the fact that he was trying to come across as non-threatening.

Garrett winced, but he said, "I'm not sure what you're talking about."

Liam walked closer to him. "One of the advantages of having a dog's sense of smell is that I can smell when someone is nervous. You were completely at ease until the messenger was brought up. I want to know why." His lips curled back in a snarl. Liam could smell the bitter tang of Garrett's fear despite him not showing a single response on the outside. "Don't lie to me. I can smell you even now."

Garrett took a moment to look at the beast that Liam resembled. Fur covered his body from head to toe, and a muzzle was starting to form on his face. The nails on his hands and feet were now as long and sharp as a dog's. His eyes were no longer human, and his canine teeth were prominent. It was discouraging to see how much he remained transformed during the times that he was supposed to be human...but in this moment, he was thankful to look intimidating.

Garrett seemed to realize that, as far as he was concerned, he wouldn't be able to get away from Liam, and if he were to attack Liam, he'd be caught right away. He said, "Alright, I'll tell you."

Liam stepped back and folded his arms.

Garrett's shoulders sagged as he said, "Someone is using the messenger to blackmail me."

Liam made sure not to show any sort of surprise and waited for Garrett to continue.

"Whoever it is, they didn't want money, but they wanted information about what you and Ravenna were figuring out about the accidents."

"You're willing to sacrifice your queen's safety by forfeiting information to someone who is a threat and could cause harm to her?" This time, Liam didn't bother smothering the growl in his voice. He wanted this pretty boy to be afraid of him. And from the smell of it, Garrett was indeed fearful.

"What are you being blackmailed for?" Liam asked. When Garrett didn't answer right away, Liam stepped closer to him and let out a low growl.

Garrett mumbled, "I was paid to look the other way whenever any of the raiders snuck around to execute an attack or transport goods."

Liam snarled.

"Don't judge me, prince! You didn't grow up wondering where your next meal would come from or having to figure out how you would survive on the streets!" Garrett glared at Liam.

"No, I didn't. But as a soldier, I know that in the army you wouldn't have needed to worry about those things anymore. You were paid well and given food and shelter. In return, you were asked for loyalty to your country." He glared right back at Garrett until Garrett looked away.

"I wasn't going to go through with it," he admitted. "I was planning on slipping a note under Ravenna's door about how to meet up with the messenger."

"That's not enough. He won't stick around if anyone besides you shows up," Liam countered. "You are going to tell Ravenna the truth, and then you are going to help us set up an ambush. Do you understand?"

"Yes, Your Highness."

"When do you have to meet him next?"

"In a week."

Liam was relieved that they weren't too late. "We'll meet tomorrow afternoon to tell Ravenna and Cress what we have to plan." Liam started to walk away, but then added, "And don't try to hide from me. Remember, I'm able to track you better than any hunting hound." He watched with satisfaction as Garrett's eyes widened in fear before going back to join Ravenna for dinner.

"Did you get lost?" she asked him playfully.

"Something like that." He smiled as he sat down on the picnic blanket.

"Don't say I didn't warn you when you find out that I ate all of the berries while you were gone."

He looked at the bowl of berries to find that it was, indeed, empty. He was slightly disappointed, but then she went over to one of the baskets that had carried their food and pulled out another bowl that she had dumped the berries into. She snickered.

"Why, you little minx!"

Without thinking about it, he reached over and tickled her. Ravenna shrieked as she tried to get away from him, but she fell onto her back and ended up pulling him down with her. He caught himself on his hands beside her head, and for a moment, stared into her eyes. She smiled up at him, which made his heart beat faster.

"I...um...sorry?" That was the only thing he could get out of his mouth as he got off of her.

"It's okay," she said as she got back up as well, but then she threw a berry at him.

"Hey!"

"That's for attacking me!"

Before she could throw another berry, he grabbed her hand and whispered, "Will you marry me?" Her smile faded, and he could feel the knot forming in his stomach. He let go before she had a chance to reply and turned back into a dog.

CHAPTER 50

Ravenna sat on the window seat in her bedroom, drinking a cup of tea as she looked out at the stars. It was past midnight, and she still couldn't fall asleep.

"Hoseenu, why can't I bring myself to love him?" she whispered. Her fear of admitting that she might actually love Liam was frustrating. He kept insisting that he loved her. With every word and deed, he'd proven it over and over again. She loved spending time with him. She could be vulnerable with him. She trusted him. Just not enough to give him her heart completely.

"I still have time, right?" she asked. He was still turning into a human during dinner. Albeit a loose definition of human...

She sighed. She was frustrated. Not only was she stuck in limbo with the curse, but she was also at a dead-end figuring out the "who" behind the accidents. She hoped - against reason - that whoever was targeting her extended family was all just some paranoid fabrication of her imagination, and it was just pure coincidence that all of them were qualified for the throne. It didn't make any sense though. Except for Lord Rivers, no one else had been killed. They had just been given warnings. Ravenna could feel a headache building.

"Please keep Lyra safe," she prayed. "I can't do this without You. I need Your help." Again, she looked out to the stars. Everything was quiet. No answer was forthcoming.

Putting her tea cup on the tray, she got up and went back to bed to try to get some sleep.

Cress burst into her room bright and early. Groggily, Ravenna peered over her covers at the tall blonde throwing open the curtains around her room, letting in the morning light.

"What are you doing?" Ravenna tried asking. It actually sounded more like a long moan. If this is how Liam felt every morning, she would never again tease him about being a grouch before noon. Cress strolled over to the bed and sat at the end.

"Rise and shine! Garrett said he knows how to find the messenger!" Cress trilled. That woke Ravenna up. She sat up and tossed the covers off and immediately went over to her wardrobe. She pulled out a lavender dress and threw it on hastily.

"Come on! We need to wake Liam." She might have decided to never tease him again, but she wasn't sympathetic enough to never wake him up early.

"I'll let you wake up your sleeping prince. See you in the breakfast room!" Cress smiled brightly as she left Ravenna to her task.

Ravenna opened the door between the king's and queen's chambers and saw Liam lying on top of his bed, snoring gently. She sighed. Sometimes she got lucky and he was already slightly awake, making it easier to convince him to get up. Today was not one of those days.

"Liam." No response. She moved toward his bed. "We've got to go. Garrett has information." This time she heard a low growl. Good. He was nearly conscious. Ravenna decided to do the same trick Cress had pulled on her and opened his curtains. If the increasing growls were any sign, it seemed to be working.

"I know it's early, but we have to go now!" she said. She watched as he rolled off the bed without even opening his eyes and shuffled toward the door, still growling. A laugh threatened to burst out, but she tried hard to stifle it. Otherwise, he might just turn around and go back to bed.

Slowly, they made their way to the breakfast room. Liam had stopped growling, which Ravenna counted as an improvement, but his eyes were still not fully open.

Cress and Garrett were already there, waiting for them. Tatiana sat at the other end of the table, drinking tea. A finished plate sat in front of her. Liam jumped onto his chair at the head of the table and then put his head down on the table and closed his eyes. Ravenna continued toward the laid out food, prepared two plates, and placed one in front of Liam. He sniffed it but didn't move to eat it right away. Cress gave them a cheesy grin, but Ravenna chose to ignore it.

"Garrett, what do you know about the raiders' messenger?" Ravenna's question stopped Garrett's bewildered stare at Liam and made him look at Ravenna.

"He should be meeting with someone next week."

Liam growled at Garrett's response, and Garrett's face blanched.

"I mean, he's expecting to meet with me next week," Garrett said, so quietly that Ravenna wasn't sure she had heard him correctly. Cress must have had the same problem, because she asked, "*You're* meeting with him?"

Garrett nodded, looked up at the ceiling, and then said, "Someone is blackmailing me to tell them what Ravenna is learning about the accidents."

Ravenna's eyes narrowed at him.

"I'm not actually going to tell them anything!" he quickly added.

"What did you do that gave someone reason to blackmail you?" she asked him.

"I'd rather not say." Garrett looked over at Liam, but Liam gave no response.

"I guess it doesn't matter right now. What matters is that you know where and when he's going to show up, so we can set up an ambush," Ravenna said.

Liam lifted his head from the table and nodded in approval before finally starting to eat the food on his plate. Before Garrett could say more, Cress raised her hand to stop him. "This time, you're not going alone," Cress told Ravenna, giving the queen a death glare.

"Fine. We won't go alone. You can be there with us." Ravenna grinned.

"You bet I'll be going with you!"

Ravenna chuckled and turned again to look at Garrett. "Where is the meeting spot?"

"It's at a small pub called The O'Malley. He set up the time to be five days from now in the afternoon when most people won't be around."

Ravenna had never seen Garrett look so defeated, including when he had come to her study to apologize. He had always portrayed himself as a carefree protector - almost invincible. Now he seemed weak and vulnerable. Her heart ached to see him like this.

You and Cress should wait in one of the back rooms long before Garrett meets with the man. I'll be lying near the fire like a pub dog. Then after Garrett and I subdue him, we'll bring him to where you are and interrogate him there. Liam's voice startled Ravenna slightly since he had been quiet for so long. She told the rest of them what he had planned out.

"Sounds good," Cress said. Then, as if she had decided that they were done discussing the matter, she started eating breakfast in earnest. It didn't seem like she wanted to talk anymore. Ravenna's brow rose at this - something was off, and she decided that sometime later she would ask about it.

Finding that she wasn't terribly hungry, and having already finished what little food she had given to herself, Ravenna decided to go for an early morning walk. She looked over at Liam and nodded her head toward the door to silently ask if he wanted to come with her. He nodded his head and jumped off his chair.

"We're going to go now. I'm sure I'll see you both later."

Tatiana had apparently left at some point while they had been talking because she was nowhere to be found when Ravenna turned to say goodbye to her.

Where are we going? Liam asked after they left the breakfast room.

"I don't know. Anywhere but near Garrett." Ravenna continued walking aimlessly in the general direction of the forest. She thought back to how Garrett had looked at Liam throughout the whole exchange.

"*You* know what he did that he's being blackmailed for." It wasn't so much of a question as it was an accusation. They walked a few more steps before Liam answered, *I found out yesterday during dinner.*

"That's why you took so long getting back," she said more to herself than to him. "How bad is it?"

Depends on when he was doing it. He looked up at Ravenna. *He could have done worse, and I'm sure he'll tell someone else eventually, but all I cared about was that he came clean about the messenger.*

Ravenna hadn't expected Liam to tell her what Garrett had done, and she wasn't sure she wanted to know just how far Garrett had fallen from the pedestal that she had originally placed him on. It was already hard enough dealing with the feelings that he brought out in her. If she was honest with herself, there was a little bit of hope that he'd admit that he actually had loved her before, just to make it feel like her previously treasured memories had value. She was sick of being heartbroken over complete lies.

When they made it outside, Ravenna looked around to see that she had just been following Liam without paying attention to where they were going. Instead of changing direction now that she was aware of her surroundings, she let him lead her to the lake.

The day was getting hotter, and as soon as they arrived, Liam ran off and pranced around the shallows, making Ravenna giggle. He gave her a doggy smile, rushed toward where she was still standing by the water's edge, and shook the water off right next to her.

Ravenna shrieked as she tried to run away from him, but he kept chasing her and rubbing his wet fur all over her legs.

"Liam!"

If dogs could look smug, Liam definitely looked it as he headed back toward the water. Ravenna quickly followed him. She hitched up the skirt of her dress and walked into the shallows. Bending down, she dipped her hand into the water. Liam came over to see what she was doing, and she splashed him. He pranced away and barked at her. Then he jumped in place to try to splash her in return.

They played like that for a while before Ravenna realized that they had actually missed a council meeting.

"We need to hurry back and get cleaned up."

When she got out of the water, she looked back wistfully. Liam shook out his fur coat and then cocked his head at her.

"I'd rather stay out here too." She patted his head. "Come on. Let's go home."

CHAPTER 51

The week before their planned ambush went by a lot faster than Liam had thought it would. When the day came to corner the messenger, it went exactly as planned. Cress and Ravenna hid away in a large storage room while he lay down in front of the empty fireplace. The last few days of summer were turning out to be extremely hot, so most people didn't bother building a fire and would rather keep their curtains closed to keep out the heat.

While Liam waited, he thought about how much of the previous week had been spent trying to cheer Ravenna up. She had opened up and told him how worried she was about her extended family, how distracted she had been during council meetings, and just how stressed she was feeling, doubting that she was a good queen.

He had learned that words of comfort and praise didn't

mean much to her as she would just brush them aside. Instead, he tried to find ways to get her to laugh, mostly at his expense. It was worth it to see her smile and look carefree during those moments. Hoseenu knew how much he loved her.

A short man walking into the pub caught his attention and pulled his mind away from thoughts of Ravenna. He made sure not to lift his head to get a better look at the man lest he draw attention to himself. From all the reports he had poured over while searching for the raiders' hideout, this man matched the description of every account given about the messenger.

Liam watched as he ordered a tankard of ale from the counter and then sat at a table in the corner near the fireplace. It was only a matter of time before Garrett entered the pub, and then they would be able to herd him toward the storage room where the girls would be waiting with rope to tie him up. He wondered briefly if Garrett would make a run for it instead of following through with his part of the plan. But before long, Garrett walked in through the pub doors.

Garrett scanned the room before spotting the messenger drinking his ale. He headed toward the man and joined him at the table. Liam could hear them talking from where he lay.

"Nice to see that you actually came," the man said. His voice was high and whiny, and it made Liam cringe upon hearing it.

"I didn't really have much of a choice, did I?" Garrett scowled.

The other man gave a long and shrill laugh. "No, you didn't. Now, what message do you have for me to send?" He flashed Garrett a toothy grin.

Liam started to slowly make his way over to their table. He caught Garrett's eye to let him know that it was time.

Garrett drew out a knife, and before the other man could react, he placed it at the messenger's throat. Liam made it to the man's other side and gave a low growl. He could see the messenger's eyes widen in fear.

"I do have a message for you, but first, I need you to come with me." Garrett's voice came out low and hard. Liam made a quick glance around the rest of the room to make sure they hadn't drawn attention to themselves. They hadn't.

Slowly, Garrett escorted their captive toward the storage room. Liam followed behind to make sure the man wouldn't try to escape. Thankfully, they were able to get him in without any trouble.

Ravenna and Cress were waiting for them with rope to tie the man up while Garrett continued holding his knife to his throat. When they were done tying him to a chair, Ravenna stood before him with Liam standing by her side. He could smell the fear rolling off of the man, and if he wasn't mistaken, urine as well.

"For someone whose clientele are mostly criminals, you are easily threatened. I'm surprised," Ravenna said. Their prisoner had definitely urinated, Liam decided.

"My clients usually provide protection." The man began sniveling.

Liam *actually* felt embarrassed by this display of cowardice. Here was a man whose whole reputation was dealing with hardened criminals and blackmailers, and he was cowering in front of two women, a man, and a dog. He was tempted to get a message to the raiders that they should find a better messenger; it was that pathetic. The rest of the room seemed to feel the same way based on the looks they gave each other.

Ravenna pinched the bridge of her nose. "Who's blackmailing this man?" She gestured toward Garrett.

"I can't tell you."

Liam perked up. At least his reputation of keeping his clients' names a secret would remain intact. He almost reconsidered his views on the man.

"Oh, I think you can with a little persuading." Ravenna nodded toward Garrett who pulled the base of his knife out again. The man trembled.

"It's Lord Damien!" he wept.

Ravenna's face blanched. Cress glanced over at Ravenna in concern, and Liam wanted to go to her right away, but he didn't want to draw unwanted attention to her.

"Tell us how you get in contact with Lord Damien." Ravenna's voice took on an impatient tone, borderline threatening, after she took a moment to collect herself.

The man seemed to sense that it was in his best interest to share everything he knew because he quickly said, "We have a system in place. If he needs to meet with me, he'll leave a red stone in a small nook in the town gate. Then, if I want to meet with him, I leave a blue stone. The place and time are different each time because we change it at the end of each meeting. We check the meeting spot every week after we drop off the stone until the other person shows up." The man was singing like a bird.

"If you were to leave a blue stone today, when and where would you meet him?" Ravenna demanded.

"On the third day of the week after sundown in the castle gardens."

That was two days from now.

"And how long have you been working for him?" she demanded.

"Not long. He knew that I worked with the men who live near the Wilderosian and Lyrian border. He said he wanted to do business with them, and ask them about who planned the attack on the former king and queen of Lyra."

Ravenna narrowed her eyes at the man in front of her.

"Did he learn who it was?" she demanded.

"He never told me," the messenger squealed.

"After we're done with our little meeting, we're going to take your blue stone, and because I'm feeling generous, you are going to leave Lyra and never come back. If you do return, I'm sure we can find enough evidence to hold you in the castle dungeons for the rest of your miserable life. Do I make myself clear?" Her tone was filled with ice.

The man nodded his head vigorously and told them which pocket held the stone. When Garrett took it from him, Ravenna put on the hood of her cloak and walked out of the room. Cress followed closely behind.

"Are you just going to leave me here?" The man sobbed.

Liam and Garrett shared a quick glance, and then Garrett stuffed the man's mouth with a piece of cloth before they both walked out.

When they made it outside, Liam heard Cress's attempts to get Ravenna to talk to her, but she wasn't having any sort of success. Ravenna just continued moving forward, acting like she wasn't even aware of her friend beside her. Liam trotted up to follow beside her when Cress gave up and fell behind.

CHAPTER 52

Ravenna wasn't aware of how she ended up back in her bedroom. Her mind was too focused on what the messenger had said. She had always thought the attack on her parents was just bad luck because the routes that the monarchs travel on were never publicly discussed. She hadn't thought that it had been deliberate, let alone that her own uncle had known that. And now he was organizing attacks on her extended family. Nothing made sense anymore.

Tears fell from her eyes as the pain of losing her parents came up fresh in her memory again. She started to wipe them away, but they were coming so fast that she gave up and cried in earnest. That's when the door between hers and Liam's room opened slightly, and Liam poked his head in. When he saw her crying, he came all the way to her and jumped on to her bed.

THE CURSED QUEEN

She had thought she wanted to be alone, but when he lay down beside her she was grateful for his presence and the fact that he didn't offer any meaningless words of comfort. She cried harder and hugged Liam when he pressed himself against her, sobbing into his furry chest.

When she had run out of energy to cry, Liam licked the remaining tears off of her face. His face was the last thing she saw before she gave in to her exhaustion and fell asleep.

Liam woke up to the feeling of something warm pressed up against him. It smelled faintly of roses. He buried his nose deeper into the smell and felt silky hair. He quickly opened his eyes to see Ravenna asleep in her bed. He was in her room on her bed.

Immediately, the night before came rushing back to him, and he let himself relax. After Ravenna had fallen asleep, Liam hadn't dared move in case he woke her up. He must have also fallen asleep not long afterward.

He looked around the darkened room and realized that they must have slept through dinnertime and well into the night. It seemed like there were still several more hours before sunrise, so he thought about getting up and going to his bed. Even though he wanted to stay with Ravenna, it almost felt like torture to stay with her as a dog. He longed to be human and hold her while she slept. He had dreamt about doing just that several times over the past few months.

Liam started to inch away from her and toward the edge of the bed when all of a sudden, Ravenna's arm shot out, and she grabbed his paw. He froze.

"Stay," she mumbled.

It's not proper for the queen to spend the night alone with her suitor. He inwardly chuckled. Did it matter since he was a dog?

She mumbled again, but this time he couldn't make out the words she said. He tried again to crawl toward the edge of the bed, but her grasp on his paw tightened. He sighed and stopped moving, and her grip eased. When he moved back toward her, she finally let go so he could curl up in a ball beside her.

Hoseenu, I love her, and I think she is falling in love with me. Please have this curse end soon so she can officially be mine and I hers.

CHAPTER 53

The sunset cast a golden glow on the gardens. Ravenna, filled with nervous energy, twiddled her skirt in her fingers as she waited for the sun to completely set so she could meet her uncle. She and Liam ate outside while they waited. It had been his idea to eat in the gardens, as her guards would be required to be nearby. If something were to go wrong tonight, they would be right there.

Liam was now practically a full dog during dinner, albeit one that wore clothes. He still stood on his hind legs, and he could still talk, but that was all that was left of his human form. His face remained completely that of a dog, and his tail didn't disappear anymore. Paw pads lined the bottom of his feet and hands, and the curse no longer provided him boots to wear...his legs wouldn't be able to stand them since they were no longer human shaped.

She could tell that with every new lack of change he

was disappointed, but he never complained to her or made her feel guilty that she kept refusing him as her king. In all honesty, that's what actually made her feel even worse.

"It's going to be fine. We'll catch your uncle in the act, and this nightmare will be over for you," Liam said when he caught her staring at him.

"You're right," she said.

He reached over and squeezed her hand. She smiled at him and was tempted to lean into him for strength, but she knew that wouldn't be fair to him.

When they had finished eating, they walked around the gardens. The sun had almost set completely when they came upon the rose bushes. A few of the blossoms were still left, and Ravenna knew that fall was just around the corner.

Liam broke one of the red roses off a bush and handed it to her.

"Will you marry me?" She saw that his eyes were filled with love for her, and yet she could also tell that he was resigned to hearing the same answer that she had been giving him. She felt a knot form in her throat as she shook her head. The rose dropped to the ground as he once again became a dog.

Instead of leaving the rose, Liam gently picked it up with his mouth and again offered it to her. Ravenna carefully took it from him and held onto it as they continued their silent walk.

They had made their way to a giant oak tree in the middle of the gardens when Liam stopped and took a sniff of the air. The hackles on his neck rose, and she could tell he was trying to hold back a growl that would give them away. She looked in the direction he now faced and saw a man standing underneath the tree. He was looking the other direction.

He hadn't spotted them yet so they slowly made their way toward him. When they got closer, she saw that the man was indeed Uncle Damien. He turned to look toward the direction they were coming from. When he saw them, he stilled, and then walked toward them.

"Good evening," Damien called out.

"Uncle Damien, what are you doing out here?" Ravenna pretended to be surprised.

"Just enjoying the summer evening."

"Were you also planning on meeting anyone tonight?" Ravenna held up the messenger's pebble.

Damien's face turned red as he blustered, "What are you implying?"

Liam growled at him.

Ravenna lost her patience and blurted out, "Tell me who hired the raiders to kill my parents." She glared at her uncle, who she had always thought was difficult, but had also chosen to believe was someone who was loyal to his family.

"I don't know what you're talking about."

"Don't you dare lie to me. I know that you are working with them. I also know that you were behind Lord Rivers's death, and all of the accidents that happened to everyone in line for the throne. I'll ask you again. Why?" It took so much self-control on her part to not tell Liam to rip Damien's throat out. She had to remind herself that murder was not justice.

"I just needed some extra coin," Damien said. But Ravenna noticed that he kept shifting his eyes away from hers.

"What do you need the coin for? Your estate has plenty." Ravenna narrowed her eyes at her uncle, trying to figure out what he had left unsaid.

"It's none of your concern." Her uncle began pacing and kept grasping at the knife on his belt.

Liam drew closer to her and looked about ready to tackle Damien, but she held out her hand to stop him. She wanted to try some other questions before asking again who had killed her parents.

"And the attacks on the nobles? Why did you arrange them?"

"They were a distraction," he whispered more to himself than to her.

"What do you mean?"

"It doesn't matter. No one can know." Damien stopped pacing and looked at Ravenna with resignation. "Including you. I'm sorry," he said as if it pained him to do what he was about to do next.

Ravenna had started to wonder where her personal guards were. They should have come after hearing her uncle imply that he planned on killing her.

It was at that moment that Liam launched toward Damien, but before he reached him, her uncle pulled out the knife.

Time seemed to slow down as she realized that Damien was going to kill Liam. It was at that moment she realized that she couldn't live without Liam and that she could never marry anyone else...because she did love him.

Right as Damien started to lunge his knife at Liam, she ran and pushed Liam out of the way. She heard Liam shout her name as he growled, and then the pain in her side took over. The world went black.

Liam stilled as he saw Ravenna's body crumple to the ground. That blow was meant for him, not her. The next thing he knew, he was attacking Damien. Rage filled him as he clamped his jaws onto Damien's neck and shook the older man. He ignored his prey's cries and didn't let go until he heard nothing but silence. Liam rushed over to Ravenna's body and howled over her. His prayer to Hoseenu that someone would intervene was too late. Something inside of him broke.

He whimpered as he lay on top of his queen's still form, not paying attention to any of the shouts coming from the distance. When someone reached out to touch his queen, he growled and snapped at the hand.

He kept it up until a soothing voice said, "Liam, we need to take her inside."

He looked up and saw a woman. No, not a woman, a fairy. He got up and watched as the fairy directed some humans to pick up his queen, but he stayed close by, whimpering as they walked back toward the castle.

CHAPTER 54

Her head hurt; a light shone behind her eyelids. Ravenna had always thought that the hereafter was supposed to be soothing. There would be no more pain because Hoseenu would meet her face-to-face, and He was all things good.

She thought she heard Tatiana's voice. But that couldn't be right. She was a fairy godmother, and as far as she knew, the conditions of her blood oath were still in effect.

Ravenna tried to open her eyes, but it made her feel *so* exhausted. She heard whimpering and realized it could only be Liam. That gave her enough energy to push through her fatigue and open her eyes.

The effort made her groan, and it was as if being able to see her bedroom made her aware of how sore her body was, especially her lower right side.

"You're awake."

Ravenna turned her head and saw Tatiana smiling softly at her. Her fairy godmother sat in a chair that had been pulled up next to the head of her bed.

"I heard Liam."

Tatiana chuckled. Liam came into Ravenna's line of view, and she felt immediate relief to see him alive. He slowly inched his way up to her from the foot of her bed. She smiled as he gently licked her hand. Then she reached over and scratched behind his ear.

"Hey," she whispered to him. The only response he gave was a tail wag, and then he rested his head on his front paws as he lay next to her. Ravenna frowned and turned to look at Tatiana. "What happened?" She couldn't remember anything after Damien had stabbed her.

Tatiana stroked Ravenna's hair before she answered. "Liam asked Hoseenu to tell me to come find you both. Apparently, when Damien found out that you were eating dinner in the gardens the night that he was supposed to meet his messenger there, he took precautions and told your personal guards that they didn't need to guard you on castle grounds. I arrived just in time to see Damien attack you." Tatiana looked furious as she recounted that last part.

"Where is he now?" Ravenna asked.

Tatiana looked over at Liam briefly before answering, "He died while Liam was protecting you from him."

Liam raised his head and thumped his tail, but then he closed his eyes and rested his head again.

It was hard for her to process that her uncle was dead. She had just seen him. Yes, he had attacked her, but she thought that he put family before everything. And now that he was dead, she realized that he wouldn't be able to provide any answers behind what he did.

Ravenna winced. Irena would have to be told about her

father's death, if she hadn't been told already. Even though they had never gotten along, a parent's death was not something she would wish on even her worst enemy.

"Is Liam okay?" Ravenna tried to see if Liam was hurt, but he seemed fine. She was still concerned though. He hadn't spoken at all since she woke up.

"He's been by your side for the last couple of days while you've been healing. I would imagine that he's exhausted from keeping watch over you."

Ravenna snapped her head up. "I've been asleep for *days?*"

"Even though Damien didn't hit anything vital, his knife did go deep into your side. The surgeon was able to close up the wound, but he and I thought it was necessary for your healing to get some solid sleep."

Ravenna didn't have anything to say to that. It made sense, but it was still jarring to know that she had been unconscious for multiple days.

"I should leave and request dinner to be brought up to you." Then Tatiana added with a smile, "Cress also wanted me to tell you as soon as you wake up that she plans on killing you for causing her to worry even more about you."

"Of course she did." Ravenna chuckled to herself, but she winced at the pain in her side.

After Tatiana left, Ravenna looked over at Liam, who was indeed sleeping. She remembered what she had felt right before she pushed him away from Damien's knife and wanted dinner to come as soon as possible so she could surprise him by accepting his marriage proposal.

She loved him.

The realization hit her again and made her feel giddy. It also made her heart flutter, and she thanked Hoseenu that he had healed her heart enough to love again.

A tray of food arrived, and she waited for Liam to transform. When he didn't, she thought that maybe it was because he was still asleep, so she gently tried to wake him up by petting him. He opened his eyes and licked her hand, but he remained a dog.

Panic started to wash away the excitement she had been feeling earlier.

"Liam, please say something. Anything."

Nothing.

His mouth remained closed. There was no voice in her head that only she could hear. He didn't even bark, let alone whimper.

"No, no, no, no, no. Oh, Hoseenu, please, no!" She started to sit up, and he scooted closer to her.

"Liam, do you understand me at all?" He cocked his head. She tried something else. "Nod your head if you can."

He didn't even move.

"Liam." She began to cry. She was too late.

He came over and started licking the tears off of her face, but that only made her cry harder.

"Liam. I'm so sorry," she sobbed. "I do love you. I want to marry you." She wrapped her arms around his neck while he continued to lick her tears.

"Please, will you marry me?" she whispered into his ear.

A bright light filled her vision, and she felt human arms pulling her close to a human chest.

"Yes, I will," she heard a human man's voice whisper. She pulled back and saw Liam's green eyes meeting her own, a wide smile on his face.

"Liam!" She shouted and then pressed her lips to his. It took a moment for Liam to recover from the surprise of her kissing him, but then he returned her kiss. She could feel the same longing she felt for him in his kiss. More tears started to flow, and he kissed them away, whispering how much he loved her between each kiss.

"I love you, Liam," she said. "Thank you for not giving up on me."

Liam pulled back to look at her. "I promised that I would never give up. I love you, Ravenna."

She smiled up at him and thanked Hoseenu again that this was the man He had provided to be her king.

EPILOGUE

Six months later

"I can't believe today is finally here!" Sophia squealed. The Wilderosian queen went over and hugged Ravenna, who was waiting for Cress to finish helping her put on her dress - one that Cress had designed and sewed completely herself. Ravenna was sure that, after today, her small dressmaking business would be swamped with orders.

"It is hard to believe that I'm getting married in a few short hours," Ravenna said as Sophia pulled away from her.

"Will you stop fidgeting?!" Cress huffed. "Honestly, you are the worst model a dressmaker could ever ask for."

Ravenna snorted at Sophia's raised eyebrows and Cress's exasperated face.

"Then it's a good thing that I'm no longer your only model," Ravenna said with a wink.

Cress broke out into a smile. "But none of them are as kind as you," she conceded.

"You should come to Wilderose," Sophia said. "There are plenty of women who would make kind models there."

Cress tapped her chin. "Well, I suppose I could go and make sure Garrett actually helps capture the raiders." Ravenna raised a brow at the mention of Garrett.

Garrett had finally told the rest of their little group that he had taken bribes from the raiders, and because of that, he knew where they were hiding. He had volunteered to make up for his crimes by helping put a stop to the raiders. Hopefully he would also learn who had hired them to kill her parents.

"Is he your intended?" Sophia asked Cress.

"No!" Cress squawked. "He's despicable and untrustworthy. Someone familiar with his ways needs to be around him to keep him honest."

Sophia and Ravenna shared a look.

Ravenna glanced at her cousin, who sat alone in the corner of the room, not even attempting to interact with the rest of the women. Ravenna still felt awkward being around Irena, especially after everything that had happened with Irena's father, but she had hoped that asking Irena to be one of her wedding attendants would show her that Ravenna didn't hold Damien's actions against her. It had been hard telling Irena about everything Damien had done. A couple of days before Damien's funeral, Ravenna asked Irena if she knew how Damien had been involved with the raiders and the accidents. "If I did, I wouldn't tell you," Irena had sneered. Ravenna hadn't pressed the issue with her since then. She wanted to give her cousin time to grieve.

Tatiana opened the door. "It's time!" she said. Then she

caught sight of Ravenna standing in her white dress and veil. "You look beautiful!"

Ravenna swore she could see tears in her fairy godmother's eyes, but when she blinked, they were as clear as day. "Thank you," she said, as she dipped her head.

"Let's go!" Cress shouted, grabbing Sophia's arm and leading her toward the main chapel hall. Ravenna followed closely behind and chuckled at the two women who had become fast friends. Irena walked past Ravenna to stand behind the other wedding attendants.

"Are you ready?" Tatiana squeezed Ravenna's arm.

Ravenna beamed. "I am!"

When they got to the door leading into the hall, Ravenna could hear the music swelling out over the room. One by one, her friends slipped in to walk down the aisle before her. First Tatiana. Then Sophia. Followed by Irena. Cress ended their procession.

Before Ravenna's turn came, she thought about how much she wished her parents could be there. *Please let them know I'm getting married,* Ravenna prayed to Hoseenu.

Finally, she walked through the doors and saw Liam standing at the end of the aisle waiting for her. He looked so handsome in his white formal clothes, his red hair standing out in contrast. She could see him beaming as he saw her for the first time. She started crying as she walked toward him. They were not tears of sadness and regret, but of joy and hope for the future that Hoseenu had for them.

THE SWAN WING

THE LYRIAN ALLIANCE

BOOK TWO

COMING FALL 2021

ACKNOWLEDGEMENTS

It's hard to believe that after all this time, I'm writing down an acknowledgement page. So many people (and dogs) helped me with this book. It would not even exist if it weren't for the following people who I need to thank.

First, I want to thank God for giving me the opportunity to even write this book. This would not have been possible without Him.

Second, I've already dedicated this book to her, but Lila really does need a lot of credit for this, even though she is a dog. If it weren't for a trip to the snow-covered dog park back in January 2019, you would not be reading this book.

Now after these first two, the following comes in no special order of importance:

Thank you to Sarah Fox, Mikael Short, and everyone at The Bookish Fox. I didn't have any idea what I was doing, but I learned so much and now have the start of a book series instead of a standalone book.

This stunning cover wouldn't have existed if it weren't for those that worked at Damonza.com. It made The Cursed Queen come alive!

To Hanna Sandvig who is the artist behind the map of "The Known World". Thank you for deciphering my horrible drawing and creating something beautiful! (Also, everyone should read her books! They are some of my favorites.)

Thank you to everyone at Enchanted Ink Publishing for doing the hard work of making the inside of The Cursed Queen beautiful.

Thank you Lauren for listening to me talk through every single detail of this book, but also this series. And for reading every single version of The Cursed Queen. You deserve all the rewards! (And all of the Miraculous Ladybug merch.)

Thank you to Amber for being a grammar Nazi. You're the reason why this book is finally finished. Also, here it is, after all the random back and forth over "lay" vs "laid", I publicly admit defeat. (I didn't run this page by you, because I wanted to surprise you, but I'm sure you'll have wished I did by grammar mistake number one.)

To all of my friends and family (hi Mom) who supported me throughout this whole entire process. I was so nervous telling y'all that I was actually writing/publishing a book, and you're now more excited than I am. A special thank you to the ones that had to read early versions. You are the real troopers and I hoped this version was a better experience.

ABOUT THE AUTHOR

Colleen Forbes is an author based in the greater Seattle area where she loves to write fairy tale retellings. After becoming a computer programmer, she tried out a few different roles before writing her first book, The Cursed Queen. In addition to writing, she is also a part-time librarian, part-time grad student in library school, and a full-time follower of Jesus. When not reading in her home library hidden behind a secret bookshelf door, you can find her having adventures with her Black Labrador Retriever, Lila.

CPSIA information can be obtained
at www.ICGtesting.com
Printed in the USA
BVHW070032061120
592469BV00004B/9/J